A Prayer for
Understanding

By Cecelia Hopkins-Drewer

ISBN: 978-0-6481160-6-6
Published by CGH Literacy Institute,
Adelaide, South Australia, 2020

ISBN: 978-0-6481160-6-6

Acknowledgements: Cover Photograph by Cecelia Hopkins,

St Mary's – Port Douglas

Fictional disclaimer:

*All characters and events in this work are fictional, and while an effort has been made to recreate
the era of the 1980s and incorporate selected aspects of history which are general knowledge; the
story was written for entertainment purposes. The characters have no existence outside the
imagination of the author and any similarity to persons or events outside the text is the result of
coincidence.*

CONTENTS

PROLOGUE: A LETTER FROM AUNT ELISABET

Allegra had started reading Grandmother's diary to her young children as a spot of rainy-day fun, but somehow, the activity had become serious. They had learned that life had been different and interesting during the mid-nineteen-eighties, and that Grandma had relationship challenges that Allegra had known nothing about. Curiosity had impelled Allegra to seek out diaries belonging to Grandmother's university friends, known as 'Aunt Kathy' and 'Aunt Cara' in an attempt to find out what happened next.

Aunt Kathy's diary had been full of surprises, as Grandma and Grandpa had broken up for a semester, but halfway through Aunt Cara's diary, Allegra and the children had been pleased to find Grandma and Grandpa reunited. Allegra knew that the diary stories would run out eventually, but she had begged Grandma to locate a diary covering the final year of university, leading up to graduation in 1987.

Grandma had to think for a while about the request, but she eventually replied that she had been busy in 1987 to keep a diary. However, she thought that her room-mate Elisabet might have kept something that year. Grandma wrote to her old friend, who took a long time to reply; but promised to search through her things and post the diary if she found anything. Allegra was very excited when a brown paper package arrived in the mail one day.

"I hope it is worth the wait," she said to her children.

"It will be," Ellie asserted eagerly.

"Perhaps you could skip the boring bits and especially the kissing," Terry suggested. Terry wasn't really old enough to mind kissing, but he had heard from the kids at playgroup that it was silly.

"Alright!" Allegra agreed with amusement. She certainly would not be in the business of reading any explicit recollections to her two children, although she doubted that the diary writer would have been too unguarded in those conservative times. "Shall I look at it on my own first then?"

"Sure," Terry ran off to play happily.

Ellie remained interested, attempting to peek over Allegra's shoulder as she opened the diary. A handful of fashion clippings fell out, evening dresses of the nineteen-eighties. Ellie gathered the pictures up in glee and began studying them. Allegra was left to read the narrative in solitude:

"I am looking forward to returning to Silver Springs University to complete my final year of study," Elisabet had written. *"I like the campus social life too, although I don't think that it has ever been as important to me as to my room-mate for the year,*

Stephanie Lowood. The boys on campus are nice, but I have not met one that might be special, the one for me!"

The diary continued on the next page: "I actually count myself lucky that I haven't experienced the heartbreak some girls have, getting serious and breaking up again. I guess the nearest thing has been my mild crush on Craig…"

There was a thoughtful doodle and something had been scribbled out. "Craig and I have been out, and I do think he is the best looking, most talented young man on campus. He has encouraged my music, but I do not think he returns my feelings."

"That doesn't matter," the scribble continued "I still dream of meeting someone really special. Perhaps a bit like Tom Randall, my English classmate, who is artistic and sporty as well? However, Tom is going steady with Joelle, and the time he asked me to a function because Joelle was busy was just an embarrassment."

"I had to say 'no'!" The chronicler had drawn a row of exclamation marks. "Luckily there was another guy, Felipe. He was too science orientated for me, and we had very little to talk about, but we had a very nice evening, nonetheless. I will have to watch out that he doesn't want to get serious with me this year."

"I will be concentrating on my studies as well," the writer promised herself. "There are plenty of guys who will ask me on dates, and none is more important than my career and dreams. At least, not until I meet the one I am sure is Mr. Right, and then, well I want career and dreams as well. I believe I deserve the whole package."

CHAPTER ONE: FINAL YEAR AT SILVER SPRINGS

It was the last Sunday in February, and Elisabet was making the pleasant drive from Byron Bay to Silver Springs University. This route took her along the Pacific Highway, through Tweed Heads and Coolangatta, and past the Gold Coast settlement.

She stopped for a meal break just south of Brisbane before skirting around the city; from there the fastest route took her along the Gateway Motorway, which had just been built, and onto the Bruce Highway. Elisabet left the Bruce Highway at Northcoast, and proceeded more gently into Silver Springs, where she turned up University Drive.

The Gemini had been Elisabet's mother's car, but her mother had decided to upgrade to an Audi 5000 CS Station Wagon. That vehicle did not come cheap, but had all the features required to be a tax deduction for her parent's organic fruit and vegetable business.

The business, which had always done very well, was currently benefiting from the paranoia arising from the outbreak of the "mad cow" disease. Since November, many meat products were suspect. Vegetarian food was popular, and organically grown produce commanded an extra premium.

Elisabet by-passed the student car park and drove right up to the door of the girls' dormitory, where she hoped she could get somebody to help with her bags. She was in luck, because she immediately saw her room-mate's boyfriend, Garrick Merton exiting the foyer. She hailed him:

"Hey Garry!"

Garry turned around in surprise. "Is that you, Elisabet?" he asked.

"Of course!" Elisabet laughed. "Could you give me a hand with the bags?"

Elisabet knew Garry was always very gentlemanly and obliging. Although he had just finished helping his girlfriend, Stephanie Lowood, with her bags, he would be perfectly willing to turn around and help Elisabet. He went around to the rear of the car and waited for her to unlock the luggage compartment.

The bags were heavy, but Garry was fit and strong. He made no complaint. Elisabet picked up a number of smaller parcels and followed him into the foyer of the girls' dormitory.

Garry nodded to the girl on reception, and she obligingly activated the public address system: "Man in the dorm, man in the dorm!"

The warning message was projected just in case some girls should be running around the corridors in a state of undress. This was unlikely on the afternoon of their arrival back at university, but every precaution was taken anyway.

Garry dropped the bags in the corridor outside the room Elisabet and Stephanie intended to share, and knocked on the door. Stephanie unlocked the door, looking surprised to see Garry back. Then she noticed Elisabet and hastened to give her a hug.

Elisabet and Stephanie had shared English classes for three years. When they had the chance to invoke 'senior privilege' and claim single rooms, they had decided to forego the honour for the pleasure of rooming together.

The two girls were from very different backgrounds. Stephanie was from Adelaide, and her family were relatively hard-up. She was a talented seamstress and designed most of her own clothes to compensate for her limited budget.

Elisabet, on the other hand, had lots of lovely shop bought clothing, because her family were doing quite well financially. Stephanie had long brown hair, which was stubbornly straight; while Elisabet had honey blonde hair with a natural wave.

Both girls were considered somewhat 'quiet' by the majority of people on campus, but in different ways. Stephanie been shy when she had first enrolled at Silver Springs; but nowadays, made an effort to be assertive. Elisabet, in contrast, was naturally confident and refused to put herself out for anyone. She was also single by choice.

Elisabet put her light bags down on the bed. "I have to shift the car," she pronounced. "I'm not supposed to leave it out the front!"

"I have to leave the dormitory too," Garry said. "I'm not allowed to hang around." He gave Stephanie a quick kiss, and then followed Elisabet back towards reception. "I hope you girls have fun rooming together."

"We should," Elisabet said. "But I'm expecting Stephanie to leave me at some stage and marry you…"

Garry grunted. He had attended summer school at the University of Wollongong in the hopes of organizing a mid-year graduation. However, when he had proposed to Stephanie, she said that she was not quite ready. It was only a little over a year since her previous boyfriend, Bradley Parker had been killed in a motorcycle accident.

"If I get work somewhere local - that might just happen," he admitted.

"I've seen the wedding dress that Stephanie and Bede made for that design competition," Elisabet said teasingly. "It is beautiful."

"Well - you are luckier than me," Garry admitted. "They kept it hidden from me."

"I expect it is meant to be a surprise," Elisabet said.

"I think Steph was planning to use the dress as a grad gown," Garry said. "But you are right. She won't want it seen before the presentation."

Monday was registration day. Having learned in previous years that it was pointless to join the queue early in the morning, because that was when it was at its longest, Elisabet slept in and then crossed to the cafeteria to enjoy a leisurely breakfast with her friends.

Stephanie and Garry, Cara and Dylan were a tight group, because they shared their biology classes together. This involved long afternoon laboratories and frequent off-campus expeditions, creating a sense of camaraderie. In addition, Cara had finally agreed to go steady with Dylan.

There were also several fourth year theology students and girlfriends at the table. Luke, who doubled as the university bus driver, and his long-term girlfriend Tess, were probably the 'oldest' couple on campus; while David and Debbie were also very well established, followed by Anita and Larry.

Andrew Grosvy was looking somewhat lonely, because his girlfriend Kathy had completed her primary teaching course and graduated the previous December. Kathy had been lucky enough to gain work in Queensland, based in Dalby, which was about three hours away. This meant weekend visits were possible, although Andrew explained that with Kathy's heavy load as a first year career teacher, she would be very busy.

After the cafeteria closed its doors for breakfast, the students remained in the lounge area, chatting and exchanging stories about their holidays. They were joined by some third year students. Bede O'Brien was Cara's younger sister, and strangely enough was dating Cara's ex-boyfriend, African-American exchange student, Kaleb Proctor. Her friends Janet and Lacy were basketball players, and had both captained women's teams the previous year. Terrance played in the more prestigious men's basketball competition.

"Did you hear how you went in the design competition?" Stephanie asked Bede.

The design competition had been sponsored by the American Fiber

Manufacturers Association, and Stephanie had helped Bede with the construction of samples. The prize was a years' all expenses paid internship in the United States, which Bede hoped to win so she could join Kaleb in America for at least a year.

Bede nodded, and her eyes were shining. "I didn't think it possible that I would win," she said. "So I was thrilled to learn I was first runner-up!"

"You deserved it," Stephanie said. "You – we both – put a lot of work into those designs."

"The good news is," Bede continued, "The grand prize winner was happy to keep the title, but declined the internship due to already having employment in the fashion industry. So the opportunity was passed on to me!"

"What incredible luck," Debbie exclaimed.

"It's providential," corrected Andrew Grosvy, who saw the hand of God in everything. "Luke eleven, verse thirteen, 'If you then, being evil, know how to give good gifts to your children, how much more will your heavenly Father give the Holy Spirit to those who ask Him!'."

Bede giggled. "I will be leaving for the United States late in July, which is when Kaleb's scholarship here runs out," she explained. "The timing couldn't be better!"

Elisabet kept her ideas to herself, merely answering others inquiries when they were directly addressed to her. Finally she pulled herself to her feet: "I think I will drop by the office and see if I can get my papers signed off before lunch."

Registration was a minor matter for seniors. They had to get their subjects approved, but most decisions had been made for them either in previous years, or by their course structure.

Elisabet had to do curriculum studies, and her compulsory education units were practice teaching, and health. Her major field of study was English and her minor field was history. The final area of choice remaining to her were two electives.

Elisabet was thrilled that she had fulfilled the pre-requisites for entry into the music progamme. The Silver Springs' Music programme was very demanding, requiring prospective students to have completed their AMUS exams to grade eight. Elisabet had not achieved this standard by the end of high school, but she had been taking private lessons, and sat her exam the previous year.

The English Professor approved her subjects, and observed that the Music electives gave her a very strong arts/humanities line-up, which would make her popular in the workforce. Elisabet then hurried on to the business office, where she paid a deposit towards her fees and signed up for a payment plan. Luckily as her parents were in primary production, she was entitled to student allowance.

Tuesday, classes commenced for the semester. In English she was studying Seventeenth Century literature. This included some of Shakespeare's later plays; the Metaphysical poets, and *Faustus* by Christopher Marlowe. Later in the semester they would be studying, Dryden, Milton's *Paradise Lost*, and *Pilgrim's Progress* by John Bunyan. Non-fiction included the essays of Bacon, Descartes and Newton.

Elisabet shared her English classes with her room-mate Stephanie, their friend Phoebe, who no longer lived in the dormitory because she had married her mechanic boyfriend Hank, and Anita. Tom Randall was the only remaining male student in the fourth year English class. His girlfriend Joelle was a talented Music major who played for most of the worships and assemblies.

After English, Elisabet had health. This subject promised to be interesting, touching on such topics as mental health, counselling, disease, exercise, and poverty. Other areas of study included: equality and discrimination, nutrition and community. One of the requirements of the subject was to complete their Senior First Aid Certificates with an independent accrediting body such as the Red Cross or St. John Ambulance society.

Wednesday, Elisabet had curriculum studies and practice teaching. Curriculum studies tended more towards understanding the subject guidelines, while practice teaching focused on practical skills. After these classes finished, Elisabet wandered over to the Music Department. Here she found Craig practicing his violin.

Craig was a tall thin young man that Elisabet had been out with several times. No relationship had developed, their friends assumed it was because they were both too quiet, but Elisabet had other suspicions. Moreover, she had immense respect for Craig, who he was vastly talented.

"I got into the music programme," Elisabet announced proudly, when Craig came to a pause in his violin practice.

Craig looked pleased. "Congratulations!" he said. "I knew you would eventually."

"I know, but it took work," Elisabet observed.

"Everything worthwhile does," Craig reflected.

Elisabet grimaced. She was no stranger to work; she helped her parents in the gardening business. However, she liked to see a healthy return for her efforts whenever she made them.

"What are you using as your second instrument?" Craig inquired. "Voice or recorder?"

"I've put down both," Elisabet said. "But I think recorder. It is very versatile."

"A practical choice," Craig nodded approvingly. "And what are you doing for performance? Choir?"

"I don't know," Elisabet replied artlessly. "Choir seems an awful big commitment for a fourth year with other studies to complete."

"What then?" Craig asked.

"I was wondering," Elisabet began tentatively, "Whether you would be open to starting a small band… then we could schedule practices to suit ourselves."

Craig grinned. "It just so happens that I have some original compositions, I need some volunteers to play for me… so that isn't a half bad idea."

"I hoped you would," Elisabet smiled happily. Things usually went her way.

"So would you be on the recorder or the keyboard do you think?" Craig asked.

"Electric keyboard," Elisabet said. "Unless your pieces are way beyond me."

"No, they are designed for the average player," Craig assured her. "Then I will be on strings – we could do with at least one on brass or wind, and a drummer. I will ask around."

"What about Joelle?" Elisabet inquired, referring to Tom's girlfriend.

"Joelle uses worships as her performance," Craig said. "I don't really expect that to change as she does so much in that area. Leave it with me – one of the guys was in here mucking around with the drums a bit last year. Vincent, I think. He had been dropped by the basketball clique over that steroid scandal and was looking for something else to do. "

"I thought he was one of the cleanest," Elisabet frowned in an attempt to remember.

"He was one of the better ones," Craig observed. "The first to admit his mistake, and hence the one that got ostracised. I'll see who else is available for the brass."

"Oh thanks," Elisabet said.

She went on her way to the cafeteria smiling. That little conversation had half of her subject requirements in the bag already. It was nice when you could get other people to help, and Elisabet had always found people very obliging.

Thursday morning, Elisabet and Stephanie had English. The first weeks were devoted to Shakespeare's final plays and looked like they would be highly enjoyable. Stephanie sat with her friend Phoebe, who she was always happy to see. Elisabet was perfectly comfortable sitting alone, but she looked up when Tom Randall slid into the seat beside her.

Tom was tall and good-looking, with hair that was just a little too long, because shag hairstyles were all the rage. He loved to surf and often went out to the beach with Cara's boyfriend Dylan.

Elisabet liked Tom, but tension had arisen between them late last year, when he had asked her to accompany him to a campus function. The invitation was probably innocent, but Elisabet had felt obliged to refuse Tom in favour of an invitation from science student Felipe, who was clearly single.

"Did you have a good summer?" Tom asked.

"I did," Elisabet said. She had helped her parents on the market stall because summer was their busy season, but that wasn't something she mentioned around university. "How was your summer?"

"Oh fine," Tom said. "Joelle was away for six weeks doing her concert tour, but when she returned, we celebrated a late Christmas."

"Did you miss her?" Elisabet asked.

Tom sighed. "I always miss Joelle when she is busy with her music," he muttered. "But the opportunity was so great – I couldn't stand in her way."

"Of course not," Elisabet said. "I think you are very noble."

Tom was clearly looking for sympathy. Elisabet concentrated on her notepad, despite the fact it was almost empty. Tom had been a good friend for three years – until he had suddenly become complicated. The English Professor entered the room just then and she was able to relax under the guise of listening to the lecture.

Thursday afternoon, Elisabet was surprised to learn that Stephanie had a biology practical, the same as she had for the previous three years. In the fourth year, it was the custom to drop your minor and pick up electives. Instead, Stephanie had chosen to strengthen her minor. Her boyfriend Garry, who had missed a biology unit the semester he had attended the University of Wollongong instead of Silver Springs, would share her classes.

Friday, Elisabet had her first music class. After all the build-up, and the high level she had to achieve to enter the programme, she was sharing the class with a small group of first year music majors. Jess reminded Elisabet of a young Joelle, because she was so earnest and dedicated. James was open and friendly, and Vivione was a little shy.

All the new students were highly accomplished. Jess played the piano and harp, James was a trumpeter, and Vivione was a cellist. At first the other class members assumed Elisabet was also a first year, but she explained she had chosen music as an elective. Then they became curious and asked her a lot of questions about the university.

Friday evening, all the students attended the Uniting Church vespers, which was a co-educational activity held in the women's assembly area. The girls did their hair and make-up in an effort to look their best, as the men were in attendance.

The girls who had regular boyfriends waited to be collected at reception and escorted across to the small chapel. Elisabet had no steady boyfriend, so she waited until Garry had Stephanie paged over the public address system, and walked across to the assembly area with the couple. Once at the vespers, they were joined on the bench seat by Cara and her boyfriend Dylan.

The speaker for the evening was the Uniting Chaplain, who traditionally opened the university year with worship. As the last hymn faded away, a soft murmur arose among the students, many of whom would hang around to socialise after the programme.

"Are you happy to be back?" Dylan asked, from his seat on the other side of Cara.

"I think so," Elisabet said. "It is the last year of our course and there will be many exciting changes."

"There will too," Dylan and Cara exchanged glances. The couple had only resolved their differences the middle of last year, so it was too soon for them to be announcing an engagement. However, Elisabet knew that they both shared an interest in the outdoors and adventure.

"Graduation is months away," Cara sighed. "And we will have horrible assignments." Cara was sporty and none too fond of book work, despite the fact that she was taking some of the most demanding science subjects available.

Andrew Grosvy was sitting on the other side of Cara. "Have you heard that the Reverse Tea is back?" he asked. "I will be inviting Kathy!"

"I thought the Reverse Tea had been cancelled because of the 'men's liberation' movement," Elisabet responded in surprise.

Andrew shrugged. "Most of the men's libbers graduated last year," he said casually. "The rest of us are pretty happy with the rights we already have!"

"It was a nasty, retrospectively conservative movement anyway," Garry observed. "I was never on-board with them!"

"It would be exciting to have Kathy back for the weekend," Stephanie said. "But you cannot possibly ask her to the Reverse Tea, Andrew!"

"Why not?" the innocent Theology Student sounded puzzled.

"The girls have to ask the guys," Stephanie explained.

"Okay, I will buy Kathy a meal ticket and then she can ask me to tea," Andrew replied pacifically.

Stephanie giggled pertly. "Who will you be asking Elisabet?"

"I don't know," Elisabet said. "I hadn't thought about it."

This added complexity to Tom's desire to sit with her during English. She sincerely hoped that he and Joelle were all good, and he had not been fishing for an invitation. She glanced around the assembly area, and noticed Joelle had left the organ and was sitting beside Tom. Her other side was occupied by a young man Elisabet did not know.

"Who is that sitting alongside Joelle?" Elisabet asked.

"I believe he is a Masters of Theology student from the UK," Andrew informed her. "Joelle met him when she was on tour."

"Hmm," Eisabet murmured.

"I think he is a very nice guy," Andrew continued. He looked obliging: "I could organize an introduction to him if you are interested."

"Maybe another time," Elisabet said. "What is his name?"

"Justin," Andrew said. "I haven't had much chance to get to know him myself, but I expect we all will by the end of the year."

"Yeah," Elisabet turned away as if she had lost interest, but she had to admit Justin was handsome. The British youth had a neater style than the average Australian, a little less of the roughness of the outdoors, but she was sure he would get a touch of suntan very soon.

Saturday morning, Elisabet was lingering over a leisurely breakfast when Felipe put his tray down beside her. "May I sit here?" he asked with Latin politeness.

"Of course!" Elisabet said. "You are welcome anytime."

"Welcome enough to get an invitation from you to the Reverse Tea?" Felipe asked, somewhat directly. His scientific mind apparently did not run towards subtlety.

"I only heard about the function last night," Elisabet objected. Her mind was racing. Felipe was nice, but he was so into pure science and she was so pure arts, she often wondered whether they had any common ground. "Perhaps we ought to get to know someone new."

"I believe that is what the function is for," Felipe agreed somewhat reluctantly. "It is a sort of mixer."

"Exactly," Elisabet said. She fiddled with her glass. "What electives have you chosen, Felipe?"

"Well as physics major, with mathematics minor, I thought the best compliment would be chemistry," Felipe said.

"It does sound suitable," Elisabet said. "You didn't think of splashing out and taking biology?"

"I cannot fit any more units into my degree," Felipe said. "And where I could, I added some computing."

"Very wise," Elisabet said. "That's like a new science isn't it?"

Felipe nodded eagerly. "A growing technologic field," he admitted. "And quite creative."

Felipe appeared to think he was claiming some common grounds as Elisabet was known for her love of the creative arts.

"You will have to tell me about it some time," Elisabet murmured.

"Yes," Felipe looked enthusiastic.

Just then Craig stopped by the table. "Elisabet," he said, "I would like to get together for band practice today. After lunch if that would suit."

"That is fine," Elisabet said. "Music room at two?"

"One-thirty would be better," Craig said.

"Okay," Elisabet said. She turned to Felipe. "I have things to do this morning then. I will see you later."

"See you," Felipe said somewhat wistfully.

Elisabet picked up her tray, placed it on the dishwasher shelf, and then followed Craig out of the cafeteria. She changed direction at the door and headed towards the girl's dormitory, where Stephanie was in their room. The scholar liked to begin her assignments early, and then finished just when everybody else had begun to stress. Elisabet sighed and picked up one of the Shakespearean plays. She might as well join Stephanie.

After lunch, Elisabet made her way to the Music Department. Truth to be told, she was excited by the idea of starting a band. Craig was already there, and Vincent was setting up the drums. Elisabet was surprised to see James was also there.

Craig gave her a huge grin. "Hey, Elisabet," he announced. "I got us a brass player."

"Cool," Elisabet said. "Hi, James."

"Hey, Elisabet," James said. "I was thrilled when Craig asked me to join the band."

"It will be good to have you," Eisabet said. She crossed to the electric keyboard and switched it on. Craig handed her a sheaf of handwritten sheet music she flicked through rapidly. "This looks good, Craig!"

Elisabet fiddled with the keyboard settings and then began to experimentally peck her way through the tunes. After listening for a few bars, Vincent began to beat a matching rhythm on the drums. James set up his own stand and tentatively sounded a few notes on the trumpet. Elisabet paused.

"Take it from the beginning," Craig said, and their practice began in earnest.

Some of Craig's tunes were acoustic and folksy in style, while a few were rhythmic and rollicking. Eisabet would have liked the chance to practice alone, but bravely pushed ahead in the group situation, becoming smoother with each repetition. After about an hour and a half, Craig called a halt. His eyes were shining.

"That sounded great guys," the composer said. "I want to make a few adjustments and then we will practice again. I'm also looking for an opportunity to let us loose on the student body!"

Vincent pulled the cover over the drums and headed off for the gymnasium. It was a new year and a new basketball season, which had the jock hoping the scandal of the previous year might be forgotten, and a place found for him on a team again. James picked up his trumpet and also left. Elisabet was alone with Craig, which was something for which she had been hoping.

"Have you heard about the Reverse Tea?" Elisabet began, but a shadow fell over Craig's face.

"If you were thinking of asking me, please don't," Craig pronounced pre-emptively.

Elisabet was puzzled. "We have been to these things together before."

"Often enough that people might talk," Craig said. "And I don't want you hurt."

"I won't get hurt," Elisabet said, but she understood what Craig was saying. It was similar to the reason she had not asked Felipe when he had dropped a hint.

"Yeah, but now we are starting a band too," Craig continued, "We will be together a lot."

"So – you want to keep things professional?" Elisabet said. "I can do that."

"Cool," Craig said. "It's not that we aren't good friends – of course we are!"

"Forgive me for suggesting this," Elisabet said gently. "But mightn't it be easier for you - if you came out as gay?'

Craig looked shocked. "Come out as gay around here? I could get expelled," he exclaimed. "Even if that didn't happen – I certainly wouldn't get employment."

"You haven't done anything to deserve expulsion," Elisabet objected. "And the other is pure discrimination."

"I know," Craig said. "But I'm not even sure I am gay. I have liked girls in the past."

"I know you started to like Cara when you were fake-dating her last year," Elisabet admitted. "That is what gave me the idea you might be gay. Cara is sort of boyish."

"Not that boyish!" Craig retorted. "I dunno - gay and straight aren't my only options - I sometimes feel like I am not built for relationships at all."

"I don't understand," Elisabet stammered.

Craig shrugged. "It's not easy for me either."

"I will respect your confidence," Elisabet whispered.

"Thanks," Craig said. He reached out to give her a tentative touch on the arm. Elisabet longed to hug him in return, but she sensed he might be uncomfortable with her touch. "Why don't you ask one of the other band guys? Vincent or James?"

"Vincent would be a sympathy invite, and I don't do those," Elisabet said. "But I might ask James when I see him in music class."

She returned to the dormitory. Stephanie was there hanging clothes in the wardrobe. The outfits were her own creations. Stephanie's designs were quirky and unusual, far from the current fashion. While they were cool, they were also far more seventies than eighties. When questioned, Stephanie said that she liked to be 'ahead' of current fashion. If the girl's predictions were right, the nineteen-nineties would be seeing a seventies revival.

CHAPTER TWO: RELATIONSHIP ROULETTE

Sunday morning offered a choice of church services. The students could attend the Inter-denominational praise service at 7:30 am or the Reform Church service at 10:30 am. The Inter-denominational praise service was lively and popular despite its incredibly early hour. Elisabet and Stephanie rose early and put on their best clothes.

They knocked on Cara's bedroom door. Elisabet was wearing a fashionable eighties dress with padded shoulders, crossover bodice and sash at the waist, while Stephanie was wearing an original design with a flowing uneven hemline. The practical Cara appeared wearing a simple skirt and blouse.

Downstairs, the girls were joined by Dylan and Garry both encased in their church suits, and they sat down in the pew behind Joelle and Tom. As Joelle frequently played the organ for both services, it was unusual for her to be sitting down. Elisabet could not help notice the graduate student, Justin, was sitting on the other side of the musician; and the warmth in Joelle's manner towards the English youth was unmistakable.

After the praise service was over, Joelle and Tom hurried out of the women's assembly area, and headed through the light rain towards the campus meeting hall. Justin followed closely in their footsteps. Elisabet turned to Stephanie and Cara.

"Tom and Joelle are still going out – aren't they?" she asked in puzzlement.

Cara looked surprised. "As far as I know," she said.

Stephanie looked thoughtful. "I see what you mean," she said. "The new guy!"

"I'm sure Joelle is just showing him around, and when he makes more friends, he will go his own way," Cara observed.

"Andrew says Justin is nice," Elisabet said.

"It doesn't mean that his presence couldn't be trouble though," Stephanie said. "Poor Tom – he is our friend."

"Tom has chosen to stick with Joelle this far," Cara observed.

"I'm sure it will work out one way or another," Dylan weighed in casually. "You girls think too much about other people's relationships."

"At least we are well-meaning," Stephanie retorted. "Some people around here just gossip."

"Gossip is wrong and can be very hurtful," Garry agreed.

The girls dropped the subject of Tom and Joelle; moving on to their plans for the coming semester. The group of friends sat talking for so long that they decided it was not worth crossing over to the campus meeting hall for the Reform Church service. As the rain became heavier, walking did not appeal. Instead they meandered across to the cafeteria to wait under the veranda for the doors to open for an early lunch.

Monday morning, Elisabet had a number of classes, including education and then music. During music, Elisabet waited for a discrete moment in which to ask James to the Reverse Tea. Her opportunity came when the lecturer assigned them into pairs for a musical appreciation activity. The other girls, Jess and Vivione chose to work together, giggling and laughing as they listened to their assigned piece.

"What are you getting from the music?" Elisabet asked James.

"Well – it's very subtle," James said.

"It is relaxing," Elisabet said. "So – meditation music or a lullaby?"

"I think it might be a relatively new form known as 'ambient music',"

James said. "The sound also has some acoustic elements."

"I was wondering," Elisabet interjected. "Have you heard of something called the Reverse Tea?"

"That's the thing in a week's time isn't it?" James said. "I'm afraid I don't know any of the girls well enough yet to get an invite."

"Would you like to go with me then?" Elisabet said.

James looked flattered. "I would love to," he said. "But you must have male friends – if not a boyfriend. You are a fourth year."

"Well I do have a few male friends," Elisabet admitted. "But I said to them that I would like to get to know someone new."

"And I'm new!" James grinned. "You have got yourself a date, Elisabet."

"Do you think one of those two were likely to ask you?" Elisabet asked curiously, glancing towards Jess and Vivione.

James shook his head. "No – I reckon they both have crushes on guys in our first year class."

Tuesday after classes finished, Elisabet hurried to lunch. After lunch, she had her student work placement. Elisabet felt quite privileged that her employment was in Student Services. She had gained the position because she had clerical experience helping her parents with their business, and it was more like a 'real job' than most student work assignments.

Her task that afternoon was to type out the upcoming campus newsletter. Elisabet enjoyed the typing, and her artistic side rejoiced in the fact that she was involved in 'publishing' in a minor way. The final bonus was that she got to see all the news before it was officially released.

That Wednesday was Ash Wednesday and the first day of lent. A few of the students joked about giving something up for lent, but most lacked the self-discipline required. All were hungry, healthy young people.

Andrew Grosvy, who had the privilege of conducting the first Convocation of the year, suggested that the students read an extra Bible text a day in-lieu of giving something up. This idea was greeted with enthusiasm by many of the theology students, who loved anything that increased their contact with the holy word.

Thursday in English, Tom sat with Elisabet again. It was a small class and Elisabet supposed grudgingly that he had to sit with someone. Stephanie liked to catch up with her married friend Phoebe, and that just left Tom and Elisabet unseated.

The undergraduate modestly tried to spread her books out and imply that she needed the space next to her for reading material, but Tom simply sat on her other side. She could hardly tell him to go away. It was his class too.

"Hello Elisabet," he said.

"Hey Tom," Elisabet responded. "How are you?"

She had learned it was usually safest to head people off by encouraging them to talk about themselves.

"I'm good," Tom said. "Are you enjoying English this year?"

"Oh yes," Elisabet asserted. She laughed, "No point not enjoying it – it is our major!"

"True," Tom agreed. "Joelle tells me that you got into music?"

The Music Department was relatively small and most of the talented students knew all about each other. Joelle would have heard immediately Elisabet joined the class.

"Ah yes," Elisabet admitted. "That took a lot of work."

"I can believe it," Tom said. "Joelle is always practicing."

Elisabet began to relax after several mentions of his girlfriend.

She giggled: "Joelle is an amazing musician."

"So she is," Tom agreed. "I am very proud. Have you asked anyone to the Reverse Tea yet?"

Elisabet wrinkled her nose. She was very conscious of Phoebe and Joelle listening from their seats, less than a stride away. "Aren't you going with Joelle?"

"Joelle is going with Justin," Tom admitted. "She met him in the UK at Christmas and is showing him around."

"Taking him to the Reverse Tea seems a little over and beyond the requirements of hospitality," Elisabet could not help remarking.

Tom nodded. "We thought I could find someone else – just for the function."

"You could have hooked Justin up with a blind date," Elisabet observed darkly. "Instead of Joelle herself. How come he followed Joelle over to Australia?"

Tom laughed. "Justin didn't follow Joelle. He had already applied to the Masters of Theology course here."

"It seems like a weird coincidence," Elisabet insisted.

"Not so weird when you factor in that he is the Music Master's nephew," Tom replied.

"Oh!" Elisabet exclaimed. A few things suddenly became clearer. Whether they improved Tom's situation, she did not know, but they did explain Joelle's intense interest in the new guy. "Well I am afraid you are out of luck with me. I have already asked James to the Reverse Tea."

"Isn't he in your band too?" Stephanie interjected.

"Yes," Elisabet blushed for no real reason.

"Band, class and now the Reverse Tea – you will be seeing a lot of this James!" Stephanie observed.

"Just as a friend," Elisabet insisted.

"Friendship is the best basis," added Phoebe with all the wisdom of a married woman.

Tom looked disappointed. "I guess I'll have to find someone else to ask me."

"What about Janet or Lacey?" Stephanie suggested.

Both girls were active in organizing the basketball program that year. They were third years, one year below the graduating class. Sporty girls often stayed single longer than the other girls, and tended to tolerate no nonsense from the boys.

Tom looked thoughtful. "Maybe Lacey - I like her."

"If this is just because Joelle is busy for the evening," Phoebe ventured. "You need to be careful."

Tom sighed. "I know – I'm not as clueless as you girls think!"

Phoebe, Elisabet and Stephanie exchanged glances. The girls were not at all sure Tom knew what they really thought of the situation, and they were not planning to tell him. At least, not at this stage. Luckily the English Professor arrived just then and began to enthusiastically conduct the lecture.

"I can't believe the way the first two weeks have flown," Stephanie exclaimed Friday afternoon. The roommate was fiddling with some fabric trying to add lace inserts to the design. Lace wasn't really in fashion, but it was Stephanie's latest craze. She kept trying to make strategic holes in the outfits and fill them with lace.

"Is that what we will be wearing in the year two thousand?" Elisabet joked.

Stephanie looked thoughtful. "I dunno," she said. "I will be thirty by then – it's incredibly hard to imagine."

"But what do you think?" Elisabet asked.

"More like stretch knits," Stephanie said. "That's one thing I learned doing the Man Made Fiber Competition. Stretch knits are very convenient and very comfortable. I reckon they will be here to stay. Except for the denim mini, short dresses are out at the moment, so they have to come back sometime."

"It doesn't sound very glamorous," Elisabet murmured. She enjoyed shopping, and next to her favourite strappy sundress, loved a neat jacket. Preferably with padded shoulders for a powerful silhouette.

"Perhaps people get tired of looking good!" Stephanie joked. "Maybe they begin to enjoy clashes and start grunge dressing. One day, my mum, who likes to pull track pants on under her skirts in winter, will actually be fashionable."

"Ugh!" Elisabet sniffed. "I can't imagine it." She pulled her prettiest summer frock out of the wardrobe. It had a sweet-heart neckline, slightly wide straps and back that ended just above her bra strap. Campus dress codes did not allow for really low backs. "I think I will wear this to vespers tonight."

"You will look very nice," Stephanie said generously. "If you didn't already have a date for the Reverse Tea, I'm sure some guy would beg you to ask him."

Elisabet grunted in satisfaction. That was the way she saw things too. As it was, she was pleased to be looking good when she was introduced to Justin. The moment came about quite naturally as Tom, Joelle and Justin joined Stephanie, Garry and Elisabet in the pew that evening. Cara and Dylan, who arrived a moment later, stopped when they saw the bench was full, and decided to keep Andrew, Debbie and David company on the next seat.

The Uniting Church vespers that evening was conducted by Larry, who was also a fourth year. Larry's theological interests swung towards the charismatic, but Silver Springs was a multi-denominational campus, so that did not matter. Larry spoke on the gifts of the spirit, and made a good case for using their talents in teaching and ministry.

Larry also made the very interesting point, that when he read the passages about spiritual gifts very closely, he came across two gifts sometimes overlooked in the excitement of reading about the other gifts. These gifts were "faith" in Romans chapter 12, verse 3; and "grace" in First Corinthians, chapter 1, verse 4.

"It is easy to think 'oh that is just a way of talking' when you read those verses through," Larry concluded. "But what beautiful gifts faith and grace are really!"

Larry's girlfriend Anita then placed a transparency upon the overhead projector, and Joelle began playing the rousing bars of a modern spiritual song. The students joined and sung the anthem with gusto. A couple of songs later, Larry called the service to a halt and closed with prayer.

"I always love it when our own classmates preach," Joelle said with a sigh. She turned to her seat-mates. "Stephanie, Garry, Elisabet – have you met Justin?"

Stephanie and Garry nodded politely. "Nice to meet you, Justin."

Elisabet looked up, and managed to catch the twinkle in Justin's eyes. They were an amazing deep violet blue, and contrasted with his naturally blonde hair. She found herself having to concentrate on her breathing.

"How are you Justin?" she stammered.

"I am very well, thank you," Justin said. "And acclimatizing to this wonderfully warm country of yours."

"You will have to go to the beach with Tom," Elisabet stammered. "He loves his surfing."

"Indeed I will," Justin replied with some amusement. "I have been waiting for my skin to toughen a little. And then – perhaps you will be coming along with us?"

"If it is a group outing," Elisabet agreed. "I don't do the early morning surfing run."

Had Justin just asked her out, or was he being polite to a new acquaintance? It was hard to tell with his British mannerisms. She decided to stick to the safe assumption that he was being courteous.

"Everything I do seems to be a group thing at the moment," Justin said. "Later on I hope to know my own way around."

"I'm sure you will settle in quickly," Elisabet agreed. "As you get into your studies."

"There are certainly some brilliant lecturers in the Theology Department," Justin granted.

"Tom and I are leaving now, Justin," Joelle called. "I will have an early morning, playing for the Inter-denominational praise service. Are you coming?"

"I was hoping to have a word with Larry," Justin said. "He spoke so well tonight."

"Come along dear," Tom said to Joelle, steering her out of the assembly area. "There is no need for us to wait."

Seeing the space on the pew open up after Tom and Joelle left; Dylan and Cara came to join the party. Elisabet introduced them to Justin, and then fell silent as the conversation flowed around her in a pleasant fashion. Finally Justin espied Larry emerging from one of the side-rooms, and rose to greet him.

Craig had scheduled band practice for Saturday afternoon once again. This gave the band members the morning to relax and rest, and left the evening free to socialize if something was on. When their leader arrived at the Music Department, he looked excited.

"I think I have scored us a gig," he exclaimed.

"Wonderful!" James enthused.

"Where?" Elisabet was more cautious.

"How would you like to be the entertainment at a staff luncheon?" Craig asked.

Vincent frowned. "That isn't really the launch of my dreams," he complained.

"Well it was that or play for the Reverse Tea – which I don't think we are ready for," Craig explained. "Really we should be playing in the RSL, but we would be suspended if we did that!"

James looked surprised. "Small town boy here," he said. "Correct me if I'm wrong, but the Retired Service League is designed to honour our returned soldiers – I know the Reform Church has a somewhat non-combatant stance – but I don't see why we would be suspended for showing our respect."

"The Noosa RSL serves alcohol," Craig observed.

"Oh!" James looked surprised. "In my town there was only an empty hall with an honour roll on the wall."

Elisabet began to giggle.

"Somewhat of a difference between branches," Vincent remarked.

"That is one reason why it is so hard to be a Christian and an artist," Craig agreed. "The venues you can't play – the lyrics you can't write, and a myriad of other artistic conundrums that make it so hard to be authentic and yet faith-filled."

"Well, tell us more about playing for the staff," Elisabet said.

"It's just a few pieces really, while the staff enjoy their meal," Craig said. "The gig will get us heard, and maybe approved for other campus functions. If Elisabet and James want to count this as their 'performance component', we need to be performing."

"The drums are just a hobby to me," Vincent said.

"Doesn't mean you can't do a bang-up job," Craig retorted.

"Ha, ha, funny," Vincent groaned.

Elisabet placed the first sheet on the keyboard, and began the opening bars. She had practiced once or twice since last week, and the new version, including Craig's minor adjustments, flowed quite smoothly from her fingers. Vincent began to tap in time to her playing. James picked up his trumpet. He really was a talented player, because he could make the trumpet sound smooth and mellow, as well as militant. Craig picked up his violin and began to play the melody.

Half way through practice, Craig put his violin down, picked up the microphone, and began to sing. Elisabet was surprised, because up until this moment, she had not realized the pieces had lyrics. Moreover, Craig had a very nice voice.

Elisabet kept playing and concentrated upon her timing, although her mind was beginning to wander. If Craig had not confided what he had to her, she would be developing a major crush on him. He was so talented, and in his own reserved way, kind and obliging. Elisabet's fingers faltered and Craig frowned slightly. She focused her mind back on the piece she was playing.

Eventually, Craig called a halt. "Very good guys," he observed. "I think we will be ready in time for the staff."

"You sing very well," James observed.

"I've been told I have a mellow voice," Craig said. "It is hard to have all eyes upon me however."

"You did a solo part for *Handel's Messiah* two years ago," Elisabet recalled.

"I had an entire orchestra backing me then," Craig said. "And for some of us, the performance nerves never die down."

Craig looked slightly anxious, even though it was only their very small group that had heard him sing. Elisabet flexed her fingers over the keyboard.

"It's okay Craig," she said. "We will be there to support you."

"I have some news of my own," Vincent said, changing the subject slightly. "I'm back on a basketball team – playing men's B grade this year."

"That is wonderful Vincent," Craig said.

"You are all welcome to come and watch me," Vincent invited. "My first match is on Monday night!"

"I will think about it," Elisabet said. That was a safe reply to most invitations. However, watching campus basketball was a popular activity, and she could see herself doing it sometime. "Can I bring a few friends?"

"Of course," Vincent said. "I would appreciate the support."

Elisabet gathered up the few items she had brought across to the Music Department and glanced at her watch. There wasn't a lot of time left before tea. For a moment she thought James was going to offer to walk her back to the dormitory, but then he looked shy. He was a first year after all, and she was a fourth year.

Elisabet said, "Goodbye," to Craig and Vincent; and "I will see you in class" to James. Then she walked herself across to the dormitory.

Sunday afternoon was fine and the Adventure Club had organized a barbeque beside the pool. The barbeque was open to everybody, because the club was recruiting new members.

Elisabet had never joined the Adventure Club, because some of their activities involved backpacking, rock climbing and abseiling, which one really had to be physical to do. Cara and Dylan were regular members, and Garry was a member too, but Stephanie was not, although she attended some events as Garry's guest. Tom was also a member.

The barbeque was typically Australian, with a choice of vegetarian or meat sausages, plenty of fried onion, hamburger buns, and cooling salads. Elisabet was sitting with her friends, when she saw James collecting his food. He didn't seem to know where to go next. She raised her hand and waved tentatively. James trotted across to her side.

"Hello," he said.

"Everybody, this is James," Elisabet said. "He is in my music class."

"It's nice to meet you James," Stephanie said.

"Are you thinking of joining the Adventure Club?" Garry asked. "It's a great way of getting out and about."

"I don't know," James said. "I have a lot of practice to do."

"James is an incredible trumpet player," Elisabet said.

"I quite like band music," Dylan observed.

James sat down with the group. Elisabet noted that he oriented himself a little more towards the guys, as if that made him feel comfortable, but he was still very friendly towards everybody.

"It's great that you came over and joined us," Cara said. "I know how snobby we must look - always sitting together – but we are not like that at all. It's just that we have known each other for three years now."

"My first year class is closing ranks and forming groups already too," James admitted.

"I think it's great you are going to the Reverse Tea with Elisabet," Stephanie remarked with a glitter in her eye. "Elisabet is the only one of us who is single and can have fun!"

"We have fun," Garry objected.

"Oh – of course," Stephanie said. "But no more surprises."

"I'm sure Garry could organize a surprise for you Stephanie, if that is what you require," Andrew observed innocently. A few nearby guys snorted and the theology student observed them with bafflement. "I didn't mean anything..."

James studied Andrew. "You don't appear to have a girlfriend either?"

"My girlfriend graduated," Andrew said with a sigh. "So I'm lonely this year. She should be coming to visit this weekend however!"

"That's good, mate," James said.

Elisabet finished her hotdog and James offered to fetch her some desert, which was fruit salad and ice-cream. Andrew got up to accompany him to the serving area.

"James seems nice," Cara whispered while the guys were away.

"Yeah," Elisabet admitted. "I needed to find someone new for the Reverse Tea. Felipe has been just a little too keen."

"Felipe seems to be doing all right for himself over there," Stephanie observed. The roommate nodded towards where Felipe was sitting; telling the exciting story of his escape from South America to several bright eyed first year girls.

"I hope he does find someone," Elisabet said. "Don't get me wrong, I really like Felipe – just not that way!"

James and Andrew returned with bowls of fruit salad. Elisabet was amused to see that James had collected a huge, man sized serve for her, as well as himself.

He whispered that she didn't have to eat it all, but she laughed. The first year had given her the perfect excuse to over-indulge in sweets, and she could always take an extra stroll around campus to burn the calories off.

Monday afternoon, Elisabet had not really meant to go and watch Vincent play basketball, but she discovered Stephanie was planning to go and watch Garry. The biology students had not played regular competition basketball the year before, because they all had afternoon practical sessions. However, with this year being their final year, and last university seasons, they had returned to the competition.

Cara had just scraped back into A grade girls, while Garry had been assigned to his old position with the B grade boys. Dylan, who was also slightly out of practice, had been assigned to the C grade men's competition. Vincent was in the same team as Garry. Tom was more usually a surfer, but he had been recruited to basketball because of his height, and was in another B grade team.

Bede and her boyfriend Kaleb Proctor were also in the gymnasium to watch. Elisabet noticed Justin was sitting alongside Kaleb. Justin was tall, so perhaps she ought not to have been astounded to hear that he played on Kaleb's A grade team. However, she was wryly impressed the graduate student had gotten away from Joelle's grasp for long enough to sign up!

There were too many teams to play on the same night; so the matches that were timetabled for that evening involved Cara's A grade girls' team, and Garry's B grade boys' team. The girls played first.

Cara's team captain was Janet, while the captain of the opposition team was another third year called Moira. The match went well, and while it was early days on the leader-board, it looked like they had a good chance of making it to the finals.

After the A grade girl's match finished, Cara, Janet and Lacey joined the group on the spectator's bench. Half-way through the boy's match, Elisabet overheard Janet asking Justin to accompany her to the Reverse Tea. Elisabet nudged Stephanie subtly, and both girls strained their ears to catch Justin's reply.

"I think I'm – um – going with someone," Justin said.

"If you mean Joelle," Janet replied practically, "What fun can you have with somebody else's girlfriend really?"

"You do have a point," Justin appeared to agree.

"I'm not in Tom's confidence," Janet continued. "But I think he would prefer to go with Joelle himself. I heard he tried asking Lacey, but she really wasn't comfortable with the idea."

"So the relationship boundaries around here are pretty rigid then?" Justin inquired.

"Yeah!" Janet was firm.

"In that case, I would be happy to go with you," Justin said. "Joelle made the arrangements sound pretty relaxed – but I guess they are not."

"Not so that you would notice!" Janet sounded amused. "Some people think who you take to the functions is a big deal."

"Hmm," Justin sounded thoughtful.

"Call for me at the girl's dormitory on Saturday, around five-thirty," Janet instructed.

Garry's team also played strongly, leading several people to comment they really ought to be in the A grade. At the end of the match, Garry and Vincent came across to the bench to be congratulated on their win. Garry walked Stephanie across to the girl's dormitory as usual, and Vincent asked whether he could escort Elisabet.

The quartet left the rest of the spectators talking in the gymnasium and walked back across campus in the gathering dark. Garry kissed Stephanie goodnight, while Vincent said goodbye to Elisabet more politely and formally.

Tuesday in class, Tom seemed much happier, remarking that it had 'worked out' so that he could go to the Reverse Tea with Joelle after all. Moreover, he remarked Justin seemed to have found his own feet, and wasn't hanging around with the couple all the time, which was giving them some long-awaited privacy. The privacy was welcome to Tom at least. He wasn't quite sure about Joelle, who seemed to have relished the distraction at times.

Wednesday a mild scandal broke out across campus, because Craig and Mathew had both decided to go to the Reverse Tea dateless, and put their names down next to each other on the seating plan. The gossip had spread because there was a new bunch of hospitality students catering for the function, and their friend Damaris, who used to help the students manage these things discretely, had left to take other employment in Brisbane, along with her husband Michael.

"They used to say that Craig was gay," Lacey exclaimed at the lunch table. "I didn't believe them, but now he and another guy are on a date."

Elisabet remembered Craig telling her that he had no intention of coming out as gay. She shook her head.

"I don't think so," she said. "The guys are going as friends."

"I think it's shocking," Cara observed. "Two girls go to a function together and they are being 'liberated' - two guys support each other, and everyone abuses them."

"The prejudice in the dorms is quite strong," Terence, who organized the men's basketball, added. "I remember last year, two male team captains hugged, and they got harassed over it, even though both had girlfriends."

"I'm sorry I said anything," Lacey admitted. "It really isn't any of our business."

"I expect Craig is trying to join in more socially, in preparation for the launch of our band," Elisabet ventured. "That is going to be exciting."

"Have you guys really started a band?" Lacey asked in excitement. "Tell us about it!"

"It is partly to fulfill course requirements," Elisabet stammered. "And partly because Craig has been composing original songs. Really great original songs – or at least I think so."

"When will you play for us?" Janet was curious.

"We have to play the pieces for the staff first to get approval," Elisabet explained. "But soon after that. Maybe at the next campus social event."

Thursday was raining heavily, as was normal for a semi-tropical climate in March. Elisabet caught up with James during the evening meal to make sure he had something to wear to the Reverse Tea. This year's function was themed around St. Patrick's Day. It wasn't strictly a costume event, as previous years had been, but was formal, with something green added.

James said that he would look through his wardrobe for a green shirt, and get back to her during music class on Friday. The next day James confirmed that he had found a green handkerchief, which his mother had packed. It was new and clean, straight out of the package, and he intended to fold it and display it from his suit pocket.

"That will look great," Eisabet said. Unlike some girls, she did not care much for costume events. She expected James would be smart in his suit.

For her part, she had many pretty dresses from which to choose. "Pick me up at the girl's dorm just before six!"

James smiled his cheeky, semi-shy country town smile. "I dunno – I've never picked a girl up from reception before. Perhaps I should take you to vespers as well for practice."

Elisabet shrugged. "Oh well, if you like. We will sit with my friends though."

"I like your friends," James agreed. "Especially the blokes!"

So James escorted Elisabet to vespers, and the student body caught sight of them as a two-some for the first time. There were a few good natured comments about 'a fourth year and a first year together', but most people seemed accepting.

Elisabet knew that she would have to be careful not to be seen with any one guy too regularly or they would be deemed a couple. Then she would lose her freedom to search for that special someone she believed was just around the corner of her life. Still it was an acceptable tradition to hang out as 'friends' before and after a function attended together.

CHAPTER THREE: LAUNCHING THE BAND

Saturday morning, Andrew's girlfriend Kathy arrived on campus. Kathy was a primary school teacher, and explained she had to work Friday afternoon. By the time she was free to leave Dalby it was raining heavily, and the three hour drive looked dismal. So she had waited until morning. This involved getting up early, which Elisabet and Stephanie both knew Kathy hated.

Kathy had elected to stay in the dorms with Stephanie and Elisabet. This meant they had to place a mattress down on the bedroom floor, but it was worth it to spend time with a friend. After settling Kathy into the dormitory, the girls went across to the cafeteria, where Andrew joined them for lunch. After the meal, Elisabet attended a short band practice in the Music Department, before going back to the dormitory to dress for the Reverse Tea.

The March evening was warm, and while the humidity was high, it was not raining. Elisabet had a dress with puffy sleeves, a tight bodice and a full skirt. It was a fashionable hot pink taffeta, and reminded her of something Princess Diana had worn. Her touch of green was a diamanté broach studded with green crystals.

Kathy had a sophisticated black dress, which was straight, but featured a deep V-neck ruffled with gold fabric. The primary teacher hadn't known she was meant to wear something green, so she had arrived with nothing. The green paper bows tacked onto the top of her shoes had been Stephanie's clever innovation.

Stephanie had sewn her own dress during the summer holidays. It was brown, which Stephanie declared was 'the new black', and featured a scoop neckline. The dress would have hung loosely on Stephanie's slim figure, except that she had created a series of eyelets and laces with which to fit it to her form. When she had heard the requirement that they wear something green, the clever girl had simply removed the brown lacing and replaced it with green cord.

"You all look lovely," Garry exclaimed when he had Stephanie called down to reception. He took Stephanie by the hand and gave her a kiss. "My woodland babe!"

Andrew hugged Kathy as if he had not seen her for hours, instead of about forty-five minutes. "Oh how I missed you!" he exclaimed. "Kathy you must never leave me again."

"I cannot match those greetings," James said uncomfortably, comparing himself to the two established boyfriends. "You do look nice though, Elisabet!"

"That will do just fine, thank you James," Elisabet said. "I understand it is our first event."

"My first ever time escorting a girl to one of these things," James said honestly. "You might have to guide me a little."

The group walked across to the cafeteria, which was decorated with green shamrocks, and even had green tablecloths. Because alcohol was not allowed on campus, the drinks were sparkling apple juice. The food was traditional Irish fare, with baked rosemary potatoes and home-made soda bread.

Some people found the cabbage pies quite strange, and a few people complained when they found that the main course was Irish stew, in a choice of either meat or vegetable options. Stephanie, however, asserted that she "loved" stew, and Elisabet also found it quite tasty. Desert was an apple and blackberry cake, served with cream and ice-cream.

The meal over, there were a few silly jokes, a couple of indoor games, and then the evening was officially finished. James walked Elisabet back to the girl's dormitory and steered her well away from the other canoodling couples.

"What happens now?" he asked.

"I don't kiss on the first date," Elisabet replied, slightly puzzled.

James flushed so red Elisabet could almost see it in the dark. "Neither do I," he said. "That's not what I meant."

"I see," Elisabet said slowly. She thought the blush was cute, and reflected that James was newer to campus life than she was. "We have music together and we are in the band together. We will see a lot of each other, and I would like it if we were good friends."

"The old 'let's just be friends' line eh?" James joked.

It was Elisabet's turn to flush. "Most times when people say that – I suspect they do not really mean it. I do. I asked you to a function because I genuinely wanted to deepen our acquaintance."

"What do friends do?" James asked.

"Hang out, talk, occasionally go out again," Elisabet was struggling to define friendship. "They don't hurt each other, or get angry if the other dates someone else."

"I think you mean 'mates'," James said.

"Except in Aussie parlance, 'mates' are usually blokes," Elisabet agreed.

"I can do that," James said. "I just needed to know the expectations, being new here and all." The first year reached out and gave her hug. It was an awkward gesture, as if he were more used to shaking hands, but felt that didn't fit the situation. "Have a good night."

"You too," Elisabet said. She climbed up the stairs to her room, where she was shortly joined by Stephanie and Kathy, who had both been forced inside by the electronic security system that locked all the doors on the girls' dormitory at eleven.

Sunday morning the three girls woke earlier than they expected. It was something to do with having Kathy sleeping on the floor, where they had to be careful not to fall over her. After ascertaining that they were all awake, and none were in danger of falling back to sleep, Stephanie decided that it was time for girl-talk.

"How have you been enjoying your job, Kathy?" Stephanie asked.

"It's okay I guess," Kathy murmured.

"Only okay?" Elisabet inquired.

"Well," Kathy said. "I like the children – but I am up to all hours preparing lesson materials. Past midnight every night. And I asked for Queensland because I thought I might get something near here. But Dalby is three hours from Andrew, and even further from my parents. I am very lonely."

"That's no good Kathy," Stephanie said. "But they do say the first year is the worst. Won't things get easier later?"

"I don't see how," Kathy murmured. "You might be able to use a few resources again, but every class is different – even at the same level. And the curriculum changes year by year."

"Would it be better if you got work nearer Andrew or your parents?" Elisabet asked.

"It would be better," Kathy said. "I've heard that something is coming up in Murwillumbah in July. But I didn't know if I ought to leave my first job so soon."

"It can't hurt to just apply," Stephanie said quietly.

"Of course not," Elisabet said. "And if you get it – see how you feel."

"I might do that," Kathy said. "But enough about me. What is new around here?"

"Tom keeps trying to ask me out," Elisabet said. It somehow just popped out, and she immediately wanted to kick herself.

"Joelle's Tom?" Kathy responded, puzzled. "I saw them together last night."

"They are having problems," Stephanie explained. "Joelle gives Tom very little attention; and this semester she has been dragging some guy she met in Britain around after her."

The girl kept talking, adding all the details she knew.

"Well, I dunno," Kathy said finally. "As someone who is not here all the time anymore, it sounds to me as though other people are propping Tom and Joelle's relationship up."

"That is something Dylan or Garry would say," Stephanie admitted. "They told us to stay out of it!"

"I can't ignore Tom in class," Elisabet said. "It would be rude."

"Of course," Kathy agreed.

"I thought you would be on Joelle's side," Elisabet was surprised.

"I would be if I thought she was in the right," Kathy said. "But it sounds to me as though Joelle is trying to have her cake and eat it too. A career, guys she fancies, and poor faithful Tom on the side."

"You didn't like it when Owen demanded you quit your course," Stephanie observed.

"Well that was a basic qualification, which I think everyone has a right to get," Kathy said. "There are levels beyond that, where I think we have a choice. Like me with Dalby or Murwillumbah."

"Do you want to go out with Tom?" Stephanie asked curiously.

"I don't know," Elisabet said. "I haven't thought about it since first year. He has been 'Joelle's Tom' ever since second year."

"Why are you single really?" Kathy asked. "I know at least six guys ask you out every year?"

"Maybe more than that!" Elisabet smiled. "I guess I'm waiting for someone special. I'm still young."

"Same age as us!" Stephanie observed.

"Some people marry straight out of high school," Kathy shivered. "That wasn't for me."

"I don't think it matters when you meet the right person," Stephanie added. "Although my first choice was probably pretty clueless!"

"Yeah, I think you are lucky you didn't end up with Jeff," Kathy said. "Both Brad and Garry have been good for you though."

"Oh for sure," Stephanie agreed.

"You need to take care though Elisabet," Kathy observed. "You could let that someone special pass you by if you are too fussy."

"I'm not planning to let that happen," Elisabet laughed.

"You know, once I thought there was no one I wanted to date – so I let the algorithm pick for me at the Computer Tea," Kathy admitted. "And do you know who the machine picked?"

"Andrew," Stephanie said with a grin. It was a longstanding joke in the group that the computer had matched Kathy and Andrew.

"Well let's see what the computer has in store for me then," Elisabet murmured.

Eventually the girls decided to get up, shower and dress in their best clothes before going to the cafeteria. A number of people who knew Kathy from previous years stopped to say, "Hello," and then the group went onto the Inter-denominational praise service.

Kathy's boyfriend Andrew was a keen church participant, so they also attended the Reform Church service. After that, they enjoyed a leisurely lunch in the cafeteria. Kathy and Andrew went for a short drive in Kathy's car to spend some precious time alone together, and then Kathy commenced the trek back to Dalby.

Andrew came into the cafeteria at tea time looking glum. He bemoaned the fact that Kathy had left already, because she had school to teach the next day.

"She only spent one night," he groaned. "She couldn't even stay the whole weekend."

"It was good to see her though," Stephanie said.

"She really needs your support," Elisabet added. "Really, really!"

"I know," Andrew said. "But with my studies – and lacking a vehicle of my own – what can I do?"

"Consult a bus timetable?" Stephanie suggested somewhat flippantly. "I don't know what the buses are like between here and Dalby…"

"I would miss worship here," Andrew said. "And as a theology student, I am judged by my participation."

"If you did something at her church maybe?" Cara suggested. "As a fourth year, you are allowed to preach in the community."

"That is a brilliant idea," Andrew exclaimed. "Why didn't I think of it?"

"You were too embedded in the situation perhaps," Stephanie observed.

"We will miss you on the weekends," Elisabet murmured. Andrew's situation was different than hers, as he was in an off-campus relationship, but sometimes the fact that neither he nor she had regular partners made the numbers in the group more even.

Monday lunch time Craig gathered Elisabet, Vincent and James together and organized an extra practice session. The staff luncheon was scheduled for the Friday, and it would take a lot of work to be ready by then. Craig was confident that they could do it, as with the exception of Vincent, all the members were part of the university music course.

Tuesday in English, Elisabet tried to relax when Tom slid into the seat beside her. She remembered the conversation with Kathy, and Kathy's assessment it wasn't really Tom attempting to two-time Joelle, but Joelle trying to have her little bit on the side. Still, Elisabet wasn't sure that Tom was dealing with the situation in as straightforward a manner as he ought.

"How are you?" he asked.

"I'm good," Elisabet said. "How are you and Joelle?"

"Both well so far as I can tell," Tom said. "Did you have a nice time at the Reverse Tea with your date – what was his name – James?"

"Actually I did," Elisabet said. "It was great that you finally got to take Joelle."

"Yes," Tom said. "That sorted itself out in the end!"

"But for how long?" Elisabet murmured.

"I beg your pardon?" Tom exclaimed.

"I mean, I sometimes wonder whether you ought to assert yourself a little more with Joelle," Elisabet said.

"I'm afraid that if I do that – I could lose her," Tom admitted.

"It's not good to be frightened," Elisabet said.

"No, it's not," Tom agreed.

Elisabet was going to give Tom a pep-talk about having confidence in himself; but just then, Stephanie and Phoebe, who had been chatting outside in the corridor, entered the room. They sat down next to Tom and Joelle, and the conversation became more general. A few minutes later, the English Professor arrived, and began leading a lively discussion of Shakespeare's *The Winter's Tale.*

Wednesday afternoon, Elisabet had curriculum studies and practice teaching, both compulsory classes that she shared with her roommate, Stephanie. In practice teaching, the focus was on discipline, and in curriculum studies, the focus was on planning. At this stage, they were learning not just to plan single lessons, but design entire units and reference them to the relevant curriculum.

After classes were over, Stephanie went off to join Garry, along with her other biology classmates, Cara and Dylan. Elisabet hurried straight up to the cafeteria, where she sat at a table with Debbie and David. They exchanged the usual greetings and enquiries about each other's health. Then Debbie remarked on the previous weekend.

"I saw you and Stephanie had Kathy over to stay," Debbie said.

Elisabet nodded. "Well, we had to share her with Andrew."

"Of course," Debbie said. "I said 'hello' briefly, but I barely got to talk to her. How is she doing?"

"Okay I think," Elisabet said. She wasn't authorized to share all Kathy's conversation, although she knew that Debbie and Kathy had been good friends, both having boyfriends who were theology students.

"That's good to hear," Debbie reflected.

"She said some thought provoking things about teaching however," Elisabet ventured.

"In what way?" Debbie said.

"Planning takes a lot of time," Elisabet said.

"I expect it does," Debbie agreed. "I'm seeing that in practice teaching."

"It's made me worried about going out teaching," Elisabet continued.

Debbie was silent for a moment. "Primary teachers are generalists," she mused. "They teach a bit of everything. It's a huge job!"

"Yes," Elisabet nodded.

"High school teachers concentrate on their subjects," Debbie said. "I think that might be easier – so long as we can deal with the teenagers."

"I hope you are right," Eisabet said.

The girls finished their lunches and both hurried away to complete their afternoon activities. Elisabet had reading to complete for several subjects, and needed to practice the keyboard for her music studies. After that, it was time to go to tea, and finally attend the evening dormitory meeting.

Thursday afternoon, Craig called for another band practice. It was their last opportunity to add polish and coordination before playing for the staff luncheon. They also had to organize practical things like how the drum kit would be transferred across to the venue that the staff were using for lunch.

"By the way," Craig said when they had finished practice, "We need to choose a name. Something to introduce ourselves by tomorrow, and Elisabet can put in that newsletter she types up for the Student Service Office."

"Good idea," James said.

"Rock of Ages," Vincent suggested promptly.

"I suspect that has been taken," Craig said with a laugh.

"Personally I like 'Gifts of Grace'," Elisabet said dreamily, harking back to Larry's sermon a week or so ago.

"And what if we are not playing spiritual songs in that particular performance?" Vincent asked.

"We are still using our gifts," Elisabet asserted.

"I kinda like it," Craig said. "Short of using our initials, I can't think of a better name."

Vincent and James actually liked the idea of using a combination of their initials, which Craig had suggested so dismissively, and the 'EJCV Band' was born. The members swore a solemn oath not to tell anyone that EJCV really stood for Elisabet, James, Craig and Vincent, and instead adopted a cheeky alternative suggested by James: "*Electronic Jive Classical Vibe Band.*"

"Now that we have selected a name," Craig said, "We can go ahead."

The Music Master was their official staff sponsor, so he was very supportive. The only problem was that because Vincent was not an official part of the music programme, the Music Master said that they would need to take out an insurance policy to cover themselves and the equipment if they ever took the drum kit off campus.

Craig was disappointed because he had hoped to run the band at no cost to the participants, even if it did not make a profit from gigs. However, he said it was a good rule to have insurance, if they were willing to put in twenty dollars each towards a policy. Twenty dollars was a lot for students on allowances, but all were keen and agreed.

Luckily, Elisabet and James' Friday morning music class finished in good time for them to go and set up in the hall. As lunchtime approached, the band members were seated, nervously contemplating their debut performance.

The various fellows of the staff filed in one by one and sat down. There were some speeches and formalities as the staff were congratulated upon commencing another fine year of tuition. Then the Theology Lecturer gave thanks and asked for a blessing on the food.

Craig nodded at the band members and Elisabet began to play the keyboard quietly. The piece was an acoustic background tune Craig had composed. It was designed to be pleasant and fill in time. The melody was light and agreeable, although it was not Craig's most sophisticated.

After the first item, the Music Master stood and addressed the other members of staff. "I am very proud," he began, "To introduce four dedicated students who have created their own band. This takes a great deal of talent, teamwork and initiative."

Several members of staff, including the English Professor and the Chemistry Doctor, clapped appreciatively. Ms. Louise, the Art Lecturer, also applauded gently. The Uniting Church Chaplain smiled encouragingly and added his tapping fingers to the ovation.

Then the Theology Lecturer leaned forward thoughtfully. "Is it Christian band?" he asked.

"It is a Christian band," the Music Master explained. "Because it is composed of Christian artists. Some of their pieces will be religious, while others will be purely artistic."

"They sound a bit rocky," the Reform Church Chaplain complained.

"I believe they are technically a blues band," the Music Master said. "With a touch of acoustic, soul and jazz."

"I heard rock and roll," the Reform Church Chaplain insisted stubbornly. "But I'm prepared to be liberal."

"Do they sing?" Ms. Louise inquired.

Craig put his violin down and picked up the microphone. "This is for you, Ms. Louise," he announced. "It's about creation… but it doesn't push the issue, so it is perfect for sharing with any audience." Craig's voice had a liquid charm, and his words about walking together through the beauties of the Queensland rainforest were perfectly respectful.

Most of the staff were smiling. "That's the boy who sung in *Handel's Messiah* a couple of years ago," someone whispered.

"Do you write the lyrics yourself?" the English Professor asked curiously after Craig had finished.

"I do," Craig admitted. "This one is a little different… it is about the pain caused by sin."

"Ooh," some staff gasped.

Craig launched into an innocent sounding song about a lamb who wandered from his mother's side. A few people smiled, as Craig sung about the lamb skipping through the field. They were expecting Craig to follow the story of the 'Good Shepherd' and have the farmer rescue the lamb. He did eventually, but not until the lamb had suffered some tribulations. When Craig had finished, several female members of the staff were wiping their eyes.

"We know the students like a bit of fun," Craig announced. He nodded to his musicians and they began a rhythmic folksy tune. "I must acknowledge I owe this to the amazing artist, Woody Guthrie." He launched into a version of *'This Land was Made for You and Me'* with the lyrics adapted to suit the Australian landscape.

"Very pleasant," the Uniting Church Chaplain mused.

"Where are you aiming with this project, boy?" The Chancellor asked.

"I want to show that Christians can form a band, and succeed without the debauchery, drugs and other abuses associated with the commercial music industry," Craig answered cleverly.

"Admirable," The Chancellor acknowledged. "And the Music Master tells me that several of your members will be using it as a component of their courses."

"Yes, sir," Craig affirmed.

"You have our approval, conditional to your following the guidance of the Music Master," The Chancellor conceded.

"Thank you, sir!" Craig said. He picked his violin up once again and nodded to the band. They played several more background pieces while the staff finished their lunch.

When they finally finished playing, Elisabet found that she was trembling from released tension. She folded up her sheet music, and picked the folio up to take with her.

The staff had not finished eating, so the band members crept out of the side door. They hurried up to the cafeteria, where the last of the student lunch was being served. Elisabet could hardly concentrate on food, but she forced herself to eat some of the lasagna, which was really good after all.

After they had eaten their lunch, Craig announced that they needed to go back and collect the drum kit, keyboard and speaker set-up. Elisabet was surprised when Tom stood up to accompany them.

"What is he doing?" she whispered to Craig.

"Oh," Craig said. "Tom was hanging around the Music Department waiting for Joelle, so I asked him to be our roadie."

"Why can't he be Joelle's roadie?" Elisabet asked.

"Perhaps because Joelle does not carry a piano or organ around with her all the time," Craig responded logically. "She plays instruments that are permanently installed in the venues."

"Oh okay," Elisabet muttered. "It's just – I wouldn't have asked him – for personal reasons. "

"I asked Tom," Craig replied sternly. "So it is my responsibility."

Elisabet felt mildly rebuked. She reminded herself that Kathy had said she did not believe Tom was the villain in the situation he faced with Joelle, and discretely concentrated on doing her share of helping pack the gear up. The equipment was valuable, so the boys carried it between them carefully.

Elisabet wound up the cords and stowed the microphones away sensibly. When the gear had been safely stowed away, James left to join his first year friends. Elisabet turned to leave the Music Department as well, but was waylaid by Vincent.

"It's good that we got the approval, isn't it?" the Drummer remarked in a conversational tone.

"It's great," Elisabet said.

"Do you think that you and James will be going out again?" Vincent asked, as James was well out of earshot.

"Probably not," Elisabet said. "We are just good friends."

"Would you like me to walk you back to the dormitory?" Vincent offered.

Elisabet was going to say that was not necessary, when she realised that having Vincent walk her back to the dormitory would save her from any risk of Tom offering to do so, which would be awkward, even if Tom was heading that way to pick Joelle up. "Thanks."

They waved goodbye to Craig and Tom, and then Vincent walked Elisabet back to the girls' dormitory. The girl was surprised to find that she really did enjoy his conversation. He was one of the few sporty types that could also relate to the fine arts. And with his return to basketball, the third year's social stock was rising around campus.

When they reached the foyer, Vincent turned to face Elisabet: "Say," he began. "You went to the Reverse Tea with James – why don't you go to the next campus function with me? The Student Service Office has organized a screening of *Cleopatra* for Saturday night."

"Fine," Elisabet agreed. "Pick me up fifteen minutes before the movie is due to commence." She reflected it would be pleasant not to be the odd single in their group. Andrew had taken the hint and booked himself a bus ticket to Dalby to see Kathy. He had probably already left campus for the weekend.

"I'll see you then," Vincent looked pleased. He walked off towards the men's dormitory and Elisabet hurried inside girls' dorm. It was turning out to be an eventful day. She still had readings and assignments to complete, so that her Saturday could be relatively free. She skipped through the corridors to her room.

"A date with Vincent is more realistic than a date with James," Stephanie remarked when she heard about Elisabet's weekend plans.

"Why ever would you say that?" Elisabet asked, although she knew she ought not to rise to the jibe.

"Well we've known Vincent two years," Stephanie said. "But James is a first year, and he will have his eye on some first year girl very soon. Mark my words!"

"I don't mind if he does," Elisabet retorted. "Sometimes I think you have forgotten what it is like to be just getting to know someone, Steph."

"I may well have at that," Stephanie admitted. "Garry and I are so delightfully comfortable. Enough! What are you planning to wear?"

"I thought my blue and white striped sweater," Elisabet said. "The evenings are getting cooler."

"Your high-waist jeans make you look very cute – and a bit sporty," Stephanie agreed. "Vincent may like that as he is a basketball player."

That Saturday evening, Vincent picked Elisabet up from the girl's dormitory and behaved like the perfect gentleman. He did not even try to slide his arm along the back of their seats. *Cleopatra* starred Elizabeth Taylor and Richard Burton. It was a delightful production from the golden age of Hollywood, where the producers spent money on lavish costumers and a cast of thousands. It wasn't a Biblical story, but it was historical, so the university had considered it appropriate to screen.

"Pretty fancy, eh?" Vincent commented. "They really knew how to make a movie in those days!"

"Why is it all the best love stories end badly?" Elisabet sighed, wiping a tear from her eye. "They both died."

"I guess it's more dramatic than 'happily ever after'," Vincent presumed. "But in real life, I could do with a bit less betrayal!"

"Sure," Elisabet said. "So could I!"

Vincent then offered to walk Elisabet back to the girls' dormitory. Half way across campus, they passed Joelle, who was walking along with a group of theology students, including Mathew and Christopher, who were Vincent's classmates.

The third years recognized Vincent and said, "Hello", but Elisabet thought that Joelle turned her head away in an effort not to be recognized.

"Wherever is Tom?" Elisabet whispered to Vincent after they had passed.

"I think I heard around the dorms that he was sick today," Vincent observed.

"Come to think of it – I didn't see him anywhere at tea," Elisabet said. "But Joelle ought not to be out with a bunch of other guys."

"Mathew and Christopher are on the worship committee this year," Vincent said. "It could all be very innocent. Forget them – we had fun didn't we?"

"Oh yes!" Elisabet agreed.

The movie had been long, and when they arrived at girls' dorm, the security door was held open by a brick, to prevent that the electronic locking system automatically activating.

Vincent turned to face Elisabet at the door. "I can't come any further," he remarked.

Elisabet giggled. "Of course not!"

"I'm going to save you giving me 'the big speech' by doing it myself," Vincent said. "Let's not risk creating any relationship dramas while we are in the band together."

"Very wise," Elisabet said. Truth to tell, she was a little surprised. She had thought Vincent might be looking for a relationship, but taking it very slowly.

"I wanted a fun night with some pleasant company," Vincent explained. "I don't need to take it any further at this stage."

"Well thanks again for asking me," Elisabet said. "I had fun too!"

As Elisabet climbed the stairs to go to bed, part of her mind was occupied by a niggling feeling something was wrong. Lately, guys were backing off from her, rather than the other way around. First James, then Vincent. She couldn't help asking herself what had diminished her usual charisma?

CHAPTER FOUR: A Second Gig

Elisabet woke up late on Sunday morning to discover that Stephanie had already been to breakfast in the cafeteria, and was preparing to go to the Inter-denominational praise service with Garry. Sometimes Stephanie could be frustratingly energetic, although she wasn't as bad as Cara, who was a sportswoman all the way.

The older girl rolled over in bed and groaned. "How can you be so cheery?"

"I can never sleep in," Stephanie replied with cheery disregard for the exact truth, as she might occasionally sleep past eight am during the holidays.

"*Cleopatra* sure was a long movie," Elisabet murmured.

"Did you have a good time with Vincent?" Stephanie asked curiously.

"Nice enough," Elisabet yawned. Her room-mate might have had a couple of serious boyfriends, but the younger girl was still naïve in some ways. And despite Stephanie being settled in a permanent relationship, Elisabet was the more assured of the two. "A movie is what you make of it. In this case – it was a casual event."

"Well Garry is outside waiting for me!" Stephanie announced, and gathered up her purse and keys.

"You look very smart," Elisabet murmured, and indeed, Stephanie did. The brunette was wearing one of her own designs, figure fitting with a ruched line down the centre front. The dress was a shiny copper fabric that was most unusual.

"Thanks," Stephanie said.

The room-mate left the bedchamber and Elisabet pulled herself out of bed more slowly. After a leisurely shower, she made her way across to the cafeteria to scrounge something for breakfast. Then she made her way more sedately to attend the Reform Church service, which was generally less exciting than the praise service, but offered at a more comfortable hour.

Justin was the speaker at the Reform Church service, and Elisabet had to admit that she was impressed by his eloquence. She could almost understand Joelle fancying the young man, even though the musician had a perfectly steadfast boyfriend in Tom.

After the service finished, Elisabet noticed that Joelle lingered beside the organ until Tom arrived to collect her, and walk her across to lunch. Her backwards glance showed that she had hoped Justin would accompany them. Justin however, had ideas of his own, hailing Janet, whom he had taken to the Reverse Tea and remained 'good friends' with ever since.

Elisabet joined Debbie and David on their way across to the cafeteria. Hank and Phoebe were also on campus for the service and had decided to eat at the cafeteria, although because they did not live on campus, they had to stop and pay at the door. Stephanie and Garry arrived with Dylan and Cara and they all sat down to enjoy an amiable meal.

Later that afternoon, Andrew arrived back from Dalby. The fourth year students clustered around, curious to hear how his trip to see Kathy had gone. Half a dozen people addressed questions to him at once.

"We had a nice visit," Andrew replied carefully. His face betrayed a mixture of his natural optimism and tender concern for his girlfriend.

"I'm surprised you didn't stay longer," Stephanie observed.

Andrew shrugged: "There wasn't a lot of choice, and the second bus would have made me very late. I didn't think I could neglect my studies like that. Besides, Kathy had lessons to prepare."

"How is Kathy doing?" Cara asked.

"A little better," Andrew reported. "I am encouraging her to apply for that job in Murwillumbah though. Being closer to her parents could really help."

"It is only one week till the school holidays," Stephanie observed, and Andrew looked pleased.

"Yes, that is a blessing," he said. "A pity our holidays don't coincide with the school ones."

"They never do," Elisabet explained, "It is because of practice teaching. We cannot visit schools during our holidays if they are on break too."

"That doesn't affect us ministerial students as much," David commented. "I guess we have to keep in line though."

"Easter *is* very late this year," Cara added, and the conversation drifted to how the Silver Springs University break had been delayed until the middle of April.

"When I'm lucky I get a holiday for my birthday," Stephanie said, "But Easter isn't until well after this year."

"I don't think I have ever known such a late Easter," Debbie reminisced. "It has pushed first semester all out of shape!"

Monday morning in music, the class was doing voice training, as all instrumental music teachers were also assumed to be able to lead choirs. Jessie, James and Vivien were a little more proficient than Elisabet, because they were music majors. Nevertheless, Elisabet enjoyed the class.

James approached her in the interval with a grin on his face. "I saw you out with Vincent on the weekend," he said.

"Oh yes," Elisabet agreed. "I had already been out with you, so I had to be fair and go out with Vincent."

"I bet you will be going to watch him play basketball tonight," James teased.

"My room-mates' boyfriend is also playing, so I somehow cannot escape the game," Elisabet admitted.

"So you say!" James laughed.

"How are you going with those first year girls?" Elisabet deflected.

"Well enough," James said. "I told you there was more than one that caught my eye?"

"Going out with more than one could make trouble," Elisabet warned, but James shrugged.

"I wouldn't do that if I got serious about anyone," he said.

The rest of the class passed quickly, as the Music Master assigned voice exercises and popular tunes for the students to learn. After lunch, Elisabet spent a couple of hours in the room practicing the piano. She could hear Joelle in the next chamber tinkling away at a much more challenging level, and tried not to consciously stop and listen. It was hard, however, not to envy someone such incredible skill.

As it turned out, back in their room, Stephanie reminded Elisabet of some urgent reading they both had to do for their compulsory education subject. Stephanie, as usual had completed the readings, but Elisabet decided to forego watching basketball that evening to catch up on study.

Tuesday afternoon, Elisabet was working in the Student Services Office. Besides answer the telephone, she had to file documents and type the newsletter. This week, she was delighted because Craig had put in an announcement regarding the *Electronic Jive Classical Vibe Band.*

Seeing the name in print made Elisabet feel so proud, she saved several of the early copies to distribute amongst the band members.

Wednesday for practice teaching, the fourth year students were transported out to the local school to observe lessons. With only two more days left in the first term, some of the lessons involved revision, and a few students were restless. There may have been more discipline issues than usual to observe as the regular teachers struggled valiantly to teach right up until Friday afternoon.

Thursday morning Stephanie and Elisabet both had English, and it was their habit to walk across to the lecture theatre together. Tom saw the girls crossing the lawn and fell into step beside Stephanie, who welcomed him happily. "How are you Tom?"

"I'm fine," Tom said. "What about you girls?"

"I'm good," Stephanie said.

"I am well," Elisabet replied with a little more reserve.

"I have been wondering whether you would join the Year Book committee," Tom ventured. "Some silly professor has put me in charge this year."

Stephanie giggled at Tom's irreverence. "I don't know whether I will have the time – this being my final year and all."

"I have the band," Elisabet was pleased to say.

"I don't expect it will be that demanding," Tom said. "Just a few meetings, looking through photographs and that sort of thing…. One of the computing guys will be doing the layout for the book."

"Hmm," Stephanie said. "I do like creative things… and publishing."

"You would be so useful, Elisabet," Tom begged. "You can type."

"Who told you that?" Elisabet stammered.

"Well that's what you do over at Student Services isn't it?" Tom demanded. "Craig showed me the newsletter."

"You got me there," Elisabet admitted. "But between the band, and Student Services and my studies, I don't know what time I would have."

"I'll take what I can get," Tom said humbly.

Elisabet laughed. "If you put it like that," she conceded.

Friday afternoon, Craig called the *Electronic Jive Classical Vibe Band* together for a practice. His eyes were shining, and he was looking more confident and assertive by the day. Elisabet slid into her place behind the electronic keyboard, and played the pieces that he had placed before her. When James and Vincent arrived, they quietly took their sheet music and began to harmonise with Elisabet.

"You are sounding good guys," Craig said.

Vincent stilled his drums and addressed Craig. "What is this all about mate?" he asked.

"I have got us another gig," Craig announced proudly.

"Swell," James said. "Where is it this time?"

"It is at the Senior Citizen's Club in Northcoast," Craig explained.

Vincent frowned. "I'm not sure that is exactly what we signed on for," he said.

"It is an audience," Craig said. "And some of the seniors are still quite lively!"

"We have to be heard by someone, Vincent," Elisabet said. "This is the citizens club and not the nursing home – isn't it Craig?"

"It is the club, so it counts as a real concert," Craig said. "The mayor of Noosa Shire has been known to drop by on occasion, so it is a real gig, with the chance of more exposure for our group."

"I suppose so," Vincent sounded doubtful.

"I would play at the nursing home if it came to that," Elisabet said. "It would cheer the elderly people up."

"It wouldn't be very exciting, but it would be a worthy cause," James agreed. "After all we are a Christian band."

Craig looked pleased to hear all this. "If you are willing to be flexible, I can get us more gigs," he said.

"All right," Vincent conceded. "It isn't exactly the glory of rock and roll, but I will go wherever you decide."

"You would be surprised at the humble gigs some of our best known bands started off doing," Craig said with satisfaction, and they turned back to practicing.

Craig had introduced one or two popular pieces from earlier in the century, because he believed that they would appeal to the senior citizens. These had been radio hits during the war, and the rhythms were syncopated and tricky. Elisabet enjoyed the challenge, but it took a little coordinating with the other instruments.

That evening, as Elisabet stood in the doorway of the women's assembly area surveying the crowd at vespers, she heard a voice just behind her. It was Justin greeting her in a friendly fashion.

"Oh hello," Elisabet returned casually.

"I'm surprised to see you alone," Justin remarked. "You usually arrive with your friends, or escorted by one of several young men."

"If you mean the boys from the band," Elisabet said, "We are just friends." She pointed to where James was surrounded by a laughing group of first years. "James is moving on already."

"I can see that," Justin said. "And perhaps Vincent too." He pointed towards the front, where Vincent was seated beside Janet. The pair appeared engrossed in earnest conversation.

"But Janet has been hanging out with you!" Elisabet exclaimed.

"Just as a friend," Justin said. "And a good friend at that – she helped me avoid a somewhat unpleasant misunderstanding working up between myself, Tom and Joelle."

"I didn't know you were aware of that," Elisabet murmured.

"I may be new around here, but I'm not stupid," Justin pronounced.

"I didn't think you were," Elisabet demurred. "But Joelle does have a history of liking ministerial students."

"So Larry told me," Justin agreed.

Elisabet sniffed. "I scarcely think that was fair," she observed. "Larry was hardly a disinterested person in that matter."

"It is a couple of years ago from what I hear," Justin concluded equitably. "Although I must say – if Joelle's goals lie in a vastly different direction than Toms'…."

"Tom is so faithful," Elisabet murmured. "But Vincent and Janet – when did that begin?"

Justin laughed. "It seems you missed an eventful night in the gym last Monday. Or maybe even a week full of eventful nights."

"I know that getting back into the basketball scene is important to Vincent," Elisabet said.

"For more reason than one it seems," Justin concluded. "Shall we find ourselves seats?"

Elisabet followed Justin into the women's assembly area, and they settled down near Debbie and David. The programme was lively, and the message was delivered by Kaleb Proctor, whose rousing and eloquent tones revealed his background as an African-American exchange student. Occasionally he glanced towards where his girlfriend Bede O'Brien was sitting with her third year friends.

Saturday, Craig had scheduled another band practice. The senior citizens' gig was scheduled for the coming Wednesday, and there were new pieces to learn, so they would be practicing almost daily in the between time. During practice, Elisabet quizzed Vincent gently about his relationship with Janet.

Vincent blushed. "I didn't think she would look my way after last year," he admitted. "But when I went to the movie with you – she seemed a little concerned."

"Concerned?" Elisabet asked.

"Worried that I might be taken," Vincent admitted. "Like you – she had been very supportive."

"I'm glad I was able to help you make Janet jealous," Elisabet observed dryly.

"It wasn't like that," Vincent said. "I was glad to get out there and socialise with you. But I never used you. Janet showing an interest came later. It was a bonus."

"It sure was!" Elisabet exclaimed. "I always thought – maybe Janet and Terence?"

"I think Terence fancies you actually," Vincent said. "He said something about your coming down and watching the basketball."

"What sort of something?" Elisabet was mildly curious. Terrance was an A grade basketball captain and something of a good catch, even if he was a third year.

"He noticed you hadn't been down last week," Vincent said.

"I had study," Elisabet said. "Between band practices and now Year Book – I hardly have time to fit everything."

"The Year Book?" Vincent was surprised.

"Tom asked Stephanie and me to help," Elisabet explained.

"Ah – Tom – our roadie," Vincent sounded as though he could say more, but he didn't.

Just then Craig, who had been coaching James on his trumpet harmony; called Elisabet and Vincent back into the general practice. They ran through the musical pieces several more times before Craig declared them finished for the day, and dismissed the band.

That evening, Elisabet went down to the recreation area, where she watched an evening television show, and then played pool with James and his first year friends. There were several girls James seemed very friendly towards, but Elisabet was unable to determine which he preferred. At the end of the evening, she went back to the girl's dormitory relaxed and happy.

Sunday morning, Elisabet woke up in time to go to the cafeteria for an early breakfast with Stephanie and Garry, Cara and Dylan. Then she attended the Inter-denominational praise service, which was always full of stimulating singing.

After the praise service, her friends invited Elisabet to go for a walk instead of attending the Reform Church service. They were joined by Craig, who had played his violin at the praise service, and was not involved in the second service. Tom was also at a loose end, because Joelle was busy playing the organ for both services.

The students walked down University Drive, towards the small settlement of Silver Springs, which was usually very quiet on a Sunday. Having time up their sleeves, they turned the corner and continued on towards the service station. When they reached the service station, they discovered that they were not alone, but had been spotted by some local Northcoast louts.

"Hey Christian fag---," called one of the louts.

"Just ignore them," advised Garry, stepping protectively closer to

Stephanie.

Dylan strode ahead, determined to pass the service station, where they could discretely loop around and return to campus using a back track. He had a sturdy arm around Cara and was steering her along with him. Elisabet skipped a few steps in order to keep up.

"Don't run," Stephanie whispered. "They will think we are frightened."

"I'm speaking to you f--s," the lout said more insistently.

The gang members were looking at Tom and Craig who had fallen behind, deep in conversation because they had developed a good friendship over the years Tom had been going out with Joelle. Tom was tall and blonde, and very good-looking in a shaggy haired surfy sort of way. Craig was also very tall, but of a lighter build, with medium brown hair and a less assertive stance. He normally dressed pretty much like everyone else, but unfortunately was wearing a burgundy cardigan that afternoon. It was the casual alternative to a suit coat, but did make him stand out from the group.

"I see you wearing pink," another gang member jeered.

Burgundy was not pink, and could be crisp and masculine, especially when paired with navy and white, but the harm was done. Homophobic jests followed the students up the path.

"We are not going to stop and fight," Garry observed grimly, but he slowed his stride a little to allow Tom and Craig to catch up. The group closed ranks and marched straight ahead until they were out of sight and sound of the local louts. They had almost made it to safety when Craig exclaimed sharply.

"Ouch," the Band Leader said. He was rubbing the back of his neck, which had been struck by a clod of dirt. Grains of muddy sand had spread across his back.

"Lucky it wasn't a stone," Tom said.

"Yeah!" Elisabet gasped. The students all knew the story of David and Goliath, which was in the Bible. A stone thrown hard enough and with sufficient accuracy could kill.

"We won't go out wearing our Sunday best another time," Garry observed grimly. "It marks us as students."

"It shouldn't matter what we are," Dylan growled.

"In an ideal world of course," Stephanie added. "But the world is far from ideal."

The incident left an unpleasant taste in their mouths, and they walked back to the main campus in a more sober mood than the one in which they had left. Elisabet dropped back to fall into step with Craig and offered him her support. It was horrible to think that the harassment had been directed primarily at him. Moreover, she sincerely hoped that it would not make the young man too nervous to perform at their upcoming gig.

Monday Elisabet and Stephanie had an education test to mark the middle of the semester. After lunch Elisabet went to band practice, and was pleased to see that Craig appeared to be able to function as normal. If anything, he was a bit more precise and exacting about their performance. There was no escaping the fact that he could be a perfectionist, but she had to admit that her skills were developing at a great rate under his mentorship.

In the evening, Elisabet visited the gymnasium briefly, just long enough to see Garry and Vincent play their basketball matches. Terrance was present as one of the organisers, and he greeted her pleasantly.

"Hey Elisabet, it's nice to see you. We missed you last week!" he said.

"I've been busy," Elisabet replied and sat down beside Stephanie, who was present to cheer Garry on. "Have I missed anything?"

"They are just about to start," Stephanie confirmed.

The game that evening was unremarkable. Vincent and Garry both put in solid performances, and their team won by a small margin. Every win put them one step up the ladder, and closer to the finals, so the boys were very pleased.

After the match, Terence suggested that they drop by the campus canteen for celebratory soft drinks and junk food. Elisabet agreed to join the group, and she noticed that Vincent and Janet had progressed to the stage of holding hands, which was generally considered a public declaration of commitment around Silver Springs campus.

Tuesday morning, the Health Lecturer announced that the following week would bring a test. This caused Elisabet some anxiety. Her room-mate Stephanie was cruising through health, because much of the material was similar to that of her minor specialty, biology. However, the scientific focus of the subject was foreign to Elisabet, who had always had a strong arts and literature focus. Stephanie promised to share some revision time with her, which cheered Elisabet immensely.

After lunch, she had to perform her duties in the Student Services Office, and in the evening, the *Electronic Jive Classical Vibe Band* had their final practice before the scheduled gig at the senior citizens. Elisabet ventured to ask Craig how he was going after the cruel incident on the weekend and he shrugged it off, observing that it was highly unlikely the service station loiterers would be at the senior citizens club.

"It is important to know where you are appreciated," Craig said. "At a gig – we are the stars, and we cannot go wrong."

"What if we make a mistake?" Elisabet asked.

"Laugh and move along," Craig advised. "After all these practices, it is unlikely that we will make a huge blunder."

Wednesday was the first of April, also known to many as "April Fools' Day". It was necessary to keep one's wits about, because a few tricks were always played during the morning. Someone had put sugar in the salt shakers in the cafeteria, with the result that a few students almost sweetened their eggs instead of salting them. Luckily, the sugar granules barely fitted through the fine holes in the salt shaker, and little harm was done. Someone else had placed a detour sign on the lawn, and some students found themselves taking an unnecessarily circuitous route to their lectures. After that, things quietened down, because the staff would countenance no interruption to classes.

After lunch, Tom and Luke met the band members at the Music Department, and helped them load all the equipment into the mini-bus. Then Luke drove them towards the Northcoast Senior Citizen's Club. Luke helped unload the bus, and then drove away. Tom remained to help set-up in the main function area. He was getting quite knowledgeable about all the cords and plugs; and even somewhat clever with the mixer.

The band had just finished setting up when the senior citizens began to arrive. They appeared to be a friendly bunch of men and women aged between sixty and eighty years old. A few needed walking frames, and one was in a wheel chair, accompanied by their carer. All expressed a love of music, and eagerness to hear what the *Electronic Jive Classical Vibe Band* had prepared for them.

The band commenced with some honky-tonk and an Andrew's Sisters number to warm the audience, then presented one of Craig's personal compositions. Elisabet had been mildly concerned that they might be wasting their talents, but the seniors proved most discerning.

After the concert finished, the organisers invited the band members to have a cup of tea and biscuits with the seniors. Elisabet found herself talking to a nice lady who reminded her somewhat of her own great-grandmother.

Craig proved to be a real hit with the older people, who praised him for being so 'refined' and so 'talented'. The men had loved James' trumpet selection, which reminded some of them of their marching band days. Vincent received the least praise, although everyone acknowledged that any real band needed a drummer.

Tom maintained a fairly quiet profile during the concert. He was doubling as sound technician, as well as roadie, and this kept him very busy. While the band members were socialising with the older people, Tom, together with Luke who arrived back on schedule, packed most of the equipment into the bus.

Elisabet was almost sorry when it was time to leave the senior citizens club and travel back to the university. She was feeling so mellow that she forgot her reservations about Tom, and sat next to him on the bus during the return trip, chatting merrily.

Thursday at lunch, Andrew Grosvy was all smiles, explaining that he had heard from Kathy, who was spending the school holidays at her parents' home in Armidale.

"Kathy sounds much happier," Andrew said.

"I'm pleased to hear that," Stephanie enthused, and Elisabet added her best wishes.

"She has also put her application in for that job in Murwillumbah," Andrew said. "From what she has heard so far, she thinks she has a good chance."

"Oh I hope she gets it," Cara cried. "It would be so much better for her!"

"That remains to be seen," Andrew concluded. "Her only concern has been that it means two different jobs in six months."

"That does sound like a challenge," Garry observed. "But the right job could prove to be so much better and easier than the wrong job."

Friday afternoon, Elisabet took her health text book to the library and settled down to study alone. Stephanie had promised to join her later, but the roommate worked as cleaner of the women's assembly area. She took great pride in having the venue spotless before the combined meetings on the weekend.

After a while, Elisabet noticed that she was not far from Justin, who was surrounded by a large number of theological tomes. As a postgraduate, Justin was expected to do a great deal of research, and his timetable was different from the undergraduates.

The girl edged her books slightly closer to where Justin was sitting. "Hello," she said. "I hadn't seen you sitting there."

Justin smiled an amiable smile. "Likewise," he said. "I was absorbed in my reading."

"I have been wondering something," Elisabet said. "I thought that because you are already a fully qualified minister you might have an opinion on something."

"Sure – what is it?" Justin inquired.

"Elisabet blushed: "What does the Bible really say about being gay?"

"The Bible doesn't encourage any sort of promiscuity," Justin said. "You know the ten commandments."

"Oh yes," Elisabet said. "But to me 'adultery' implies multiple partners."

"It generally does," Justin agreed. "What brought this on? Something in that health text?"

"Not exactly," Elisabet admitted. "It's my friend Craig. Last week some creeps threw a clod of dirt at him. They shouldn't have done that!"

"God loves everybody," Justin commented. "John 3:16 tells us that Jesus died to save the whole world. The text doesn't specify any limitations. You can be assured that God loves Craig – no matter what he might be struggling with."

"Isn't that a lazy answer?" Elisabet challenged.

"I don't think so," Justin said. "The Bible is clear we should not make assumptions about things we don't understand. James 4, verse 12: 'There is one Lawgiver, who is able to save and to destroy. Who are you to judge another?' Then there is the difference between inclination and action. Even Jesus was tempted – but he didn't sin."

Justin sighed. "Between you and me – I also have a problem in the dating department this year. If I ask a girl out – I might have to go back to the UK at the end of the year. And it might be too soon to ask a girl to go with me… she would be a long way from her family too."

"Bede is going to the United States with Kaleb," Elisabet said. "She has even won an internship over there to have a career when she goes."

"That is excellent – but not everybody can be so flexible," Justin said. "Or so lucky!"

"So if I asked you to come to a video night at Hank and Phoebe's house Saturday you wouldn't come?" Elisabet joked.

"On the contrary – I would come!" Justin declared.

"Whoa?" Elisabet exclaimed.

"Well, to be invited to your friend's place would be an honour," Justin said. "It's after that things get confusing."

Stephanie arrived at the table just then, and the conversation turned towards less personal matters. In fact, Elisabet was honestly surprised when Justin had her called over the public address system a few hours later in order to go down to vespers together. She decided it felt good though, as Cara and Stephanie, Debbie and Tess, all had steady beaux that escorted them down to the combined services and social events.

Saturday afternoon Elisabet started her small car, which was hesitant after its long stint idle in the car park, and drove Stephanie, Garry, and Justin over to Hank and Phoebes' tiny house. Cara and Dylan arrived just ahead of them, having driven across in Dylan's light Jeep.

Hank had bought the house a little over a year ago, so that he and Phoebe could get married. Phoebe showed them through the building proudly, highlighting the changes she and Hank had made since the wedding.

"This was an enclosed veranda," Phoebe explained to Justin. "Now you can see it is fully walled and lined, making a second bedroom."

"The kitchen is still tiny," Stephanie joked.

"I like it that way," Phoebe asserted. "But you will see, Hank is building a pergola outside so we can enjoy outdoor dining."

"Oh, I love a pergola," Elisabet gushed.

Phoebe's house reminded her of home, and the relaxed, sunny lifestyle of Byron Bay. She had a good relationship with her parents and loved them very much, although neither she nor they were big letter writers.

"What movie are we watching?" asked Cara.

"Crocodile Dundee," Phoebe said with a grin. "It's freshly out on VHS."

"I don't think I have heard of that one," Justin said, looking puzzled.

"It is an Australian production," Elisabet explained. "Starring Paul Hogan. He used to have a funny show called the 'Paul Hogan Show'."

"It has romance for the girls, plus humour and action for the boys," Hank added with a grin.

The group settled down to watch the movie. As hostess, Phoebe had provided oven-popped popcorn, and mixed a punch using pineapple juice and lemonade. Everyone enjoyed the film, including Justin, who occasionally needed the Australian humour explained to him. After the movie was over, the boys fell into conversation, while the girls retreated to the tiny kitchen.

"Justin seems to be getting along well with the other guys," Phoebe observed in a whisper.

"Of course – that is what I date a man for!" Elisabet giggled.

"Seriously," Phoebe countered. "Men are fairly good judges of other men. Justin is looking like one of the best you have considered."

"Except he is going back to England at the end of the year," Elisabet murmured.

"We do worry about you," Stephanie whispered. "You get lots of dates – but no one regular."

"Please don't," Elisabet said. "I've been alright alone – honestly."

"I was a bit like you last year," Cara admitted. "I was only dating Kaleb for fun really… then I realised I was better suited to Dylan."

"And you passed Kaleb to your little sister," Phoebe surmised. "I always wondered how that one came about."

"Bede was very determined to get her man," Cara admitted. "In the end, I didn't mind. There was no way I was going to the United States with Kaleb."

"Would you go back to England with Justin?" Stephanie asked curiously.

"Shush!" Elisabet hissed. "I'm interested, but it's way too soon to think about that."

"You must know whether the country appeals – if not the man," Phoebie mused.

"England seems a long way away from Byron Bay," Elisabet admitted. "And it sounds very cold."

"You would get a 'white Christmas'," Stephanie sighed. "I've always wanted one of those."

Around ten-thirty half the visitors piled into Dylan's Suzuki light jeep; and drove quietly through the backstreets until they reached University Drive. Elisabet followed carefully with Justin in her car. The student parking lot was situated just before the check point, so both cars stopped, then the students all piled out and walked the final distance to the dormitories.

By the time the girls reached their dormitory, the automatic door had locked, and they had to use their swipe cards to get through the security system. This would alert the deans, but all the girls had filled out appropriate leave forms, claiming that they would be under the chaperonage of a married couple.

CHAPTER FIVE: ALL MY FRIENDS ARE GETTING MARRIED

Sunday morning, Elisabet woke up earlier than her usual and dressed with care before descending to breakfast. She knew that she always looked nice in her well-fitting, fashionable clothes. However, her interest in Justin made her more self-conscious than usual. The dress she chose was a pretty one with a scoop neckline and lace collar. A light cardigan protected her shoulders from the autumn breeze.

Justin was at breakfast along with Dylan and Garry, and it seemed perfectly natural to organise for him to pick her up for the Inter-denominational praise service the same time that the other boys collected their girlfriends. It also seemed natural to hang around together as a mixed group until lunch, which was generally relaxed and jovial on the weekends.

After lunch, Justin regarded Elisabet quizzically. "I feel that I ought to return your hospitality in inviting me to your friend Phoebe's place. What is the next university special event?"

"The next major special event is the Champagne Breakfast," Elisabet replied. "It is two weeks into the second half of the semester. Almost five weeks away."

"Two of those weeks are holidays," Justin observed. "I hardly think that they count."

"Perhaps not," Elisabet was blushing. "Are you asking me to the Champagne Breakfast?"

"I would like to escort you," Justin replied formally.

Elisabet usually had plenty of invitations, but she reflected that it might be nice to have things organised in advance – like the other girls.

"I would be pleased to go with you." she whispered.

"Thank you," Justin said. "It is a date!"

Elisabet glanced around self-consciously to see whether anyone had noticed the personal exchange, but the other students all appeared absorbed in their own interests. The meal concluded, and Justin made a direct line for the library to do more post-graduate research. Elisabet retreated to the girl's dormitory to study for her health test. Stephanie joined her in the room for the promised tutoring session, and the afternoon passed quickly.

Monday's classes were mildly boring, and Elisabet found that the highlight of her day was running into Justin at meal times. He had always been a friend to Joelle and Tom, but now he appeared to have joined the inner circle of their group.

In the evening, Stephanie insisted that Elisabet take a break from study and accompany her to watch Garry and Vincent play basketball. The team the boys faced this week represented a greater challenge than the team they had faced the previous week, and Stephanie thought they needed moral support.

The opposing team won the toss, and although both ends of the gymnasium were roughly equal, the captain chose the direction thought to confer an advantage. They also played quite assertively, and pushed Garry's team into a defensive game. At half time, the score stood even, but by full time, the boys had lost by two baskets.

"I do hope they do not face those guys in the finals," Stephanie moaned.

Terrence, who had been hovering nearby, laughed. "If they do not face those guys, they will have to face a team who beat those guys and is potentially even better!" he exclaimed.

"Ah well," Elisabet sighed. "It is only university basketball."

"Only university basketball!" Terrence exclaimed, choosing to take Elisabet's statement as a challenge. "Some people take it seriously!"

"I mean, whoever wins – we will have friends on each side," Elisabet elaborated.

"There is that," Terrence agreed, sliding onto the bench beside her. Elisabet looked at him quizzically, and he stretched out his long legs, attempting to appear casual. "Did you know Elisabet – I had been working my way up to asking you out?"

"Of course I didn't know," Elisabet said. "A girl clearly doesn't know if a guy doesn't say anything."

"Now it looks as though it is too late – you have started a regular thing with Justin," Terrence continued.

Elisabet sighed. "It is the first half of semester still. I would hardly call it too late."

"You know what I mean," Terrance retorted.

"I do like Justin," Elisabet mused. "He seems mature."

"In contrast, I am a third year," Terence reflected.

Elisabet giggled. "I'm not like that!"

"Of course you are," Terence said. "Everybody here is – the whole university is very stratified."

"Ask me again later," Elisabet advised. "I don't want to disrupt things with Justin now – we are in the 'getting to know each other' stage. In a few weeks' time though – I reckon we will know one way or another."

"Sure," Terence grinned and bounced off to referee the C grade men's basketball game that was about to commence.

"That was a bit odd," Elisabet observed to Stephanie. "Why would Terrence wait until Justin had asked me out to say he liked me?"

"Perhaps he was hiding from rejection by having the conversation once you appeared taken?" Stephanie suggested psychoanalytically.

"Nah! Terrance is a good bloke," said Garry, who had settled down on the bench to rest after his match. "He captains an A grade team and is quite competitive. I don't think he would be particularly intimidated by another suitor."

"Confident then," Elisabet murmured. "I like that!"

"It seems you like them both," Stephanie observed. "Justin for his maturity; and Terence for his confidence."

Elisabet had intended to walk back to the girl's dormitory with Stephanie and Garry, but she noticed that the young couple's body language was unusually exclusive that evening. Elisabet remembered that Stephanie's birthday was approaching on Thursday and smiled. Garry had no basketball victory to celebrate, but he clearly wanted to be alone with his girlfriend to plan something. After that she cheerfully bid her friends goodnight and strode across campus alone.

The health test on Tuesday proved challenging, as it was terminology and fact oriented. The paper contained a combination of short answer and multiple choice questions. Elisabet reflected that if the test did not trick her in one section, it might well trick her in another, but she did her best. She felt very grateful for Stephanie's tutoring the previous weekend.

Wednesday afternoon, Craig called a band practice. He announced that he had arranged with the Café Proprietor for the *Electronic Jive Classical Vibe Band* to present a small concert to the students on the final afternoon before the Easter break.

"Not the Wednesday," Craig explained, "As everyone will be trying to rush off. However, Tuesday afternoon seemed appropriate."

The members of the band were very excited, as this would be their first opportunity to play to the student body. They perceived young adults as their target audience and wanted to impress their peers.

"What will we be playing?" James exclaimed.

"A combination of the songs we have already practiced," Craig said. "There is less than a week to practice, so I will select pieces we are already proficient at. And of course – I want to present some of my original compositions."

"Nice," Elisabet murmured, thinking it was time that Craig's talent was appreciated more widely. He had played the violin during worship many times, but it was considered a specialised and highbrow instrument. The band music was more modern and accessible.

"It sounds like fun," Vincent added. He was looking forward to showing Janet what he could do, and why he spent long hours over in the Music Department when he wasn't really a music student.

The band settled into productive practice mode. They were performing pieces they knew, but they still needed rehearsal to make sure everything went smoothly on the day. It was almost tea time when Elisabet left the music rooms, and she only had a few moments to freshen up and tidy her hair before going across to the cafeteria.

Thursday was Stephanie's birthday. Elisabet had a small gift prepared for her room-mate, and presented it to her in the interval between breakfast and class. The gift was an elegantly bound blank journal, for she knew that Stephanie loved to write. It was an interest that both girls shared, as they were jointly English Majors.

"Do you and Garry have any special plans for today?" Elisabet asked.

Stephanie blushed. "I think so," she said.

"Tea in Northcoast perhaps?" Elisabet suggested.

Stephanie shook her head. "Actually Garry has to go to Yandina," she elaborated. "He has an interview with the Queensland Rail Depot there."

"Oh," Elisabet said. She remembered that Garry had done extra technical subjects at summer schools through both Silver Springs and Wollongong Universities, and was due to complete his course requirements six months early. "I hope that the interview goes well."

"If he gets the job, he will be able to stay close to here until I graduate," Stephanie confided.

"That would be best for you," Elisabet observed.

Stephanie giggled and blushed once again: "Garry plans to pick up a cake at the bakery in Eumundi and we will be having a small celebration in the cafeteria lounge after tea. You will be welcome to join us."

"I will make sure that I am there," Elisabet promised.

When Elisabet arrived at the cafeteria lounge that evening, she quickly realised the event was much more than a birthday party. Garry was celebrating a successful interview, and reporting there was a good possibility of a six month contract with the rail works. Stephanie was also showing people a ring she was wearing on the third finger of her left hand.

"It is pretty," Elisabet said, squinting to view the vintage garnet trilogy closer. "But it's not a diamond?"

"Garry needs to use his savings for a car," Stephanie explained. "And this was his Grandmother's gift. I love it!"

"As long as you are happy, nothing else matters," Dylan remarked with masculine indifference to the niceties of jewellery.

"It is for an engagement – not friendship?" Justin, whom Elisabet had invited to accompany her, sounded mildly puzzled.

"Of course it is an engagement ring," Stephanie said merrily. "Some of you already know Garry asked me late last year – but the time was not right. It seems right now."

Debbie and Tess bent over the ring, cooing ecstatically.

"Congratulations mate," David said. "A job and a fiancé – all in one day."

"I hope it works out," Andrew said earnestly, if not optimistically. "I'm referring to the job of course, the engagement is surely blessed."

"Have you set a date?" asked Cara.

"We are thinking the New Year," Stephanie said. "I want to enjoy graduation…"

"Will the wedding be here or in Adelaide?" Luke inquired.

Stephanie and Garry exchanged glances. "In Wollongong actually," Stephanie said. "And we hope to move back there eventually."

"Why?" Phoebe exclaimed. "It is lovely around here."

"You know that Garry's Mother had breast cancer," Stephanie elaborated. "She is in remission – but we do not know how long she will be safe. Garry would like to be close to his parents for that reason."

A dark shadow briefly crossed the happy proceedings, but it was quickly dismissed. Love and marriage were the predominant business of the day. Moreover, there was a good chance that Garry's mother would stay in good health for some years, and see her grandchildren born.

"Wollongong is beautiful too," Garry said. "It is built between the National Park and the ocean, on the side of a hill. You are all welcome to come and visit for the wedding."

Garry had purchased a dozen bottles of non-alcoholic grape drink, and he poured it into plastic cups for a toast. Stephanie blew out her birthday candles and cut the cake, which was also portioned out and handed around on paper plates. Everyone had already eaten tea in the cafeteria, so this made the perfect evening social gathering.

Friday morning classes ran smoothly. Throughout the day, word of Stephanie's engagement spread across campus. Elisabet was asked to convey congratulations to the roommate, while several senior girls gave their men gentle nudges.

Bede O'Brien arrived in their room soon after lunch and begged Stephanie to allow her to help make a dream wedding dress, as the roommate still planned to use the competition dress for graduation. The two girls were soon lost in discussion of fabrics and styles.

"I was thinking of breaking with tradition and having the wedding on the beach," Stephanie said. "So I would want something long and flowing."

"Lovely," Bede breathed. "I know that you love seventies styling and princess panels suit you because you are so slim."

"I think I will go with an empire line bodice and a slim fitting front," Stephanie said, "But I want something that can float behind me and make a showing in the wind. I do love seeing that in photos!"

"A train could be attached to the yoke," Bede speculated. "And flowers, or plaited ribbons. Were you thinking lace or satin or both?"

"Satin for the foundation," Stephanie said. "With a layer of something light like georgette for the train."

"White or cream?" Bede asked.

"A little on the cream side I think," Stephanie said. "It is so much richer. I know what people might say…"

"I think that cream has to be very beigey to not count as white," Bede observed.

"That is the way I see it too!" Stephanie exclaimed.

Elisabet left the room and went across to the library, where she hoped to find Justin and study side-by-side. She presumed the other girls continued planning the wedding in her absence.

Saturday the *Electronic Jive Classic Vibe Band* had another practice scheduled. Vincent had brought Janet along so that she could have a preview of their show, and she seemed very impressed. Tom was also in attendance to receive his instructions as their sound technician and roadie.

After the practice, Tom hung around in the Music Department waiting for Joelle, who was busy with Larry organising worship music for the weekend. The next day would be Palm Sunday, and a special service had been planned, including a children's parade. The procession would involve the offspring of the lecturers, local residents and married students.

Finally, Joelle stuck her head through the doorway and advised Tom to go ahead without her, as she would be some hours longer. Elisabet had been deep in conversation with Craig, but she took pity on Tom and allowed him to walk her back to the girl's dormitory.

"What do you think about Stephanie and Garry getting engaged?" Elisabet murmured as much to make conversation as anything else.

"I think it is great!" Tom looked enthusiastic.

"Perhaps you ought to ask Joelle to marry you then then." The suggestion escaped her lips somewhat carelessly.

"I don't think she would say 'yes'," Tom replied with brutal honesty.

"By all accounts, Stephanie did not say 'yes' the first time Garry asked either," Elisabet murmured.

"This is different," Tom said. "Joelle and I have been heading in different directions for some time."

"Most of us can see that," Elisabet said. "But you still say you are together…"

"Neither of us wants to be the bad guy, I think," Tom admitted. "But I can tell Joelle is livid about you and Justin."

"Joelle doesn't own Justin, even if she did meet him back in the UK," Elisabet said.

"Very true," Tom agreed. "And I don't think Justin sees her 'that way', but I cannot quite tell if that is simply because he would never mow another guy's grass."

"Well why don't you set Joelle free and see what she does?" Elisabet said. "I don't know if anyone has told you – but a few weeks ago, when you were sick, she was hanging out with Mathew and Christopher. They are all on the worship committee together, but sometimes I think that is just an excuse."

"I have been thinking about ending things with her," Tom said. "And the half-semester is as good a time as any."

"Holiday break-ups," Elisabet groaned. "They are such a cliché."

"But practical somehow," Tom said. He was looking determined now.

"Once you are free, I'm sure girls like Lacey would be more comfortable accepting your invitations," Elisabet observed. "Not me," she added hurriedly. "There is already a queue to date me."

"Oh?" Tom sounded vaguely amused.

"Justin and then Terrence," Elisabet admitted.

"That doesn't bode so well for your relationship with Justin," Tom observed.

"I am giving things with Justin a fair chance," Elisabet said. "It's just that he has told me he's due back in the UK at the end of the year..."

"You could be serious by then," Tom suggested.

"Perhaps, perhaps not," Elisabet said.

"That is pretty much like any new relationship," Tom observed.

They had reached the girl's dormitory by this time and were loitering around the foyer. Tom said goodbye and Elisabet went inside. She felt a little guilty and hoped that she had not been responsible for triggering Tom's decision to break-up with Joelle. Surely it had been in the works for some time?

The Palm Sunday celebrations went off smoothly, and Elisabet enjoyed watching the children carrying the palm leaves down the aisle during divine service. Andrew and David suggested some special passion readings for Holy Week, and Kaleb was helping them organise an evening meeting.

David's girlfriend Debbie was a friend, so Elisabet found herself conscripted to play the keyboard. Apparently, Joelle had been asked, but Debbie reported Joelle was in a bad mood, because she and Tom had finally broken up. The split was being touted as a mutual decision, but most of the friendship group expressed themselves on Tom's side, because it appeared he had been the one making all the effort for months.

Like most things the talented young Theology students organised, the prayer meeting was a success. Each attendee left with a schedule of readings to complete in their own time throughout the week, because there would be regular dormitory worship on the other nights, and the term actually ended Wednesday afternoon.

Monday at tea, Stephanie was all smiles, because it had been confirmed Garry was offered a six month contract at Queensland Rail, commencing the first of July. It seemed that everything was falling in line for the couple to go ahead with their wedding plans. Elisabet was pleased for her room-mate's sake.

Tuesday at lunch, the *Electronic Jive Classical Vibe Band* made its much anticipated debut to the student body. The cafeteria had been rearranged to create a staged area, and the band played pleasant background music while the food was being served. Many of the diners chatted as they ate, but gradually, they began to pay more attention to the entertainment.

When the majority of the students were assembled, Craig began to introduce his own compositions. He even dared to sing his solos, as he had previously at the staff luncheon. His melodious voice filled the cafeteria with a little help from the microphone, and his annunciation was excellent. The words were very touching, especially when he sang his song about the little injured lamb.

The applause that followed was thunderous. The students welcomed any change to their somewhat regimented campus routine, and enjoyed the slightly rocky rhythm of a few songs. Those who did not know Craig well were astounded, because he was generally thought retiring.

Elisabet was thrilled. When she had first suggested the idea of a band to Craig, she had been looking for an easy way to fulfil the performance requirements of the university music programme. Now the band was becoming something she could share with friends, and she was getting hooked on the adrenaline rush of performing.

Wednesday morning at breakfast, another engagement was announced. The lucky couple was Debbie and David, who had been going steady for over three years now. David had received a small scholarship, which was assisting him with his education costs, and subsequently had been able to save towards a modest engagement ring. The betrothal token was gold, with a small diamond set in an illusion setting, but Debbie was well pleased.

Classes finished by lunch time and the students began to migrate towards Northcoast station, which was a transport node from where they could catch the train to Brisbane and the airport, or the bus down the coast towards New South Wales. Elisabet was one of the lucky students with her own car, which she would be driving back to Byron Bay, arriving in comfortable time to spend Easter with her family.

Elisabet was happy to be home, and attended the various Easter church services including Maundy Thursday evening meditation, Good Friday solemn morning service and the joyful Easter Sunday celebration. She also enjoyed spending time with her Mother, Father, and older brother who had chosen to go into the family business, rather than attend university.

Holiday Monday Elisabet received a surprise telephone call from Justin. Her heart beat fast as she answered the telephone. "Hello?"

"I asked for your number," Justin observed in amusement when Elisabet expressed her astonishment that he had actually called.

"But most guys hate the telephone," Elisabet stammered.

"I've been a parish Pastor in England," Justin said. "I had to become comfortable reaching out using the telephone then. I'm also sitting here in boy's dorm with very little to do."

"Oh – I'm sorry," Elisabet gushed. "I didn't think about you having nowhere to go."

"That is alright," Justin said. "It would have been too soon to meet your parents anyway. Even under these circumstances. When the library opens again tomorrow I will get back to my research. A masters' thesis does not write itself."

"I guess not," Elisabet agreed. They talked about a variety of things, until Justin ran out of coins and then they had to say goodbye before they were cut off.

The next week and a half flew by in a haze of helping out in her parents' office, lazing on the beach, and a trip to Coolangatta for shopping. Elisabet read a few novels, which were not the sort studied at Silver Springs University. There was little harm in the stories, but they would hardly qualify as 'classic' literature.

On the second day of May, Elisabet had to turn around and drive back up the Bruce Highway to Silver Springs. Stephanie had already arrived at the dorm, and was keen to talk about the wedding suppliers she had checked around Wollongong. Elisabet resigned herself to months of conversation about minute details, before telling her room-mate about Justin's call.

"Actually, he called not once, but twice," Elisabet clarified.

"Keeping in contact during the holidays – that is serious," Stephanie observed.

Elisabet shrugged. "I think he was lonely. There wasn't anyone much here."

"But it was you that he called," Stephanie cooed.

"Yes it was," Elisabet sounded satisfied, even to herself. "And we had a very nice chat each time."

Monday was a holiday in some states, but Silver Springs University operated independently of such things and classes commenced on schedule. The students were excited to be back, rushing around, greeting each other in the lecture theatres and corridors.

It was lunch time before Elisabet encountered Justin, because they had no classes in common. However, when she saw him waiting for her in the cafeteria, she could not help blushing.

"What colour is red?" chortled Cara, who was beside her.

It took a few minutes to settle back into the easy companionship they had shared before the holidays, but Elisabet soon relaxed. Justin invited her to study in the library with him that afternoon, and even though none of her assignments were that pressing, Elisabet agreed just to spend time sitting together.

Tuesday when Elisabet was working in the Student Services Office, she had to type a number of engagement announcements in the newsletter, including that of Debbie and David. Anita and Larry were also announcing their engagement, as Larry had proposed during the second week of the holidays.

"I expect all the fourth year theology students will have proposed to their girlfriends before the middle of the year," whispered Tess, who was visiting the Student Services Office at that moment, and had been going out with Luke even longer than Debbie had been going out with David. "With graduation and work placements coming out in December, everyone will want to appear stable and committed."

"It doesn't sound very romantic when you put it that way," Elisabet observed, but Tess merely giggled.

"Trust me, it will be romantic, whenever and however Luke asks me," she said.

Wednesday morning, Elisabet had education and practice teaching classes. In the afternoon, Craig called the band back together for a practice and to plan the coming semester.

Thursday Elisabet and Stephanie both had English, and it was Stephanie's turn to deliver a tutorial on her chosen text. Stephanie presented a rousing reading of *Pilgrim's Progress,* which she had chosen because although the text was not listed as a drama, it was written in a very script-like manner. The story was also an adventure, and an example of the 'popular' literature of the time, which was religious in orientation. Stephanie also recognised a number of modern gaming elements in the tale's quest-like structure. As usual, Stephanie was thoroughly prepared and did very well.

Friday was the last day to get cards and letters into the mail and postmarked before Mother's Day on Sunday. Most of the students had seen their mother's recently, but there was still the traditional scramble at the student stationary shop and post office. Then there was the queue in the reception area of both dormitories for the use of the pay phones. All the students hoped to place at least one call home sometime over the weekend, and evening telephone rates were always the cheapest.

Saturday, it was Elisabet's turn to slave over an English text, because she was listed to present her tutorial topic the following Tuesday. At lunch, she overheard the boys talking about something they wanted to go and see. Garry and Dylan were deep in enthusiastic conversation, and they were doing a good job of convincing David, Justin and Andrew.

"What is a SN1987A?" Elisabet asked curiously.

"It is a naked eye supernova," Dylan answered.

"What?" Elisabet screeched. "That sounds dangerous!"

"It simply means a celestial feature that we can see from earth without magnification," Garry explained. "We would like to drive up the mountains, away from street lights and view it."

"We thought tonight would be a good night," Dylan suggested. "It is supposed to be visible throughout May."

"There is only one problem," Stephanie interjected. "You would have to go at night."

"Of course," Garry exclaimed. "And tonight is not going to be cloudy, so it would be ideal."

"Between Elisabet and me," Dylan suggested. "We have two cars and could carry eight passengers."

"I've never driven up the mountain before," Elisabet said nervously.

"Someone could drive for you," Garry suggested. "What about Justin?"

"I'm on an international license," Justin said. "I would prefer not to risk Elisabet's car in the mountains at night thank you!"

"I'm confident then," Garry said. "If Elisabet will allow me."

"If the girlfriends come, we could get locked out of the dorms by the security door," Stephanie repeated. "I expect you are going to want to wait until it is really dark to see this thing – and by then our curfew will be expiring."

"Oh!" There was no security system on the boys' dormitory, presumably because boys were considered to be at less risk from community violence. Therefore, the boys were inclined to forget the restrictions their girlfriends operated under.

"Do you think you could get permission?" Garry asked.

"We would have to speak to the deans personally," Cara said. "It might be possible."

"It would help if a lecturer was coming along," Stephanie said. "Then it would be an official excursion."

"It was the Physics Lecturer who told us about SN1987A," Garry said. "I will give him a call using the number in the campus directory."

"Let's hope he answers, or we might have to do it another weekend," Cara said.

"Next weekend is the Champagne Breakfast," Elisabet murmured.

Several of the young men looked as though they thought supernovas were more important than social events, but none dared to say that. They knew that their girlfriends loved formal functions, and the Champagne Breakfast was considered the romantic highlight of the year. Moreover, it would be Justin and Elisabet's first event together.

Garry placed a call to the Physics Lecturer, who happily agreed to come along and bring his vehicle. That meant with three vehicles and a professor in attendance, the girls could approach the deans for permission on the grounds that it was an educational outing. Permission was accordingly granted, and the cavalcade set out after tea. The plan was to drive to a convenient lookout and watch the gathering dark. Once the dark was dense enough, the supernova might begin to show itself.

The Physics Lecturer had brought a telescope, which he fussed around setting up. He argued that while the supernova would be visible with the naked eye, a much better view would be available through the telescope. He cleverly attached a SLR camera body to the telescope tube, so that they could photograph the phenomena. Photography would require a slow exposure, so the Physics Lecturer asked the students not to shake the camera when they took a turn peering through the viewer.

Elisabet and Justin wandered a little way by themselves, seeking some privacy. Elisabet thought that star gazing was an incredibly romantic activity, and was hoping for something like a first kiss from Justin.

"What mountain is this?" Justin asked.

"It is Glasshouse Mountain," Elisabet murmured. "Our friend Bradley used to love this mountain."

"I don't think I've met Bradley," Justin sounded mildly puzzled.

"He used to be in my English class, and he was Stephanie's boyfriend," Elisabet murmured. "He was killed in a motorcycle accident about a year-and-a-half ago."

"Sad," Justin mused. "But Stephanie and Garry seem like they have been together for years?"

"They have," Elisabet explained. "Except Garry left Silver Springs University for a while… you might have heard talk about his mother's health?"

"A little I think," Justin turned to face the stars. He was standing slightly behind Elisabet and laid an arm across her shoulder. "It is beautiful out here."

"It surely is," Elisabet murmured, and lifted her chin.

Justin got the hint and laid a small peck on her curved lips. It was sweet, but far too brief. "I don't know whether I ought," he whispered.

"I need a little affection to make a decision," Elisabet replied. She stood on tiptoe and attempted to return his kiss, and Justin bent his head politely. Their lips met once again, but the contact was still short.

"Let's take things gently," Justin whispered.

Elisabet flushed in the dark, wondering whether Justin thought she was wanton with her kisses. "I have dated before," she whispered, "But I have been saving myself for someone really special."

"It's not you," Justin whispered comfortingly. "It's me. I'm already a minister and ought to behave myself."

"Alright," Elisabet agreed, slightly disappointed. A steady boyfriend who was holding back wasn't her idea of a steady boyfriend. And it was not what she observed in her friends, who were all heading towards marriage with their steadies. However, she had to admit, many of them had known each other three years already.

"I'm not familiar with the stars of the Southern Hemisphere, but I think I see the supernova," Justin remarked. "It is beautiful!"

Elisabet followed the line of sight where Justin was pointing. She could see a round blur of light, vaguely larger and more noticeable than the regular stars. "It might get stronger later in the evening," she whispered.

Elisabet was not an expert on Astronomy, but she pointed out the Southern Cross, the Saucepan, and 'the evening star' or Venus, which really wasn't a star but a planet. Venus was also sometimes called 'the wishing star' and Elisabet made a little wish that Justin would one day kiss her properly. Wishing was silly superstition, of course, and Christians did not really believe in luck; but it seemed harmless.

CHAPTER SIX: MORE THAN FRIENDSHIP

Monday morning, James slid into the seat beside Elisabet in music class as was his custom. Elisabet smiled and greeted him absently. Jess and Vivione entered the room and sat down together as they had become great friends.

"Craig told me to tell you he had booked us another gig," James whispered.

"Oh – did he say what it was?" Elisabet asked.

"An afternoon assembly at Northcoast High School," James replied.

Elisabet was pleased. "At least that is a youth audience," she reflected.

"I'm a tad concerned that the high school students could be critical," James murmured.

"Teenagers can be hard to impress," Elisabet agreed. "But I think we are fairly safe. Our performance will represent a change from classes, and students always love that."

"Which attitude really bodes well for our teaching careers," James scoffed.

"School has its moments," Elisabet murmured. "And routine is good – most of the time."

"In the country," James observed, "School and church provided most of our social life."

"Where I come from," Elisabet said, "There was a strong tourist industry… and a somewhat alternate lifestyle. It was fun."

"Where was that?" James asked curiously.

"Byron Bay," Elisabet said. "Tent city or hippy-ville, however you wish to name it."

"You don't seem like a hippy," James reflected.

"We are not all barefoot and raggedy," Elisabet giggled. "My parents run an organic fruit and vegetable business."

"Are they doing well?" James, who was from a farming area himself, asked.

"Well enough," Elisabet admitted and subsided into protective silence. Some Silver Springs students had nothing but their student allowances, so she tried not to spread word about her family's affluence.

The class had moved on from musical appreciation and voice training, to simple instruments that could be easily presented in the classroom. These included the percussions, like triangles, castanets and shakers. A kettledrum was also suitable for classroom use. The recorder, which was Elisabet's second instrument of choice, was also popular for classroom instruction.

Tuesday Elisabet's English tutorial presentation was due. She had chosen to focus on poetry by Dryden, partly because she had thought that the poems would be shorter, and less work to analyse. She had regretted her decision when she came to read the poems through and noticed that they were very complex.

Interpretation and analysis was subsequently challenging, but Elisabet blundered her way through a couple of samples, using impressive sounding literary terms and making cultured observations. She must have succeeded, because the English Professor awarded her seven-and-a-half out of ten, which placed her in the running to obtain a distinction.

Wednesday afternoon, Justin had invited Elisabet to watch his basketball match. Elisabet wanted to avoid the appearance of being a basketball girlfriend, so she prevailed upon the sports-loving Cara to accompany her.

Cara was always happy to hang around in the gymnasium, so she agreed easily enough, bringing her boyfriend Dylan along for company. Cara's sister Bede came along because Kaleb was also playing.

By some coincidence, the team that included Kaleb and Justin was facing the team captained by Terence that afternoon. Terence immediately noted Elisabet's presence, and enhanced his game accordingly. Most of the spectators were unaware of this by-play, but it made Elisabet flush and avoid looking directly at him.

Justin was a very good athlete, and a solid all-rounder. His team captain, African-American born Kaleb, was even more impressive, running up and down the court at lightning speed and dunking the ball whenever possible. The defenders from the opposing team got quite puffed attempting to counter him.

Terence however, was not the president of the Silver Springs Basketball League for nothing. He was also a very good athlete, and he lengthened his stride to keep pace with Kaleb. Several times, he managed to acquire the ball at a key moment and pushed it back towards his team, encouraging them to go on the offensive.

The ball was passed back and forth, while the score mounted steadily on both sides of the board. Kaleb's team appeared to have an advantage, but Terence's team made them work for every goal. Terence employed every substitution that the rules allowed in order to reduce fatigue amongst the defenders. At half time, Kaleb and Justin's team were ahead by two goals, and at full time, they were ahead by three. Both teams had scored well into the double figures.

Cara was glowing with excitement. "That was a great game," the girl exclaimed. "Kaleb and Justin – you were wonderful."

"Kaleb is always wonderful," Bede O'Brien said possessively, giving Kaleb a conqueror's kiss.

"Your team sure made them work for it," Elisabet remarked to Terence, who had shouldered his way through the crowd to stand in front of her.

"Good work man," Justin said maturely, extending his right hand for a friendly shake.

Terence accepted the handshake with good grace. "You guys were better today," he admitted generously.

Elisabet exhaled a sigh of relief. The boys were not going to fight over her, flattering though that would be. A fight or even an argument would be embarrassing and make her the subject of campus gossip.

"I have study to do," Justin said. "Elisabet – if you will allow me to walk you back to the dormitory?"

"Sure," Elisabet agreed. Terence, Kaleb and the O'Brien sisters were making plans to visit the campus canteen, but Elisabet understood Justin had his thesis to write. Stephanie might well be back in the room by now, and Elisabet would have company studying.

The walk back to the dormitory was pleasant, and Justin gave her a brief peck when they arrived at reception. Elisabet was pleased to note that while Justin was reluctant to linger intimately over his kisses, he was not afraid to show affection in public.

Thursday afternoon, while Stephanie was busy at her biology laboratory, Elisabet sorted through her wardrobe, looking for her prettiest evening dress. The Champagne Breakfast would be her first formal date with Justin, and she wanted to make a good impression. Finally, she settled on something that she had bought in Coolangatta during the recent holidays. The dress had a sweetheart neckline, puff sleeves and full skirt. It could almost have been a bridesmaids dress, except that it was a sophisticated black.

Tea time Elisabet asked Justin what he would be wearing, and upon hearing that he had a nice black suit, was thrilled. They would match beautifully, and there would be sure to be an amateur photographer or two taking photographs.

Friday after classes had finished, Stephanie came rushing into their room. "Have you heard the news?"

"What news?" Elisabet reflected.

"Tom has asked Lacey to the Champagne Breakfast – and this time she said 'yes'!" Stephanie exclaimed.

"I think that was something the point of his getting single," Elisabet murmured.

"I know – but how will Joelle feel?" Stephanie cried.

"I think you will find Joelle has an escort of her own," Elisabet said. "The last rumour I heard – it was Mathew."

"Joelle always did fancy Theology students," Stephanie conceded. "But I cannot believe she would be fully over Tom. Not so soon."

"She probably is not," Elisabet observed. "But you are forgetting – Joelle was never as sentimental as you."

"I would like to see my friends happy," Stephanie mused.

"Well, be patient and it might happen," Elisabet advised.

"I think I will go and talk to Joelle," Stephanie said virtuously. "No matter how preoccupied she has been lately – she was part of our group once."

Elisabet felt that it was wisest not to accompany Stephanie on her visit to Joelle's room. Joelle might have a suitable date to the Champagne Breakfast, but she could still feel some resentment that Elisabet was going out with Justin. The master's student had been Joelle's wonderful holiday discovery after all.

The morning of the Champagne Breakfast dawned fine, if a little dark. The girls had set their alarms for a ridiculously early hour, so that they could shower and then help each other blow-dry and style their hair. Then they had to apply their make-up.

Justin and Garry must have arrived at reception at a similar time, because calls for Stephnie and Elisabet came over the public address system simultaneously. The girls trod carefully on the stairs in their high heeled shoes and minced their way out into the foyer. Stephanie and Garry greeted each other ecstatically. Elisabet looked at Justin more tentatively.

"I got you this,' Justin said, producing a small rose corsage.

"It is lovely," Elisabet exclaimed.

"I'm afraid I had to store it overnight," Justin said. "This function commences before any florist shop would open."

"I think it was incredibly thoughtful of you," said Elisabet, very aware of the fact that a few other girls were eyeing her enviously. "And you look very fashionable in that suit."

"European fashions must be ahead of Australian ones then," Justin observed, because this suit is several years old."

"Aussie guys rarely look comfortable dressed up – but you look relaxed," Elisabet continued.

"It is nice of you to say so," Justin conceded. "Let us follow your friends, or they will reach the cafeteria well ahead of us."

When they reached the cafeteria, the first thing Elisabet noticed was all the candles. They gave the room quite a romantic glow, and threw warm patches of light across the white table cloths. The hospitality students were moving amongst the tables, looking smart in their white uniforms, and serving the students the sparkling grape juice that was used as a substitute for wine at Silver Springs University functions.

"Yes, please," Elisabet said, holding up her glass.

"This is a special day for Garry and I," Stephanie announced. "Our first formal event as an engaged couple!"

"Did I ever tell you that Stephanie could be corny?" Elisabet moaned.

"I rather like it," Justin said, and clinked his plastic glass against hers. "Here is to Stephanie and Garry… and us!"

"And us," Elisabet murmured, her eyes shining.

The food was refined, as befitted such a gala event. They started with little savoury scrolls, and then enjoyed a bowl of cream of cauliflower soup. Elisabet had expected to hate the soup, but the cauliflower was pureed and blended perfectly with the cream and cheese.

"How have your band practices been going?" Justin asked politely as they finished their soup.

"Very well thank you," Elisabet replied. "How is your thesis going?"

"Slowly," Justin answered. "Very slowly. There is just so much material to cover. Luckily, I have a few more months."

The main course was a delicious quiche and side salad, with vegetarian and meaty options.

"I think the cooks are improving," Elisabet observed. "Did you know that the hospitality students prepare these special meals as part of their training?"

"No, actually, but now you mention it, that does make sense," Justin said. "Experience."

Having exhausted the small talk, Elisabet dug her spoon into her confection. The desert was a strawberry mouse, topped with fresh whipped cream, and filled with real strawberries. It was sweetened to just the right blend of tart and syrup.

"Have I told you that you look nice this morning?" Justin murmured.

He spoke in a low voice, his mouth close to Elisabet's ear. His arm was laid casually across the back of her chair.

"No you haven't," Elisabet responded. She was no stranger to flattery, but a compliment from Justin clearly meant something special, even if it came a little late. "Thank you, that is what a girl likes to hear."

As they finished their desert, the sun rose and flooded the cafeteria in pink, then orange and finally, yellow. A few students blew their candles out, because they were beginning to drip wax anyway.

"Walk me back to the dormitory," Elisabet murmured, hoping that if his current mood lasted, Justin might forget himself and kiss her deeply. Her hopes were not entirely disappointed, because before Justin left, he gave her not one, but two kisses that were a little more than his usual brief pecks.

The rest of Saturday passed like a blur after the Champagne Breakfast. A lot of girls removed their finery and went back to bed for a few hours. The lunch table was full of gossip about potential new couples, and post-mortems of the less successful dates.

Craig had called a band practice, and the *Electronic Jibe Classical Vibe Band* met after lunch to prepare for their scheduled gig at Northcoast High School.

"Which one of the first year girls did you take to the Champagne Breakfast?" Elisabet asked James at practice. "I was busy with Justin and did not look around much."

"Minding your own business as should be," Vincent commented. "And as no one actually does around here."

"I took Ella," James admitted. "She is really sweet. I don't know whether to ask her out again – or choose one of the other girls."

"Hang out in a group situation," Craig suggested. "That will let you learn more about her without getting tied down. I have to collect some sheet music – I seem to have forgotten a couple of pieces."

Craig left the room and the others continued chatting. They knew that if Craig was going all the way back to men's dorm, it would take him a few minutes. Vincent grinned at James.

"Relationship advice from Craig," he observed. "Well I never!"

"What does that mean?" Elisabet asked suspiciously.

"It is just that Craig has never had a steady girlfriend," Vincent returned. "At least not since I've known him."

"He can still have an opinion," Elisabet declared staunchly.

"I've seen the way you look at Craig when you think us other guys are not watching," James observed, glancing towards Elisabet. "Have you two ever?"

"We have been out once or twice," Elisabet admitted. "He has a sort of artistic charisma that I admire - but I am with Justin now."

"You and Justin make a cool couple," Vincent agreed.

After that Craig returned, and the serious musical practice commenced. The *Electronic Jibe Classical Vibe Band* were working up a few more modern spiritual pieces to please the high school students, and James was even going to do a trumpet voluntary.

Sunday Elisabet attended both church services with Justin and enjoyed the way people looked at them as if they were an established couple. Which is exactly what she thought they would be, if they did not encounter any set-backs on the path to true love. Elisabet had never yet allowed herself to fall in love, but she had begun to admit that what she felt for Justin was far more than mere friendship.

During both services, special prayers were said for the plight of the Indians in Fiji, who were being treated badly under the military government. Elisabet knew little about the history of Fiji, but she learned that Indians had been transported to the islands to use as cheap labour under the British colonial government. Now the Indigenous Fijians were demanding their independence, but there was no one to advocate for the rights of these displaced people.

Australians were advised not to travel to Fiji in the next few months, despite it being a popular tourist destination. Several international students expressed fear of returning home at the end of the year, and the Silver Springs University churches promised an attempt to sponsor them for visas that would allow them to stay in Australia longer.

Monday morning was full of classes, and in the afternoon, the band had one final practice before the upcoming gig. In the evening, Stephanie insisted Elisabet accompany her to the gymnasium to watch Garry and Vincent play basketball. They were joined on the spectator benches by Vincent's girlfriend Janet, and Tom's recent date, Lacey.

It just so happened, that Garry and Vincent's B grade team had climbed their way up the competition ladder, until they were facing Tom's B grade team, who had also climbed their way up the leader board.

"It's exciting to have so many friends playing at once – isn't it?" Stephanie whispered to Janet, who looked at her in mild amusement.

"As I play basketball myself," Janet observed. "Most of the regular players are my friends. So I always see friends playing friends."

"Well. When you put it like that…" Stephanie subsided.

Lacey, on the other hand, looked at her with more empathy. "But when one of them is your boyfriend," she said. "I expect you have the right to be excited."

"How are things going for you and Tom?" Elisabet asked curiously.

Lacey shook her head. "I do not believe Tom is over Joelle yet," she said. "We had a nice enough time at the Champagne Breakfast and remain good friends, but that is the limit."

"I didn't expect him to rush straight into another relationship," Stephanie said slowly and thoughtfully.

"Where's Justin tonight Elisabet?" Janet inquired.

"Library as usual," Elisabet reported. "Where I ought to be really."

The umpire blew his whistle and the girls transferred their attention to the basketball court. Garry, Vincent and Tom were all playing very well. The teams appeared evenly matched, and at first, it looked as though it would be a deadlocked game. Then Vincent scored a basket and everybody cheered. Tom scored the next goal, although Garry was very active in defence, attempting to block him.

There was a lot of intense ball work, but the game remained low scoring, due to the equality of the teams. At half-time, Vincent's team was one goal ahead. Immediately the second half commenced, Tom scored a basket, evening the score. Towards the end of the game, Tom's team began to lag. Although they always clawed their way towards evening the score, Vincent's team regularly scored first. When the final whistle blew, Vincent's team were the winners.

After exchanging handshakes with the other players, Vincent, Garry and Tom crossed over to the girls to receive their congratulations. Although Lacey had said she did not think anything was happening with Tom, Elisabet noticed that the third year girl was lavish with her praise. Elisabet said goodbye to the others after a discrete interval and hurried back to the dormitory. She needed a good night's sleep before the band performance on the morrow.

Tuesday, Elisabet raced up to the cafeteria the moment it opened for lunch in order to grab an early bite. Craig, Luke and Tom had already driven across to the Northcoast High School in the university mini-bus with the equipment to set up in the hall for the band. The performance was scheduled for two pm, soon after the students returned from their lunch period, and lasted until they would be dismissed at three.

After they had eaten, Elisabet drove across to the High School with James and Vincent in the Gemini. It had turned out to be handy she owned a vehicle, and Luke did not have to return for them. They found Tom and Craig in the school hall tuning the mixer to allow their amplifier to communicate with the school sound system.

Craig immediately instructed the other musicians to pull out their instruments and go through their scales. A few high school students heard the band tuning-up and collapsed into ignorant giggles, but the group were ready to give a professional presentation by the time the majority of the schoolies filed into the room.

The school music teacher, a Mr. Donell, introduced the *Electronic Jive Classical Vibe Band* to the staff and students. Craig had chosen to commence with Woody Guthrie's '*This Land was Made for You and Me*' and Craig's special lyrics, which had been a hit everywhere it had been played. Then they performed Craig's '*Rainforest Creation*' song, followed by his '*Little Lamb*'.

They followed these songs with several modern worship anthems that were always popular at the Inter-denominational praise service. With a cautious glance at the music teacher, Craig directed the band into one of his new instrumental compositions. It was jazz-based and a little quirky, throwing in odd syncopated beats and finishing on a crescendo. Vincent loved drumming for this particular piece and worked away at the percussion with inspiration.

"Well, that was different," exclaimed Mr. Donell after the band had finished.

The school principal rose to his feet and thanked the band for coming. "We especially appreciate your sharing some of your original compositions with us," the Principal said. "Hopefully they will be an inspiration to our music students."

"If I may," Craig ventured, stepping up to the microphone. "I still remember how difficult my early practices were. If anyone is struggling, I would advise them to persist."

"I was not as advanced as Craig and James when I finished High School," Elisabet testified. "I've spent the last couple of years working to catch up, but I can tell you it was well worth it!"

"I just play the drums for fun," Vincent said. "I started around the middle of last year, because I was being bullied elsewhere. I would like to thank Craig for believing in me, and allowing an amateur to join such an accomplished band."

The student body broke out into thunderous applause at this statement. A few found Craig too specialised for their taste, but it was clear that everyone could relate to Vincent. There was a question time, when Craig fended questions such as "What is it like to write your own music?" and "How do you start a band?" Then the school students filed back to their home classes for housekeeping and dismissal, and the band members were free to pack up.

Wednesday Elisabet was pleased to have a fairly normal day on campus. She had assignments to do, because a few deadlines were near. In the evening she watched Justin and Kaleb's team play basketball in the gymnasium. This week, their opponents were not Terence's team of course, but another team.

Towards the end of the match, Justin slipped and went crashing down onto the gymnasium floor. He knew that he ought not put his hand out to save himself, but he instinctively reached out, resulting in a sprained wrist. The first aider on duty in the gymnasium rushed Justin across to the bench and supplied him with an ice pack, and gave instructions to change its positioning every ten minutes. This was to help prevent swelling and yet avoid freezing the area.

The university nurse was pretty sure that it was not a break, and recommended keeping the wrist strapped for a few days. However, she also suggested Justin see a doctor and get an x-ray just in case.

Thursday afternoon, Elisabet drove Justin into Northcoast to see the doctor and get the x-ray done. The news at the medical centre was good, and Justin was advised to keep his wrist in a sling for a few days, and then he would be able to go back to normal activities. They returned to campus in a hopeful mood.

However, by Friday, Justin was feeling sore and frustrated. Unfortunately, the wrist he had sprained was also his writing hand, and while he could do reading for his thesis, he was unable to take notes. Elisabet decided to go to Northcoast to purchase some menthol liniment from the pharmacy, and also distract Justin from his worries.

Craig was not normally a keen shopper, but he elected to go along with the couple for the ride. Once their business at the chemist was complete, Justin and Craig went to browse through the cassettes in the music store, while Elisabet looked through women's fashions at a local boutique.

The trio had agreed to convene at the alfresco eating area behind the Northcoast delicatessen. Justin ordered Elisabet a thick shake, and a lemonade for himself. Craig ordered green tea, a novelty that was not available on campus.

They were waiting for their order, when Craig stood up. "I'll just be going to the men's for a moment," he said.

Elisabet and Justin sat at the table, talking between themselves. The drink orders arrived and they began to wonder why Craig was not back.

"I had better go and see where Craig got to," Justin said at last.

He rounded the corner, and gave a shout of alarm. Elisabet ran forward to see what was up, but Justin tried to push her back with his good arm. "Call the police," he cried.

Craig was down on the ground and two heavy-built boys were standing over him. He was barely conscious, and blood was spreading across his jaw from a cut in his lip. More blood was streaming from his nostrils, and there may have been a trickle of fluid from one ear. Two other youths were standing by jeering, and Elisabet thought she vaguely recognised them from the day local ruffians had thrown the clod of dirt. To her horror, she realised they appeared to be kicking Craig.

"Hurry," Justin urged. "I've only got one arm and besides I don't believe in violence."

Elisabet raced into the deli and begged permission to use the telephone. The shopkeeper was horrified to realise what was happening on his premises and insisted on making the call himself, giving the address concisely and accurately to the police. The police station was just down the street, and a group of officers arrived within minutes. They took the thugs into custody and called an ambulance for Craig.

The ambulance arrived and Craig was lifted onto a stretcher. "He has to go to hospital," one Ambulance Officer said to Elisabet. "Are you his girlfriend?"

Elisabet nodded, "Yes I am," she said.

Justin had bravely hung around in an attempt to deter the guys from beating Craig in front of a witness, and was very lucky that they had not turned their hate on him too. He frowned when he heard Elisabet claim to be Craig's girlfriend, but did not contradict her.

"If you go in the ambulance, I will follow in the car," Justin suggested.

"Ought you to drive with that wrist?" asked a Police Officer.

Justin shook his head regretfully. "Probably not."

Then the friendly policeperson offered to drive Elisabet's car the short distance to the hospital car park before re-joining their squad. Elisabet nodded numbly and handed over her car keys. Up at the hospital, it was determined Craig was suffering from concussion and cerebral compression. The ambulance officers told Elisabet that he appeared to be the victim of a 'coward punch'. It was a particularly nasty blow from behind that had been known to result in death.

"Do you know what they had against him?" someone asked.

Elisabet shook her head. "Nothing as far as I know," she said. "But I think they considered him effeminate – whereas to me, he is just elegant."

"Ah – a gay bashing," the other Ambulance Officer concluded. "They are not uncommon."

Elisabet was boiling over with anxiety for Craig, and a sense of the injustice of it all. When they reached Northcoast Hospital, Craig was rushed into an emergency examination cubicle and Elisabet was asked to wait outside. Some moments later, a doctor appeared and told Elisabet that Craig was being moved to theatre in an attempt to relieve the pressure on his brain.

"After that, we just have to wait for healing to take place," the Doctor said. "If you are one of the Christian students, you might like to pray."

Elisabet stumbled out of the Emergency Department and was pleased to see that Justin was sitting in the corridor waiting for her. The master's student had a sober expression on his face.

"How is Craig?" he asked.

"He is critical," Elisabet sobbed. "In fact, the doctors said we ought to pray."

"I need to go back to campus," Justin said. "I am sure that the hospital will ring the university with a report on his condition. Moreover, if we stay here, we will miss vespers, but if we go back there, we can get the whole student body praying for Craig."

Elisabet left her name and the number of the girl's dormitory at the triage desk and begged the nurses to call her if there was any change in her 'boyfriend's' condition. The nurses were extremely sympathetic and promised Elisabet every assistance they could provide.

Once again, Justin listened to the conversation and did not interfere. He understood Elisabet was doing what she could in order to be kept informed about Craig's condition. He too was anxious about Craig, whom he considered a friend. They drove back to campus in silence.

Saturday afternoon, the students were relieved to finally receive the news that the excess fluid in Craig's brain was beginning to subside, and there was no sign of an infection. He was being placed on precautionary antibiotics in any case. If everything went well, with no further complications, Craig ought to live.

Elisabet and Justin drove out to the hospital, where only Elisabet was allowed to visit Craig due to the seriousness of his condition. The band leader was propped up by pillows and blue bruises had developed across his face, neck and arms.

"I managed to save my hands," he croaked, displaying their delicate whiteness.

Elisabet choked in dismay. "I am glad you are recovering," she whispered.

After Elisabet emerged from Craig's room, Justin took her by the elbow and steered her towards the small non-denominational chapel provided for visitors. It was deserted and anything they said they would not be overheard.

Elisabet thought Justin wanted to pray, but instead he looked serious. "We have to talk," he announced. "You told the hospital a lie when you claimed to be Craig's girlfriend."

"Girl who is a friend," Elisabet asserted. "It was not really a lie."

"You knew they thought you meant girlfriend in the romantic sense," Justin declared. "I understand why you did it – but it was still wrong."

"Are you jealous?" Elisabet asked.

Justin shook his head. "No – I'm more like concerned for you. Are you hopelessly in love with Craig?"

"More like hero worship I think," Elisabet admitted.

"I don't want to see you sacrifice yourself in an attempt to save Craig from the consequences of being perceived as gay, or effeminate, whichever really applies. You have to allow Craig to be himself."

"What about the 'not inheriting the kingdom of heaven' part?" Elisabet inquired. "I looked it up after our last conversation on the subject."

"If you continue with the text – the writer explains we can all be 'washed white' through God's grace," Justin explained. He reached out and picked up a Bible tucked conveniently in a pocket on the back of the pew. "First Corinthians chapter 6, verses 9-11: 'Or do you not know that wrongdoers will not inherit the kingdom of God? ...But you were washed, you were sanctified, you were justified in the name of the Lord Jesus Christ and by the Spirit of our God'."

"That's nice," Elisabet mused. "And very comforting."

"To be honest, only Craig can help Craig. After he recovers from this of course," Justin said.

"What do you mean?" Elisabet asked.

"There is never any excuse for a crime like this," Justin said. "But perhaps – if Craig took a martial art class – he might walk more confidently. Bullies look for individuals that fit the victim profile."

"Christians don't believe in fighting back," Elisabet objected.

"I'm not suggesting that Craig fight," Justin said. "Just walk more assertively. It's the little things - although, none of this is Craig's fault. Those guys even looked at me funny because I spoke with a British accent."

"I see," Elisabet mused.

She allowed Justin to lead her back to the car and steered quietly during the short drive back to Silver Springs' campus. "I'm curious," Elisabet finally said. "Why did you allow me to lie to the hospital staff?"

"Because I had compassion," Justin said. "I understood why you were doing it, even when I did not approve. And calling you out at that point would have achieved nothing."

"Will it affect our relationship?" she asked.

"I sincerely hope not," Justin replied.

CHAPTER SEVEN: TRIAL BY ERROR

Sunday, Elisabet attended worship and was content to remain on campus with Justin, so long as she received good news about Craig from the hospital. Monday afternoon, Justin had an appointment to see the doctor in Northcoast, as he wanted to have the wrist checked over and get approval to play basketball again.

Elisabet went to visit Craig in hospital, while Justin was at the medical centre. She was thrilled that he was now recovered enough to talk to her, but horrified that he appeared to be blaming himself for the attack.

"It's not your fault," Elisabet cried indignantly. "Those guys had no right to hit you, no matter what they thought. And you are not rotten inside to attract this sort of thing to you. You are one of the nicest people I know!"

"Nevertheless, I think I must be inherently flawed," Craig persisted patiently.

"No," Elisabet exclaimed. "You must be experiencing some sort of depression resulting from the attack. I think you ought to get counselling."

Craig looked genuinely frightened. "I do not want to do that," he admitted. "A counsellor will pressure me to choose an orientation. A Christian counsellor would pressure me to date girls, and a secular counsellor might pressure me to date guys. I just want to be let be myself."

"Perhaps you could see a counsellor to help deal with the trauma and shock of the attack, and leave the rest alone," Elisabet suggested.

"I don't know if they would let me leave the rest alone," Craig cried desperately.

Justin had arrived while they were talking, and was standing outlined in the doorway. He cleared his throat discretely. "I hope I'm not intruding."

"Of course not," Craig said. "Come on in, Justin."

"If you don't want a counsellor – perhaps you could find some comfort in prayer," Justin suggested. "Matthew chapter 11, verses 28-30: 'Come to me, all you who labour and are heavy laden, and I will give you rest. Take my yoke upon you and learn from me, for I am gentle and lowly in heart, and you will find rest for your souls. For my yoke is easy and my burden is light'."

"You could talk to Justin, because he is already a minister," Elisabet suggested.

"I may do that, Elisabet," Craig said. "Because I liked the text he just quoted to me. However, I would want everything to remain confidential, and not be repeated even to you."

"I can promise you that," Justin said. "It is a little easier to be objective when I have my own parish, but I would do my best."

"Thank you," Craig said.

"Did the doctor say you could play basketball this week?" Elisabet asked, changing the subject.

"He said to wait a few more days," Justin said glumly. "So Craig and I are both still invalids."

Tuesday it was Phoebe's turn to present an English Tutorial. Phoebe had chosen to study *Paradise Lost* and presented a scintillating analysis of its combination of theology and mythology, pedagogy and artistry. *Paradise Lost* was a very long poem, so Phoebe's close readings of necessity focused on isolated sections. After Phoebe's presentation finished, Elisabet was more motivated to read the poem than she had been before.

Wednesday, Elisabet was studying in the dormitory room when Stephanie entered with a concerned look on her face. Stephanie had been visiting Joelle again, attempting to draw the girl back into their group. Elisabet did not expect that to happen, because there had been too many disagreements over potential partners, but Stephanie was blessed with naïve optimism.

"You would never guess what I saw when I was visiting Joelle," Stephanie exclaimed.

"What?" Elisabet asked. Unless it was more piles of sheet music than ever before, Elisabet was all out of ideas. Joelle was a one dimensional person in her estimation. Nice enough, but with very specialised interests.

"There was a chemist's paper bag on her desk, and in the bag was a long thin box. I think it was a pregnancy test!" Stephanie exclaimed.

"Joelle is pregnant?" Elisabet was all ears. "I think Tom ought to be told."

"If it is his – would they get back together for the sake of the baby?" Stephanie mused.

"I don't know," Elisabet said. "I've heard that often doesn't work. But it would seem the right thing to do. And Tom does have a right to know."

Thursday after English class, Stephanie and Elisabet drew Tom aside. He looked at them quizzically. "What is all this about? If you are wondering when we will begin on the Year Book, I will be calling a meeting in a couple of weeks' time."

"It's not that," Stephanie said. "Joelle ought to really tell you herself."

"Tell me what?" Tom was impatient and still raw over his ex-girlfriend.

Stephanie and Elisabet exchanged glances.

"When Stephanie was in Joelle's room," Elisabet ventured. "She saw a pregnancy test."

"A pregnancy test?" Tom was deadly pale. "Are you sure?"

"I am sure," Stephanie said. "I was a little surprised Joelle had left it out, but she couldn't have expected me to visit."

"Was it positive?" Tom's tone was urgent.

"I don't know," Stephanie looked helpless.

"It must have been another guy then," Tom gasped. "Because Joelle and I were waiting until we got married."

Tom dropped his face into his hands and began to sob. Elisabet and Stephanie looked at each other in consternation.

"I'm so sorry," Stephanie stammered. "We didn't know."

Elisabet put her arms around Tom and cuddled him to her. He leaned his head on her shoulder and continued to cry.

"I knew that she had moved on," he sobbed.

"It just seems a little soon for a pregnancy scare," Stephanie said. "That is why we were sure it would be yours if Joelle was pregnant."

"You would think so wouldn't you?" Tom choked.

"It's a wicked old world," Elisabet murmured, stroking Tom's hair. "What are we going to do about our other morning classes?"

"I'm going for a walk in the bush," Tom said. "It doesn't do for a guy to be seen crying around here. You can tell the others I am sick."

"I will come with you," Stephanie offered, but Tom shook his head.

"I just want to be alone," he muttered.

Normal classes had been suspended on Friday because the health students had been booked into a two-day Senior First Aid Course, which would last through into the weekend. The fourth years were all required to assemble in the Education Department, where the workshop would be run.

Elisabet and Stephanie felt horribly guilty about telling Tom that Joelle was pregnant, so Elisabet offered to partner with Tom throughout the training. Tom was too nice to hold a grudge, and accepted her offer at once. The first morning was mostly theory, and in the afternoon they practiced bandages.

It was late by the time they were released from training, so Elisabet had to hurry to eat her tea and dress in something attractive, before Justin arrived to take her across to vespers.

The next day, the first aid participants completed their theory tests, and then rehearsed their resuscitation skills. After their resuscitation proficiency was marked off, they had to complete field scenarios and accident role plays. When they were deemed competent an official certificate would be issued, to arrive in about ten days' time.

The students left the training rooms feeling victorious, and most proceeded to spend their Saturday night either in the recreation area or the gymnasium. Justin's wrist was feeling much better, so he challenged Elisabet to a few games of pool in the recreation area.

Sunday morning, Elisabet and Justin attended the Inter-denominational praise service. Joelle was playing the organ, and Mathew was operating the overhead projector for the songs. They appeared very relaxed and familiar together, setting Elisabet's mind awhirl. She knew that Joelle was seeing Mathew now, but how long had they been seeing each other really? Elisabet caught Stephanie's eye further down the pew and knew the other girl had the same thought.

"Mathew could be the father of Joelle's baby," Elisabet said, when she and Stephanie were alone in their room after lunch.

"We need to be more careful about approaching him," Stephanie said.

"You know how badly we blew it with Tom."

"He is a third year," Elisabet mused, "And that makes it more difficult… unless… we can get another third year to speak to him."

"Perhaps - but whom?" Stephanie exclaimed. "We would have to tell a third party, which is getting mighty like spreading gossip."

 "What about Bede O'Brien?" Elisabet suggested. "She is a third year and is going out with Kaleb, who is friends with Mathew."

Bede was due to visit their room to help Stephanie design her bridesmaids dresses, which created the perfect opportunity to brief the third year girl on the situation. Bede agreed that Mathew should be approached cautiously, and undertook to pump him regarding how intimate he had gotten with Joelle; without necessarily letting on that a pregnancy test existed.

"If Mathew says that he and Joelle have not been intimate," Bede declared, "I would be inclined to believe him. Kaleb and I have always found him to be very truthful."

"Like you say, it would be best if you could package the inquiry as just friendly concern," Stephanie said.

"Rather nosy friendly concern," Bede giggled.

Monday Elisabet and Stephanie concentrated on their classes and tried not to fret too much about the inquiry they had commissioned Bede to make. The girls were exceedingly curious to know the answer, but had learned the value of discretion. They steeled themselves to wait a day or two if necessary, because they knew that Bede would have to find just the right moment to ask her questions.

Craig was allowed out of hospital Tuesday, and in the afternoon, Elisabet and Justin drove across to Northcoast to pick him up. There had been some talk about sending him home, but Craig was keen to complete the semester if he could. Besides, the doctors doubted the wisdom of his catching an aeroplane to Tasmania so soon after a bout of cerebral compression.

Wednesday evening, soon after dormitory worship, Bede knocked on their bedroom door. Stephanie and Elisabet welcomed her inside eagerly.

"I've done it," Bede giggled. "I pretended I wanted Mathew's advice about me and Kaleb… and then asked him about him and Joelle."

"Very clever," Stephanie said. "What did you find out?"

"Well," Bede said. "You may be disappointed to learn that Mathew and Joelle are just good friends. They haven't even gotten to first base."

"And you are sure you believe Mathew?" Elisabet asked.

"Of course," Bede said. "You should have seen him trying to advise me. He was so comical – I do not think he even knows what first base is. Some guys need drawing a map you know!"

"Well, thank you for your help," Stephanie said. "And it's just as well that Mathew knows nothing about why you were really asking."

"Well, I better get back to my room," Bede said. "I have plenty of projects of my own to complete. Let me know when you have found the right material for the bridesmaids, Stephanie."

Stephanie closed the door behind Bede and leaned upon it.

"That is the end of the obvious leads," she said. "We cannot go around suspecting every guy on campus that Jolle has briefly spoken too."

"No we cannot," Elisabet agreed. "As you said – there is no one else obvious."

"Forget it," Stephanie said. "Joelle may not even be pregnant. The test might have read negative."

"Oh no," Elisabet cried. "Oh no, no!"

"What's wrong?" Stephanie inquired.

"Justin!" Elisabet exclaimed.

"That was weeks ago," Stephanie observed logically.

"But doesn't a pregnancy take about six weeks to show up?" Elisabet exclaimed. "The girl doesn't even suspect anything until her period is late."

"Let it be," Stephanie said sternly. "Tom was our friend and Joelle's ex. If the baby had been his, he had every right to know. Justin is with you."

"I wouldn't want a guy that had gotten another girl pregnant," Elisabet said rigidly. She recalled the way Justin held back from kissing her properly, and this ought to have made her feel better, but somehow it didn't. It made it worse. What if his restraint was because there really was someone else?

Thursday afternoon, Elisabet asked Justin to go for a short walk with her. They strolled down to the site of the suspension bridge and sat upon the grass. Justin had known there was something serious by the tone in Elisabet's voice when she had demanded the stroll, but he was flabbergasted when he heard exactly what she had to say.

"I do not think I like you like this, Elisabet," Justin said. "This is not you – all suspicious and jealous. Why can't you trust and believe me?"

"I don't know," Elisabet said. "Maybe because the evidence that there was something between you and Joelle from the beginning is too overwhelming."

"I have been with you for over two months now," Justin said. "I cannot possibly have been messing around with Joelle."

"I am sorry," Elisabet whimpered. "But there is the pregnancy test."

"There is only a chemist bag and a box, neither of which you have seen yourself," Justin thundered. "And then you come accusing me. That does it – we are finished!"

Elisabet dragged herself back to the girls' dormitory in tears, but she did not completely regret the outcome. Justin was a very nice guy, and usually wonderfully understanding, but his reserve had prevented her from growing in trust towards him.

Friday afternoon, Kathy arrived for a weekend visit, and to spend time with Andrew. She was staying in the dormitory room with Elisabet and Stephanie once again, and Elisabet sincerely welcomed the distraction. The primary teacher had been lucky because Queensland day was coming, and her school had closed around one pm. This allowed Kathy to make the three hour drive, and arrive just before the cafeteria had finished serving tea at six thirty pm.

Elisabet, Stephanie and Kathy found some time for girl talk in the interval between tea and vespers. Kathy had a shower and freshened up after her long drive and then asked what was new on campus.

"Well I suppose you have heard about all the engagements?" Elisabet replied.

"Mostly," Kathy said. "Stephanie and Garry's in particular. Many congratulations Stephanie."

"Thanks!" Stephanie said.

"It seems that you and Andrew are amongst the few not engaged yet," Elisabet observed.

"We are engaged to be engaged," Kathy mused. "That only requires a small reclassification of status. Most likely when Andrew hears where he is assigned for work."

"And I had a steady boyfriend for a couple of months," Elisabet admitted. "Justin and I have just broken up."

"I'm sorry," Kathy reflected. "How did that come about?"

Stephanie and Elisabet explained the complicated history of Justin and Joelle; and then Joelle and the pregnancy test. Kathy frowned.

"I know you two meant well – but I somehow doubt Joelle is pregnant," Kathy observed. "She is far too deliberate a person. And it seems anomalous that she would leave the preg test out where someone could see it."

"I did think about that," Stephanie said. The room-mate flushed, because she had been responsible for starting the debacle.

"Anyway – it sounds as though Joelle has got exactly what she wanted out of the fiasco," Kathy continued.

"What?" Elisabet asked.

"Justin is single," Kathy asserted.

"Do you really think that was her goal?" Stephanie puzzled.

"I don't know exactly," Kathy said. "Joelle has always been a little difficult to understand, but the pieces all seem to fit."

"Joelle is hanging out with Mathew at the moment," Elisabet objected.

"That could be for appearances," Kathy suggested. "And for how long?"

"Hmm," Stephanie mused.

"Anyway, Justin was stupid to allow himself to lose you over it, Elisabet," Kathy concluded.

"I think it just wasn't meant to be," Elisabet admitted. "I liked him more than I had anyone before… yet it wasn't going anywhere."

"It's difficult when that happens," Kathy sympathised.

A few minutes later, it was time to go down to vespers, where Kathy and Andrew were proud to be sitting together. Stephanie and Garry, Cara and Dylan filled the rest of the pew with Elisabet sitting unaccompanied at the end.

Phoebe had invited the friends across to her house for lunch on Saturday. She understood that Kathy would not automatically receive her meals at the cafeteria, and was eager to entertain her friends. Elisabet drove her car across to Hank and Phoebe's place, with Stephanie and Garry as her passengers. Dylan drove across in his Suzuki LJ with Cara, Debbie and David onboard.

Elisabet was surprised when Kathy and Andrew arrived with Joelle and Mathew as their passengers.

"Joelle said Phoebe had invited them," Kathy whispered after they had piled out of the car.

"It's Phoebe's house," Elisabet admitted. "She can invite who she likes."

"I'm sure she didn't know it would be awkward," Stephanie whispered.

"I won't let it be awkward," Eliabet said determinedly.

The new pergola was complete, and Hank had installed a barbecue, so they were having vegetable skewers, sizzling sausages and onions, with grilled fruit for lunch. Elisabet had never seen fruit cooked on the barbeque before, but Phoebe assured her that juicy fruits like peaches and pineapples made a sweet treat.

After lunch, the girls were cleaning up in the kitchen, when Joelle drew a package out of her pocket. It was the suspiciously oblong shaped chemist bag. The one Stephanie thought contained the pregnancy test.

"I'm sorry it has taken me a while to get this to you," Joelle said, and passed the package to Phoebe.

"I don't need it anymore – I've been to the doctor," Phoebe said casually and popped the chemist bag away on a shelf. "But thanks."

"What was that all about?" Elisabet inquired casually, although she thought that Joelle gave her a smug smirk.

"You know that Hank and I have been married for over a year now," Phoebe said. "We decided to let nature take its course and we have some great news!"

"You are pregnant? Stephanie exclaimed.

Phoebe confirmed that she was indeed expecting, and the girls literally jumped up and down in excitement.

"It is a good thing though, that nobody saw you with that pregnancy test Joelle," Phoebe finally concluded. "They might have gotten the wrong idea."

"Indeed," Stephanie said meaningly.

"Indeed," Joelle agree darkly. "It could have led to anything – even my expulsion if word got around."

"You know that none of us would do that to you," Elisabet murmured.

"I would like to think you are still all my friends," Joelle said. "Despite the break-up with Tom."

"Of course," Debbie assured her soothingly. "Break-ups in the group are awkward – but not insurmountable."

Although the afternoon had been highly informative, and Phoebe's pregnancy news was very exciting, Elisabet was glad when it came time for her to drive back to campus with her friends. Hank offered to drive Joelle and Mathew back to campus, so that Andrew and Kathy could have some alone time.

Sunday morning, the girls slept past the Inter-denominational praise service, which an understanding Andrew and Garry attended solo. They were loitering over the remains of breakfast in the cafeteria, when the boys caught up with them.

"You sleepy heads are planning to attend the Reform Church service aren't you?" Andrew inquired.

"I don't know," Elisabet admitted. "I've heard Justin is preaching."

"I wouldn't freak out over that," Andrew said sturdily, although he did understand Elisabet's situation. Justin was a high profile speaker, admired and respected by the other theology students because he was already a minister. "If he is a true gentleman, he won't attempt to prejudice anyone against you."

"We will all be with you," Stephanie said. "And knowing you, Elisabet, you will soon find someone else to hang out with."

So Elisabet attended the Reform Church service supported by her friends. Justin preached a sermon that he had obviously been preparing for weeks, because it touched on his masters' thesis topic, and everyone breathed a sigh of relief.

According to the liturgical calendar, the day was also Pentecost, and many of the students wear wearing red, while the meeting hall had been decorated with festive banners. Joelle played the organ as usual and Mathew operated the overhead projector displaying the song lyrics.

After lunch, the friends decided to hang out around the pool area. Even June was not too cold for the occasional bracing dip in sunny Queensland, and lazing on the sun lounges in the winter sun was quite pleasant.

After a while, Elisabet reluctantly excused herself. "I have assignments due," she said. "There are only two more weeks in the semester."

"Plus stu-vac and exams," Stephanie corrected her lazily. The girl did not get up to follow, having brought a text book across to the pool area for light revision.

"I will see you later," Elisabet concluded. Her studies required more than light revision, as she still had material to prepare.

The following Monday was known as the Queen's Birthday, which was a national holiday in every state except Western Australia. Silver Springs University ignored public holidays, but the school system acknowledged the public holiday, so Kathy had been able to sleep over. This allowed her to enjoy an unusually leisurely visit with Andrew, and drive back to Dalby after lunch.

That evening was one of the men's basketball semi-finals. According to Bede's boyfriend Kaleb, Justin would not be playing, because when he had tried out for the game, the ball had jarred his wrist.

"I could not risk having an injured player on the court under finals conditions," Kaleb pronounced responsibly.

"Justin must be disappointed," Elisabet murmured.

"I think he is giving basketball up to concentrate on his thesis," Kaleb said. "I've been looking to replace him in second semester. I'm considering either Vincent or Tom."

"Vincent would love that," Elisabet said. "It is his aim to be back in A grade."

"Tom is actually fitter, because he loves to surf," Kaleb said. He glanced towards Terence, who administered the university league. "I will have to talk it over with Terence."

So that evening, Kaleb's team played with a substitute instead of Justin. Elisabet did not go to the gymnasium to watch, but she heard that they won, due to their captain's outstanding skills. However, it was not as spectacular a victory as usual. Terence, whose team would likely be facing them in the finals, seemed pleased.

Tuesday, Tom presented the tutorial topic in English. He had taken on the philosophical essays, which were far less interesting to the girls than fiction or poetry. The period under study was an era of thought, and even scientific development, which involved not only Britain, but stretched across Europe as well. Stephanie said that Tom did very well, and hurried on to her next appointment.

Elisabet had been giving the pregnancy test mistake some thought, and had been feeling the need to apologise to Tom. He appeared somewhat surprised to see her waiting for him after class.

"Did the Professor say how you went?" Elisabet asked.

"Yes – eight out of ten," Tom reported.

"That's great," Elisabet said. "Listen Tom, I've been feeling bad. Stephanie and I were wrong about that pregnancy test belonging to Joelle. It actually belonged to Phoebe."

Tom laughed cynically. "It's all right," he said. "You were correct in believing that I would have had the right to know if it had been Joelles' pregnancy test. I think the incident helped me process some of my bitterness about the relationship."

"I'm still sorry," Elisabet faltered.

"You were looking out for a friend," Tom said. "And I was flattered that you would go to battle for me like that."

"Really?" Elisabet said.

"Yeah," Tom concluded. "I think you got played by Joelle – in fact, I think we all got played!"

"She said she wanted to be friends again," Elisabet reported.

"She can be friends with you girls," Tom suggested. "I'm out. Tell Stephanie we will be having our first year book meeting on Friday please."

"But it is almost the end of semester," Elisabet exclaimed.

"Most of the work will be done next semester," Tom said. "I just need us to make a plan before then."

"Okay," Elisabet was relieved Tom had taken things so well. He also appeared to be recovering his equanimity since the break-up with Joelle.

Wednesday evening was the women's basketball finals. Elisabet went down to the gymnasium to watch Cara and Janet play. Terence was on the spectator bench as well, and finally asked her how things stood with Justin.

"I haven't seen you two together for about a week now?" Terence probed. "Does that mean you are no longer going out?"

"Unfortunately, yes," Elisabet admitted.

"Perhaps you would like to come to the Basketball Tea with me next week then?" Terrance asked.

"Yes, I guess," Elisabet said.

"What fantastic timing," Terence crowed.

"We aim to oblige," Elisabet said glumly.

Terence gave her shoulder a squeeze. "Cheer up, Justin was a fool to let you go."

A newsflash reported an earthquake that stretched across the mid-western states of North America. It shook buildings, caved in a roofs, broke windows and disrupted telephone services. Kaleb was intensely concerned and began scanning reports to find out whether anyone he knew might have been affected.

"Some sources are saying the damage was restricted to Illinois," he testified. "Although others say the quake was also felt from Kansas to Carolina." He gestured towards a map. "Some say that shocks and tremors occurred in Ohio, Minnesota and Ontario."

"Isn't Ontario in Canada?" Bede exclaimed

Kaleb nodded, "Minnesota is up by the border too."

"It is only a couple of weeks until you will be able to return to the US," Elisabet observed. "The semester here is almost over."

"I would like that," Kaleb said. He frowned. "But I don't want to be taking Bede into danger."

"Surely the probability of it happening again is quite low?" Stephanie inquired.

"There are fault lines right across some sections of America," Kaleb reflected. "Another earthquake is not desirable, but would be very possible."

"Oh, I hope not," Bede exclaimed.

"By all the reports I can locate," Kaleb continued. "Washington and New York have escaped. I've been on the telephone and my friends at American Catholic University are all right. Your contacts at the Man-Made Fiber Producers' Association should be secure too, Bede."

"That's a relief," Bede said. "But the quake came close didn't it?"

"A little too close for comfort," Kaleb said. "Happily, my family are all safe too."

"I'm so glad," Bede said. "I am looking forward to meeting them all."

"Not long to wait now," Kaleb said. "They want to meet you too."

Friday afternoon, Elisabet and Stephanie attended the first of the Year Book committee meetings. Besides Tom, the other committee members were Moira, Felipe and Christopher. The staff member involved was Ms.

Louise the Art Lecturer, although the committee ultimately reported to the English Professor.

Tom explained that early next semester; he planned to launch a poetry competition, and also a photography competition in order to gather additional materials. The competitions would be open for about a month, then they needed to process the entries and produce the book.

"I would like Christopher to write a devotional introduction," Tom said. "Stephanie to do a 'year in brief' summary, and of course, Moira will have several sports pages. Elisabet – I want you to help me with selection and organisation."

"It sounds as though you know what you want," Stephanie observed.

"Sort of," Tom admitted. He opened an orange envelope and spread out a collection of photographs. "These are a few of the photographs that our official campus photographer, Ms. Louise, has taken already. I thought we could look through these to generate ideas."

It was heaps of fun looking through the photographs and reminiscing about the events represented.

"I think I would like to write something about our band," Elisabet said. "And – I would report about the music programme in general."

"Good idea," Tom said.

Felipe suggested that he also take the camera through the Science Department one afternoon, because there were no science photos in Ms. Louise's collection. Tom announced that he was pleased with their progress for the afternoon and closed the meeting. Ms. Louise made a few notes, because she would be responsible for ensuring people completed their tasks.

Saturday morning, Elisabet managed to have a few quiet words with Craig in the Music Department. The young man reported that he had been spending a lot of time resting in his dormitory room, and was excused from campus activities whenever he felt fatigued.

"That includes the band," Craig said. "At the moment, it is all I can do to keep up with my violin."

"I understand," Elisabet said. "I'm just pleased to have you back."

"I was sorry to hear about you and Justin," Craig said. "I was wondering, Elisabet – would you mind very much if I continued counselling with Justin as we discussed?"

"Of course not," Elisabet exclaimed. "I think it would do you good. And Justin is a good enough bloke – at least towards other men."

"It could be that there always was something deeper to his friendship with Joelle than Justin would like to admit," Craig observed with the wisdom of one who avoided involvement themselves.

"That is what I suggested, and Justin dropped me for it," Elisabet said despondently.

"Well it was no good going ahead with the relationship under the circumstances," Craig said objectively. "Harsh though that sounds."

"I know," Elisabet sighed.

CHAPTER EIGHT: THE MIDDLE OF THE YEAR

That Sunday was known as Trinity Sunday, and Andrew Grosvy preached at the Inter-denominational praise service. As usual for him, Andrew's sermon was full of textual references. At lunch a deep philosophical discussion continued between Andrew, David and Larry. The girls left the Theology students to their debate and chatted amongst themselves.

In the afternoon, Stephanie and Bede pushed the beds aside and covered the bedroom floor with fabric. Stephanie had found the exact shade of taffeta she had been seeking for the bridesmaid's dresses. She referred to the colour as 'apricot', and it represented a subtle blend of colour. The fabric was stiff and prone to rustling. It would be lined with a silky polyester.

Cara and Kathy were going to be Stephanie's bridesmaids. Both girls were young and had good figures, so they had agreed to wear any design Stephanie chose. She had gone with an empire-line bodice to match her dress, but had allowed the bridesmaid dresses to be shaped below the waist to bell out in typical eighties' fashion. The dresses also featured small puff sleeves and Elisabet thought the sketches looked very pretty.

"I'm sorry that I won't be here to help you finish them," Bede muttered regretfully, her mouth full of pins.

"Don't worry about it," Stephanie said. "Once they are cut out – I will be able to machine them up okay."

"How is the wedding dress coming along?" Elisabet asked curiously.

She had been invited to be a bridesmaid in honour of her being Stephanie's room-mate for the year, but she had declined. Elisabet had been a bridesmaid for her cousin the year before, and it wasn't as much fun as it looked.

"It's almost there," Bede said. "Luckily I am a fast seamstress. I might show the Home Economics Lecturer. Stephanie, I hope you don't mind. I may as well get a grade on it after all!"

"So long as it is only the lecturer that sees the dress, I am fine with that," Stephanie conceded.

"How are the earthquake reports?" Elisabet asked.

"Kaleb watches the international news all the time," Bede said. "He says the area we are going to is still safe. Some of the surrounding states face millions of dollars of repairs."

"I'll bet," Stephanie said. "I don't know how people face natural disasters like that – I really don't."

"The human spirit is a wonderful thing," Elisabet said. "Justin would say that was evidence of our divine origin." She had not meant to remind herself of her ex-boyfriend. She sighed: "It's been a week and a half since we broke up."

"Try not to think about it," Bede advised.

Monday evening, the men's basketball finals were played. Elisabet would have been tempted to stay away from the match, except Terence had persuaded her to watch. Moira had also been ordered to write a report for the year book, so the girls walked down to the gymnasium together.

When the girls arrived at the gymnasium, they saw the A grade teams were warming up before the game. Kaleb had decided to add both both Tom and Vincent to his team, because when he went back to America, the team would need another player.

The match began, and it seemed as though Kaleb's team was just beginning to bond with its new members. They played well, but Terence's veterans excelled in both attack and defence. By half-time, Terence's team was several goals ahead.

Kaleb counselled his members to increase their cooperative strategies, and the second half of the game represented a more even challenge. At full time, Terence's team was victorious, but all the spectators agreed that Kaleb's team made a good effort.

Terence accepted congratulations from all the guys, before crossing to the spectator bench where Elisabet was seated. He flopped down on the seat and fanned himself. He had worked up a sweat despite the mild June evening.

"You will be coming to the Basketball Tea with me on Wednesday night then?" he observed casually.

"I was hoping you might have forgotten," Elisabet joked, but it was a flirtatious little untruth. Every girl would enjoy the attention of a winning A grade captain. Well, every girl without a steady boyfriend that was.

"I never forget anything," Terence said earnestly.

"Pick me up at a quarter past five then," Elisabet said, calculating that would give them fifteen minutes before the presentations began.

"Five would be better," Terence said. "I'm one of the organisers you know."

"Oh, of course," Elisabet agreed. "Five then. And congratulations on the win!"

"Thanks," Terence said. He would have lingered longer, and maybe even walked Elisabet back to the dormitory, but Kaleb called him to assist in packing up the equipment.

Elisabet walked back to the dormitory with Stephanie and Garry, Moira, Janet and Vincent. Garry and Vincent said goodbye at the door, and the girls continued inside to their rooms.

Throughout Tuesday and Wednesday, most of the students were preoccupied with completing last minute assignments. Everything had to be handed in by five o'clock Wednesday evening. Even Stephanie had one or two reading reports that she had not finished, as some readings were announced progressively. Elisabet considered herself an efficient worker, and was able to walk across to hand her material in at the same time as her room-mate.

Wednesday evening, Terence called at the dormitory a few moments before five o'clock. Traditionally, the students wore neat casual to the Basketball Tea, while the players wore their team colours. Elisabet thought Terence looked very attractive with his oversize team shirt hanging over his denim jeans. She had spent some hours curling her blonde hair into a tangle of perfection.

"You look great," Terence exclaimed.

"I'm just casual," Elisabet said coyly. She knew that the tight jeans outlined her naturally fit legs to perfection, however.

"I like the sporty look," Terence said. "But if you don't mind – we need to hurry a little."

They reached the cafeteria and Terence led Elisabet to a seat on the A grade table. Then he went and checked the microphone set-up, and counted the trophies. Everything appeared to be in order and he returned to sit beside Elisabet.

"There is a rumour that Kaleb will announce who is to replace him as captain," Elisabet said.

Terence nodded. "It's true," he said. "And the choice may be a little controversial – but well deserved I believe."

"Hmm," Elisabet poked at the dip placed in the centre of the table, and lifted a liberally coated potato wedge to her mouth. The sweet chilly was spicy and she coughed.

"I like to get some sour cream and some sweet chilly at the same time," Terence said. He grabbed a chip and demonstrated. "It doesn't count as double dipping if you have not taken it up to your mouth yet."

"Oh of course," Elisabet smiled. "How silly of me!"

Tom slid into the seat on the other side of Elisabet. "Hello Elisabet," he said.

"Hello Tom," Elisabet said. "No date tonight?"

"I don't need a date for a function like this," Tom said. "I've got my team to sit with."

"Oh of course!" Elisabet agreed.

Janet arrived with Vincent and sat down on the other side of Tom. Lacey was with Justin, and they sat with the girls' A grade teams. Elisabet tried to turn her head so that she was not looking at Justin, but Janet gave Lacey a wave. The rest of Terence's team filed in and sat on Terence's other side with their dates.

The hospitality students brought out some hot dogs dipped in a corn batter. Students reached for the dippy dogs and spread them liberally with that Australian favourite, tomato sauce. There were lettuce cups to add a little healthy green to the meal.

Terence rose and presented the trophies to the boy's teams. It would have been silly for him to present the A grade trophy to himself, so Kaleb rose and made a show of handing it across to Terence.

"Well done mate," Kaleb said, the Australian colloquialism sounding strange with his American accent.

"Thank you, Kaleb," Terence said. "We will miss you when you leave for the US in just over a week's time."

"I will miss you all too," Kaleb said warmly. "But at least I get to take the missus with me!"

"You had better do the right thing by Bede and make her your missus for real," Cara O'Brien, Bede's sister called from amongst the girl's A grade seating.

"Fiance Visa already applied for," Kaleb said smugly.

Stephanie began clapping from her seat beside Garry on the B grade boy's table. The applause spread as the rest of the cafeteria took up the ovation. It was a strange way to announce an engagement, but everyone seemed happy.

"Now to my other big announcement," the African-American youth said. "I have discussed this at length with Terrance and he has agreed that Vincent should take over as captain of my team."

Some people looked surprised, because Vincent had not even been included in the university league at the beginning of the year. However, he had worked hard to win a place back in competition basketball and even moved back into the A grade.

"I suggested this because Vincent is a talented player," Terence said. "We all know what happened last year. Some people were passed supplements that they did not know were dangerous. Vincent was one of the first to admit his mistake. We are Christians and we believe in forgiveness. I want to see what he can make of the captain's position."

"And I am proud to be playing under his direction," Tom said, rising to his feet. Now Kaleb, Terence and Tom were all standing. One by one, all of Kaleb's team stood up to join them.

Vincent rose to his feet and thanked the guys for their support. "I will try to be a good captain," he said. "Please sit down everyone."

After the business involving the men's basketball competition was completed, the presentations were made for the girls' basketball competition. Cara and Janet both received trophies, Cara for 'Best and

Fairest' and Janet for leading her team so well. The hospitality students brought out a cake that the captains cut together.

When the tea was finished, Terence lingered with the other players, discussing the season, and planning logistics for the coming semester. Elisabet sat and waited patiently. It was pleasant to hear all the sporting talk, even though it did not involve her. Finally, Terence turned to Elisabet and apologised for his pre-occupation.

"I will walk you back to the dorms," he said.

Elisabet nodded. She rose to her feet and followed Terence towards the cafeteria door. He reached out a hand to steady her, and Elisabet allowed him to hold her hand for a moment, before discretely sliding it out of his grip.

"You know what people will say," Elisabet murmured.

"I was just being a gentleman," Terence said.

"I know," Elisabet murmured. "I understand, I really do… but public demonstration of affection…."

"Has implications around here," Terence sighed. "Nobody does it before they are ready."

"Exactly," Elisabet agreed.

The distance between the cafeteria and the girl's dormitory was not very great. The couple reached the front steps and Terence turned to face Elisabet.

"Good luck with study and exams," he said. "And I'll be seeing you around."

"I wish you good luck too," Elisabet said. "Don't be a stranger!"

"Of course I won't," Terence said. "Next semester, when the social calendar is back on, and you are over Justin, I might try inviting you to something again."

"I would like that," Elisabet said.

Terrance gave her a peck on the cheek and then left. Elisabet stepped inside the girl's dormitory and headed towards her room, where she expected to face Stephanie's curious questioning.

Thursday and Friday there were no classes because the 'study vacation' had commenced. During this time, the students were expected to manage their revision and thoroughly prepare themselves for exams. Elisabet found that rooming with a conscientious student like Stephanie was highly motivating. The two girls were able to spend time discussing the material and quizzing each other on relevant readings.

Elisabet had shared the majority of her classes with Tom as well, and during the periods that Stephanie was studying for biology, or indicated a preference for individual study, Elisabet organised to meet Tom in the library. There the two discussed poetry and commiserated with each other about the demands of their compulsory health studies.

Friday evening, the Uniting Church Vespers was offered as usual, and the students descended upon the meeting with relief, as it offered an opportunity to relax and socialise. In recognition of the fact that the Theology students were preparing for exams, the Uniting Church Chaplain had elected to organise the service himself. He spoke about the importance of prayer and Elisabet listened in amusement, because she was sure many prayers would be raised to heaven as the students entered the exam period.

Elisabet was sitting with Stephanie and Garry, while Cara and Dylan were on the far side of Stephanie. Terrance approached politely and asked to sit on Elisabet's free side. She granted him permission with an easy assurance that there was no one she would rather have sit beside her. Vincent and Janet also sat down and the pew was full to capacity.

Saturday afternoon, Elisabet wandered into the Music Department. The music exam would mostly cover theory, but she somehow felt that a few moments practice would help her. It would also ensure that she was not too rusty to fulfil the next semester's practical requirements.

Craig obviously had a similar thought, because he was in one of the practice rooms with his violin. Elisabet was glad to see that the young man looked much better than he had a couple of weeks ago.

"How are you doing?" she asked.

"Pretty good considering," Craig replied.

"I have been wondering something," Elisabet said. "Will the band be getting back together next semester?"

"I had every intention of calling the band back together once I felt better," Craig said. "However, something has happened."

"What?" Elisabet felt a shiver of alarm.

"Nothing bad," Craig assured her. "Just Vincent could be too busy managing his basketball team to join us."

"I still need a performance component for my studies," Elisabet murmured.

"We all do," Craig said. "I thought – maybe you could ask your first year music class and see whether one of them would consider taking up the drums."

"I think Vivione has a good sense of rhythm," Elisabet said. "And with her – we would still be the *Electronic Jive Classical Vibe Band*."

Craig laughed. "Replacing Vincent with someone who has the right initial is the least of our aims," he said. "But a full music major would be an asset to the band. Vincent was only ever a casual member."

"He brought so much energy to the role," Elisabet reminisced regretfully.

"Well – now he plans to channel that energy into his basketball," Craig said. "Our loss is the sport's gain."

"I guess so," Elisabet agreed. She crossed to the keyboard and began to play one of the band's regular pieces.

Craig picked up his violin and joined her with a smile. Soon after that, it was time for tea, and Elisabet crossed to the cafeteria to linger over her meal.

On Sunday there was one combined worship, instead of the usual early praise and later services. After church, the students ate in the cafeteria and then dispersed to their respective dormitories. The tension was beginning to mount, because exams would be commencing that week.

The first exam Elisabet sat was health. When the exam timetable had been released, Elisabet had gotten a fright because first year music had been scheduled to clash with fourth year health, both on Monday morning. However, she reported the clash, and the music exam had been moved to the afternoon. Two exams on the one day were quite stressful, but after Elisabet had finished, she was very relieved.

Tuesday brought Elisabet and Stephanie's English exams. Both girls wrote furiously throughout the exam period and hoped that they had done well. Stephanie had felt 'inspired' during the exam, and Elisabet had felt confident. English exams were not difficult aside from the first few moments, when one feared the dreaded 'writer's block'.

Wednesday Stephanie had biology. Elisabet had a free day, but tried not to flaunt in front of her roommate, who was stressing. Elisabet and Stephanie both had an education theory exam on Thursday, and curriculum knowledge assessment Friday. Practice teaching would be assessed by portfolio and practical exercises, so there was no exam for that subject.

By Friday afternoon, many of the students had already left campus, and the rest were finalising their travel connections. Andrew caught a bus from Northcoast to Dalby, in order to help Kathy pack her things and move to Murwillumbah. Cara and Dyan piled into Dylan's light jeep and began heading down the Bruce Highway towards Newcastle, because Dylan's home there.

Stephanie and Garry would be lingering on campus for a few days, and Stephanie had permission to enter the boy's dormitory to help pack Garry's things. After completing his units that semester, Garry, who had attended several summer schools, had achieved enough credit points to graduate. He had accepted the offer of a six month contract from the Queensland Rail, and was moving out into share accommodation with another railway employee.

After helping Garry move his things, they would be catching the train to Brisbane, and from Brisbane airport, to Wollongong, via Sydney to visit Garry's parents. Stephanie had arranged to complete her practicum at one of the high schools in Illawarra Shire, near Wollongong.

Elisabet didn't mind the drive back to Byron Bay, but she did find it a bit lonely driving in the dark. The end of semester had seemed more rushed than usual, because Easter had been late and compressed the second half of the semester. She decided to stop and visit her cousins in Tweed Heads and spent a night at her uncle's house before finishing her journey home.

The first week of the university vacation was the last week of the school holidays. During the second week, the children returned to school. Elisabet only had one week free in reality, because she had to complete a practice teaching placement.

This placement involved taking almost full responsibility for lesson planning and running the classroom by herself, with the supervising qualified teacher observing her performance. It was never a really good idea to return to one's former school for practical experience, so she had elected to teach at nearby Ballina instead of Byron Bay.

Elisabet was confident, and enjoyed the sense of authority that teaching gave her. She had two senior English classes, one middle-school English class, one middle-school history class and first year music class to teach each day. She was also expected to take homeroom and Bible lessons.

During the lunch hour, she cultivated the friendship of her supervising teachers, gathering hints from them. She was happy to follow most suggestions that they made, because this made preparation and planning easier.

The Education Lecturer visited from Silver Springs University to see how Elisabet was going in her final week. He was positive and supportive, expressing pleasure at her integration into the school system. He made a few notes on her lesson plans, and promised that he would debrief her back at university.

Elisabet arrived back on campus on the second Sunday in August. The second semester would follow a similar pattern to the first. The main differences would that they would be studying modernism in English, and that counselling skills would replace health as a house requirement. Elisabet planned to continue her music electives; and her curriculum and education subjects were compulsory.

Monday morning at breakfast, Craig went out of his way to remind Elisabet that she needed to recruit one of the girls from her music class into the band. The class met later that morning, and James helped her explain the situation to Jessie and Vivione. Both girls had seen the *Electronic Jive Classical Vibe Band* perform in the cafeteria and admitted that they were mildly interested.

Jessie said that she was following in Joelle's footsteps using the worship committee as her performance component. Vivione had been participating in choir, but she was open to more experience. Elisabet invited her to attend the *Electronic Jive Classical Vibe Band*'s next practice, which would probably be towards the end of the week.

Tuesday afternoon Elisabet had to work in the Student Services office. She answered telephone enquiries as well as performed filing duties. It was also her task to type out the first student social calendar for the semester, and she noticed that Tom had submitted the announcement of the two Year Book competitions, one for poetry and one for photography. These competitions would be open immediately and would close on the first day of September. This gave the students approximately one month to participate if they wished.

The first major social event of the second semester was traditionally the Computer Tea. This was a fun event in which each student was assigned a 'match' by a computer database matching program. The event was designed to ensure any students who had just enrolled were not left out of already solidified friendship groups.

In reality, the students had learned how to 'rig' their computerised dates. The computer simply picked out similarities and hence regular couples who filled out their forms with exactly the same answers, were usually put together. The only time the system had been known to fail had been the previous year when the computer put Cara with Vincent, instead of Dylan.

Wednesday morning after convocation, Terence asked Elisabet if she would 'rig' the Computer Tea and attend with him. Remembering that she had practically agreed to a second date after the Basketball Tea, Elisabet happily said 'yes'. Moreover, she was comfortable with Terrance. He was good looking and a team captain, generally too busy to make an embarrassment of himself, and yet very pleasant company when they were at mixed events.

By tea time, that day, Terence had procured the forms and the pair had filled them out. Elisabet giggled as she wrote her height down as six-foot-two, but Terence strictly refused to mark himself as five-foot-nine. Elisabet had no regular sport, so they both selected basketball. Terrance also put the English Professor down as his favourite lecturer, even though it had been a year since he had taken an English unit.

The pair chose green as their favourite colour, and listed watching television and playing pool as hobbies. There were a few other random questions to which the answer did not matter, just so long as their responses matched. The forms completed, they dropped the sheets of paper into the box in the cafeteria, and exchanged 'high fives' with open palms.

Thursday afternoon Stephanie had her biology practical, so Elisabet had the dormitory room to herself. She took advantage of the opportunity to rearrange her wardrobe, exchanging some of her winter clothes for festive spring clothing she had purchased during the holidays. The ruffles and frills of puffy, eighties styling filled the wardrobe to capacity, and Elisabet had to fold some garments back into the suitcase.

Friday, Tom had scheduled a Year Book committee meeting. They met in one of the art rooms because that was most convenient for Ms. Louise. After everyone was seated, Tom marked them present and opened the proceedings.

"I received your article on the semester one basketball season Moira," he said. "It was excellent and so were the photographs!"

"Thank you," Moira murmured.

"Felipe, your Science Department pictures were also interesting," Tom said. "Using a few of them will help the yearbook convey the fact that Silver Springs University offers a fully supported science programme. It is our job to advertise the university to a certain extent, as well as create student memories."

"Have you had any responses to the competitions?" Stephanie asked curiously.

"There hasn't been enough time for the processing of prints," Tom said. "I don't have any photographic entries yet."

"A few students have asked to borrow the Art Department SLR," Ms. Louise said. "I've instituted a security deposit and borrowing system."

"Very good," Tom said. "I do have one or two poems. Not very hopeful so far, I'm afraid."

"Most of the students are not accustomed to writing imaginatively," Stephanie observed.

"We can't enter," Elisabet murmured regretfully.

"Your best pieces will be published anyway," Tom said. "And you will be able to put having worked on the book on your resume."

"Along with the Student Services Office and helping in my parent's store, I will look more like a secretary than a teacher," Elisabet complained.

"At least you will have options!" Moira grinned.

"There is that," Elisabet admitted.

"A couple of guys have asked whether they are able to submit devotional poems," Christopher said.

"By all means!" Tom exclaimed. "Promote the competition amongst your fellow Theology students. I don't mind if they see God in every sunrise, this is a Christian publication."

"How very pantheistic!" Stephanie began to giggle at the thought of theology students seeing God hovering in the sky every morning, and Tom gave her a stern look.

"Now, now, Stephanie! Well – if that is everything, I think we will close our meeting. I will see you next week, same time, same place. Hopefully we will have more to discuss."

Tom dismissed the meeting and the students walked across to the cafeteria to have their tea. After that, the girls retreated to the dormitory to make themselves pretty, before attending the Uniting Church Vespers gathering that evening.

Saturday the *Electronic Jive Classical Vibe Band* convened for its first practice for the new semester. As Elisabet had hoped, Vivione turned up to join them. The first year was a full music major. She played the cello, had a nice voice, and was also skilled with the bass guitar. Her presence made Elisabet feel obsolete.

"A bass guitar will make us more rocky," she objected. "We already get accused of being a rock band!"

"But the students love that," Tom observed. The roadie was not really required at practice, but he had been bored and decided to tag along.

"The staff don't," Elisabet explained. "Being too rocky risks our approval."

"We won't be rocky without a drummer," Craig said regretfully.

"About that," James said. "I'm taking over the drums. I've been practising over the holidays."

"I don't want to lose the trumpet," Craig was doubtful.

James laughed. "With two voices, you won't need the trumpet!"

"Having a second singer does introduce more possibilities," Craig agreed. He began to discuss how the revamped line-up would work. "We have lots of options. I would like to utilise them all."

The band settled down to playing music, and aside from a few miscued notes, all was harmonious for the next hour. The composer looked very pleased with the result.

CHAPTER NINE: COMING UNRAVELLED

On Sunday, the campus was rife with rumours that Mathew and Joelle had broken up, if indeed, they had ever been a serious couple. Joelle remained tight-lipped, her face inscrutable as she played for both worship services. Mathew, on the other hand, confirmed the truth.

"We have stopped hanging out," Mathew said. "We have such different timetables, and we are at different stages, with Joelle graduating and all that."

"I wonder if Joelle will get back with Tom," Stephanie speculated. "He was her faithful boyfriend for two years."

"I sincerely hope that Tom won't take her back," Elisabet said. "I think he ought to have had enough of her self-serving ambition."

"Don't talk about one of our classmates like that!" Stephanie said sharply.

Elisabet remembered that Stephanie had roomed with Joelle during their first year at Silver Springs. The girls had never become best friends, but perhaps some residual loyalty remained. "I'm sorry," she said.

"I think Elisabet just wants Tom to be happy," Garry added in an attempt to smooth the situation over.

Garry was on campus because it was the weekend. He had settled in to work at the Engine Works and was feeling very proud of his achievements. One of his first purchases had been a small car, a Datsun with a sloping roof and sporty lines that let him drive back to visit.

Elisabet nodded. "Of course that is what I want," she said. "I think that if Tom and Joelle are not suited, they ought not to get back together."

"You might have a point," Stephanie admitted grudgingly.

"I hope it works out for the poor fellow," observed Terence, who had accompanied Elisabet to church.

Elisabet glanced at Terence gratefully. He was proving to be good company. Friendly, charming, and not too possessive at this early stage. Elisabet had no intention of treating him like a rebound boyfriend, but he was good for her current mood.

"What shall we do this afternoon?" she asked.

In the end, it was decided they would go for walk with friends, as the weather was cool and fine.

Monday in music, Jessie was full of questions regarding the band practice. Three of the members of the class were now part of the *Electronic Jive Classical Vibe Band.* It seemed to have brought them closer together, although Jessie was still adamant that the worship committee took up her spare time.

"I will just listen and bask in your reflected glory," she laughed.

"You do that," James joked and flicked her playfully with a rubber-band.

Jessie squealed and giggled. James had dated a few of the first year girls, and Jessie had been out with one or two of the first year boys, but neither had formed a serious relationship with anyone yet.

Tuesday, Elisabet was working in Student Services when something gave her pause. She was typing an announcement that Jeffrey Mannington would be relieving the Computing Lecturer for a few weeks, because the regular faculty member was going to an overseas conference.

"Now, where have I heard that name before?" Elisabet mused. Then she remembered. It was the name of Stephanie's ex-boyfriend, the weird one who graduated years ago. Perhaps she ought to warn her roommate.

A chance came that evening after the co-ed vespers service had finished, when the girls returned to their dormitory room.

"Do you still have an issue with Jeffrey Mannington?" Elisabet asked curiously.

Stephanie shook her head, but she seemed to be walking a little slower. "No," she said. "I am happily engaged to Garry."

"I've learned that Jeffrey will be replacing the Computing Lecturer for a while," Elisabet explained.

Stephanie was silent for a moment. "I don't have an issue with Jeff, but he can be a jerk," she said finally. "It's a good thing I took computing last year."

"It shouldn't affect any of us," Elisabet agreed.

"Unless Ms. Louise," Stephanie continued thoughtfully. "She seemed to have a soft spot for him. I hope that she takes care."

"You never reported him for anything, did you?" Elisabet asked curiously. She had not learned the full story, but most of the group knew Jeffrey had been bad news for Stephanie.

"Oh no," Stephanie said. "His official record is clean enough."

Wednesday the fourth years had their first counselling skills lecture. It was introductory, covering the theory and issues surrounding therapy, along with the responsibilities of the counsellor. Apparently there were a number of methods and schools of thought regarding helping others. The course would cover a few of the major methods and the students would also work in pairs to counsel each other.

Thursday afternoon, Stephanie had her biology practical. Cara dropped by the room to pick her up, as with Garry gone, the class was down to three members. Elisabet wished the girls luck, and then walked across to the music building, where Craig had scheduled another band practice.

Craig was already there. He handed each member the sheet music in the order he had planned. They played the pieces through, feeling more comfortable than the previous session. However, at one point, Craig stopped and looked at James.

"You are not Vincent," he said with a sigh.

James grimaced. "I'm better than Vincent," he announced proudly.

Craig appeared to think about it for a while. "You are right," he admitted. "Your sense of rhythm is near perfect. And yet – I liked Vincent's imperfections - his drumming breathed with us."

"Perhaps when I am more accustomed to the role I might try experimenting," James said. "But for now, I'm concentrating on getting the beat right."

"I guess that will have to do for now," Craig said.

Friday afternoon, the Year Book committee met again. Tom had organised a selection of previous year's volumes for them to compare for design and layout. They choose one of Ms. Louise's photographs for the cover, and finalised a coulour scheme.

Christopher also submitted his devotional, and Tom was very pleased. He concluded that the project was on schedule and thanked everyone for their contributions.

Saturday evening brought the Computer Tea. Stephanie and Garry had elected not to attend, because Garry had a social club gathering at the Engine Works, where Stephanie would be introduced as his fiancé. This meant that Elisabet had the dormitory room to herself while dressing.

Terence had her paged a few minutes before the Computer Tea was due to begin. Elisabet picked up her room-key, and the little purse containing her handkerchief. She walked out to the foyer to greet him.

"You look gorgeous," Terence was complimentary as usual.

"Thank you," Elisabet said. The evening was formal, and she was wearing a full skirted red satin dress that might have been too bright for some girls, but was just right for her. Terence was wearing a suit. "You look elegant too… sort of James Bond."

Terence looked pleased to be compared to James Bond. The new actor playing James Bond was Timothy Dalton, who had brought an additional level of refinement to the character. "Thanks," he said.

Terence and Elisabet walked across to the cafeteria, where they discovered their ruse had worked, and the computer had matched them together. They were also seated near Cara and Dylan, Vincent and Janet. Tom had drawn Lacey, Elisabet could not tell whether it was by accident or design. Perhaps it was deliberate, as the two were good friends.

Terence and Elisabet were enjoying the finger food, which was composed of tiny sandwiches, when Elisabet happened to glance across the room. Her eyes locked on Justin's and she flushed. Then she noticed his companion. It was Joelle. After all his denials!

Justin lowered his eyes, as if he felt a moment of guilt, and then he turned his attention towards his companion. His manner was solicitous, and the thought the pair might be 'just good friends' vanished from Elisabet's head. She drew a sharp breath.

"What is wrong?" Terence inquired kindly.

"Over there," Elisabet whispered.

Terence knew that Elisabet was not ready for public display of affection, but he placed a protective arm across the back of her chair. "Hadn't you heard?" he whispered.

"Heard what?" Elisabet asked.

"It is all through the boy's dormitory that Justin and Joelle have become a couple," Terence replied.

"No, the ex-girlfriend is always the last to be told," Elisabet whispered glumly. She was swamped in waves of humiliation.

"Please try to forget them," Terence whispered. "You are with me tonight."

Elisabet tried to listen to Terence, but she was distracted, and also grateful that he had Vincent for company. Cara looked sympathetic and attempted to offer comfort, but Elisabet could not snap out of her state of shock.

When the soup was served, she could barely swallow it. 'Justin and Joelle'! It was a constant chorus in her mind. She glanced across at Tom and saw that despite his friendship with Lacey, he was doing it tough too.

"I need to go outside," Elisabet whispered. The main course was a choice of beef or vegetarian schnitzel, with garlic and pumpkin mash. Normally Elisabet would have loved the food, but her throat was tight and furry.

"I will come with you," Terence said. He stood and gently steered her towards the balcony, where they could stand overlooking the bushland. The moon was rising and the stars twinkled mockingly.

Elisabet rested her face on his shoulder. "I'm sorry," she whispered as the tears threatened to break.

One of the staff chaperones came outside to check on them, thinking that they were sharing a passionate and forbidden embrace. Terence quietly indicated that Elisabet was upset, and the staff member went back inside.

"Let your grief out," Terence murmured. "Don't bottle it up. They are just not worth it."

"I think I'm okay now," Elisabet said finally. "I know you would like your main meal."

"It is not about me," Terence said, but he allowed himself to be persuaded to return to the cafeteria.

A few moments later, Cara arrived to keep Elisabet company on the balcony instead. The girls chatted for a few moments, and then Elisabet returned to the cafeteria. Her main course was cold and she asked the hospitality students to remove it.

Desert was served, and Elisabet plunged her spoon into the strawberry flavoured confection. A sweet would always slide down the digestive tract. Terence, Vincent and Janet kept talking about the new season's basketball, and Elisabet was thankful she could just listen.

At least Terence seemed to be having a good time, but Terence was an optimist and would likely always make the best of things. It was an endearing quality.

After the event wound to a close, Terence walked Elisabet back to the girl's dormitory. "I am sorry about tonight," she whispered as he bade her goodbye.

"Don't worry about it," Terence said. He looked hopeful. "Perhaps now you can get over Justin."

"Perhaps," Elisabet was relieved that Terence put such a promising spin on things. "I will see you sometime tomorrow, but don't look for me if I decide to miss church."

"You have to eat lunch," Terence said wisely. "If you don't come to that, I will come looking for you!"

Elisabet nodded. "Okay," she said.

Terence's prediction that Elisabet might soon overcome her break-up from Justin proved to be unrealistic. After the shock wore off, she began to feel anger at his betrayal.

The Masters in Theology student had broken up with Elisabet because she had accused him of harbouring feelings for Joelle, and it appeared that she had been right all along. Justin *had* lied to her. He *had* strung her along. Perhaps he had been trying to do the right thing at one stage, but Elisabet's mind was determined to place the most incendiary interpretation on all his actions.

When Stephanie returned to the dormitory, she was most concerned. Elisabet was pacing the room, even though it was late. The girl would not lie down to sleep, and could barely be persuaded to take off her make-up and indulge in a soothing shower.

In the end, Cara lent them a forbidden transistor radio, and Elisabet lay down with the earphones tucked into her ears, listening to the top one hundred count down of popular songs. The next morning, Elisabet was exhausted enough to sleep, and went back to bed after eating a small breakfast.

Stephanie and Cara went to the worship services and returned to wake the sleeping girl for lunch. Remembering Terence's threat to visit the dormitory if she were not at lunch, Elisabet brushed her hair and agreed to accompany her friends.

Monday, Elisabet didn't want to attend her classes, but Stephanie persuaded her the gossip would get worse if she didn't.

"Besides, you can only afford so many absences before you are disqualified," the roommate said practically.

Elisabet was normally very ambitious, but at that moment she did not care about academic performance. She had opened her heart to someone, and it had been disrespected. She understood couples broke up, but how could she - pretty, popular Elisabet from Byron Bay, have made so little impact on someone?

Life didn't make sense and nor did classes, but Stephanie's logic prevailed enough to get Elisabet out of the dormitory room. Joelle was in a few of her classes, but Justin was postgraduate and had a very different timetable, luckily.

Tuesday, everyone had something different to think about, as Ms. Louise was seen lunching in the cafeteria with Jeffrey Mannington. Sometimes, lecturers chose to slum it and eat the student fare. Jeffery and Ms. Louise appeared to have decided to make a date out of it. Stephanie rolled her eyes and predicted it would not last very long.

Wednesday, Elisabet almost failed a test because she had not done the reading. She achieved fifty percent using her general knowledge, and making up answers. It was better than failing completely, and she might be able to pull her grade up by doing well in the rest of her assignments, but the incident stunned her. Unfortunately, it did not make her care any more about doing well. Instead it convinced her that she was entering a downward life spiral.

Thursday Terence tried to cheer Elisabet up by inviting her to watch him play basketball. Elisabet agreed, because she knew Terence was being kind, and she would appear extremely surly if she refused. However, she took very little interest in the game, and primarily gained satisfaction from the fact that Justin did not show his face in the gymnasium.

Friday Tom had scheduled another Year Book committee meeting. By now, a few more competition entries had been received, and the team were able to sort them. They divided the submissions into non-starters and entries worthy of round two judging, which would commence as soon as the competition closed.

Elisabet had expected Tom to understand her listless mood. However, she was surprised to find he was strictly opposed to her descent into despondency.

"You have to snap out of it," he said.

"Why?' Elisabet demanded. "Justin double crossed me. Lied to me. Perhaps used me to shield himself from his feelings for Joelle. Maybe even while she was going out with you!"

"I have been betrayed too," Tom said. "From the beginning of the year, if not over the Christmas period. I am not allowing it to rule my life."

"So how do you bear it?" Elisabet demanded.

"I try to think positive thoughts – like how to my knowledge, they waited until after our break-up to get together," Tom said. "Instead of dwelling on ill, I like to think their feelings were innocent. I doubt they touched or kissed while either was going out with another party."

"I don't see things that way," Elisabet moaned.

"I know that you don't," Tom said. "And perhaps I didn't at first either. Do you know who was instrumental in helping me come to terms with the break up?"

"Who?" Elisabet demanded.

"You!" Tom declared. "Do you remember caring that Joelle might have been pregnant with my child? Do you remember apologising to me for your mistake and insisting on partnering me during the first aid course?"

"I do," Elisabet admitted.

"Perhaps us miserable, discarded exes should get together," Tom joked. "To form a relationship of our own in revenge."

"I cannot do that," Elisabet said. "I love you too much for that."

A funny look crossed Tom's face. "What did you say?'

"I love you, but…" Elisabet began to repeat. "Oh!"

"You love me?" Tom queried.

Elisabet nodded. "I think I do. We have been classmates for three and a half years, dated briefly in our first year, moved on to other partners and remained best friends ever since. I could not possibly use you to get revenge upon Justin and Joelle."

"I could never use you either," Tom's voice was choked.

"No revenge relationship then," Elisabet said. "Besides Terence is being so supportive. I am seeing him at the moment."

Elisabet said goodbye to Tom tenderly, and continued back to her dormitory room.

Saturday morning, Elisabet attended band practice, which was becoming serious, as Craig had announced he had a gig booked for the new band line-up. The gig was at Northcoast Reform Church, where they would only be able to perform songs of a religious nature, and the audience might be critical of anything rocky.

"It's a good thing James' drumming is more brass band style," Craig observed wryly.

James laughed. "Being a trumpeter – I am brass band!" he declared.

Craig continued, speaking of the adjustments they might have to make to ensure all their pieces were sacred. Aside from the strict religious aspect, it was a very good booking.

After practice, Elisabet returned to the dormitory room, where she found Stephanie was in something of a dilemma.

"Working closely with Ms. Louise like we are on the Year Book committee," Stephanie began, "I don't know whether I can stand by and watch her get hurt by Jeffery Mannington."

"Perhaps he will treat her better than he treated you," Elisabet suggested. "They are both adults. Ms. Louise is not a vulnerable teenager like you were once."

"You don't understand," Stephanie said. "Jeffrey Mannington is very manipulative, and almost compulsive in his propensity for mischief."

"I still say leave it until he actually does something," Elisabet said. "I think Jeff's presence is getting to you slightly – and you ought not let it."

"Garry is coming over to pick me up and take me over to Yandina for the afternoon," Stephanie said. "So I will be able to forget all about it hopefully."

"You will be missing the baptism at Noosa then?" Elisabet asked.

"Yes," Stephanie said. "It's not anybody I really know – just a couple of first years."

"Terence has asked me to drive him across," Elisabet said. "And we are taking Janet and Vincent."

"It sounds lovely," Stephanie observed absently. "I am glad that you are feeling better now."

Elisabet was surprised to hear Stephanie say that, and performed an emotional self-check upon herself. She was indeed feeling much more positive. Either the talk with Tom had performed wonders, or one week had been long enough to stew over something that was out of her control.

"I will see you later then," she said. "Have fun!"

"You too," Stephanie declared and raced down to the foyer eager to meet Garry.

Sunday during the Reform Church service, Elisabet found herself sandwiched between Tom and Terence. She had come to terms with her declaration of love for him on the grounds that it was 'just as a friend', and she trusted that was the spirit in which Tom had accepted it. There certainly seemed to be no awkwardness.

Church finished and Terence leaned closer to Elisabet. "Shall we do something this afternoon?" he whispered.

Elisabet considered. She and Terence had hung out a lot lately, but it was mostly as part of a group. She licked her lips nervously. "I'll let you know after lunch."

"Very good," Terence said easily.

Elisabet peeked at Tom, but he did not appear to be listening. He was talking to someone on the other side.

By the end of lunch, Elisabet had decided that she fancied the idea of visiting Phoebe and seeing how the girl's pregnancy was going. It would give her a suitable destination to put on her leave form, and provide her with some chaperonage. Terence agreed, although once they were on the road, he insisted they approach Phoebe and Hank's house by a somewhat circuitous route.

Elisabet didn't mind a little sight-seeing, and when Terence suggested that they pull into a tree-lined park, she knew that he was going to try to kiss her.

She submitted with good grace and allowed him to linger on her mouth. She was not really into the kissing. Terence's caress was pleasant, not earth-shattering. She didn't long for more as she had with Justin.

After the business of kissing was over, Elisabet started the car once again. She drove directly to Hank and Phoebe's place, and spent the afternoon in a very pleasant visit. Phoebe invited the couple to stay to tea, and Elisabet telephoned campus to amend her leave form appropriately.

Later that evening, Elisabet drove back to campus. She parked the car in the student car park, and allowed Terence to walk her to the dormitory.

He kissed her goodnight at the door and appeared completely unaware of the fact that the earth was not moving for his companion.

Elisabet decided that she would have to think things through before enlightening him. "I will see you tomorrow," she whispered.

"Sleep well tonight," Terence said solicitously.

"Thank you," Elisabet murmured. "You too."

Terence strode away towards the boys' dormitory and Elisabet continued inside the girls' dormitory. Stephanie had returned from her visit to Yandina, and the two girls chatted as they prepared for bed.

Monday morning, Elisabet concentrated in class. She felt as though she had ground to recover after her week's depression and neglect of her studies. After lunch, she returned to her room to catch up on reading assignments. Stephanie was also in the room studying. The two girls sat in quiet companionship.

Eventually, Elisabet decided that she had enough of thinking on her own. She decided to indulge in girl talk. "Steph," she ventured. "You have had two serious boyfriends haven't you?"

"Yes," Stephanie said. "Garry, Bradley, and then Garry again."

"Was kissing both boys the same?" Elisabet ventured.

"Now I come to think of it," Stephanie said, "No."

"Can you describe the differences?" Elisabet asked curiously.

"Well, with Bradley it was sort of divine," Stephanie said. "I thought that I would explode with joy."

"And Garry?" Elisabet asked curiously.

"Kissing Garry is warm and comforting, like I have found my forever home," Stephanie said. "I cannot say which is better really. Passion and fireworks or feeling like you have found your soul-mate."

"I see," Elisabet said slowly. "And if you did not feel a lot when kissing a guy?"

"I have heard of a slow burn," Stephanie said. "And feelings that grow – but generally speaking, I would say feeling nothing is a bad sign. Not as bad as hating the kiss though."

"I don't hate Terence's kisses," Elisabet said slowly. "I'm just not that into them yet."

"It may develop – or it may not," Stephanie deduced. "I wouldn't recommend stringing him along too long if it doesn't develop."

"It hurts to be strung along, I know that," Elisabet sighed. "I've never strung guys along, one or two dates and I make my mind up. Occasionally guys were angry I didn't take longer to decide."

"I think Terence has been making allowances because of the timing," Stephanie said. "But he won't forever."

"I get that," Elisabet said soberly.

Tuesday in counselling skills, the students were assigned partners for their major project, which would be a case study. They would be required to conduct a number of sessions with their peer, make notes during these sessions, and present a portfolio of reflections about the counselling process.

The lecturer warned the students to observe confidentiality, and suggested that if something very personal and sensitive arose during session, this material was not to be recorded. Also if someone became distressed, they could choose to debrief with the lecturer.

"Your assignment for this week is to tell each other your life story," the Counselling Lecturer announced. "Like a mini-autobiography. Next week, I will set another area for discussion."

Elisabet was assigned to work with Cara, and Stephanie was paired with Debbie. Joelle and Phoebe were partnered, while Tom was working with Dylan. David and Anita were working together; Andrew was paired with Larry. No one was assigned to work with their romantic interest, as the lecturer suggested these relationships might be too close for objectivity.

Wednesday afternoon, Craig had organised another band practice, in preparation for Saturday's performance at the Nortcoast Reform Church. Their intended recital was gentler than usual, as Craig had selected some songs that were adaptations of psalms. Presented in concert form; these pieces would likely seem fresh and interesting to the congregation.

Vivione practiced toning the bass guitar down to the level of an accompaniment, because the guitar was a strong instrument that could easily take over a performance. James was practicing a gentle touch on the drums, and Elisabet's keyboard playing would be integral to the presentation.

At the end of the practice, Elisabet and James left Vivione and Craig alone because the two were working on a duet. Vivione's eyes were bright and she was clearly enjoying Craig's mentorship. The first year appeared to be well on the way to developing a case of hero worship, similar to the one Elisabet had once harboured for Craig. Elisabet hoped that Vivione did not become too emotionally involved, because she doubted Craig had changed his position on relationships.

Thursday evening, Elisabet entered the gymnasium to watch Terence play basketball. Since the kiss, she supposed that she was considered an official basketball girlfriend. She slid onto the spectator bench beside Janet, who was there to support Vincent.

Vincent's team was facing Terrence's team. This represented a serious challenge, because the team was newly configured. Vincent was also the least experienced captain amongst the A grade. Terence's team, on the other hand, were a group of vintage players, and Terence was easily the most respected captain in the Silver Springs University basketball league.

Elisabet found her eyes drawn to Tom, who was playing on Vincent's team. He was tall, and even though they had just been through winter, he sported a slight tan and his hair was sea-bleached from early morning surfing expeditions. His fringe was just a bit too long, and kept getting in his eyes.

Afraid that Terence might fathom her attention to Tom, Elisabet glued her eyes firmly to his athletic form. Terence was also very good looking, with muscle definition because he worked out using weights. They were both very attractive, fit young men.

Elisabet realised that Janet had been talking to her. "I'm sorry," she said. "I wasn't listening."

"You were lost in a dream world," Janet said. "I said that Vincent is proving to be a very good captain."

Elisabet nodded. "Terence is a good mentor to him," she said.

Janet laughed. "And this match is amusing because they have to play against each other!"

"Exactly," Elisabet agreed.

"The look on your face before showed that you were truly in love," Janet said.

Elisabet flushed. "I don't think I am in love with Terence just yet," she said truthfully.

"Maybe a little crush then," Janet said.

"Maybe," Elisabet was thoughtful. Janet had surely observed her watching Tom, not Terrence. Elisabet knew that she ought to make a decision soon, before things got too complicated.

CHAPTER TEN: OUT OF THE FRYING PAN

During the Year Book committee meeting the next day Elisabet realised the flaw in her thinking. She had told Tom that she loved him 'as a friend' and he had apparently accepted it 'as a friend'. She had no evidence that he cared for her as a girl.

His manner on the committee was completely business-like, and even in class he treated Elisabet exactly the same way as he did Stephanie. It was ages since he had tried inviting her to a function, and of recent times, he had shown more interest in Lacey.

It was Terence that Elisabet was going out with, and Terence who had been so supportive and attentive lately. Therefore, it was Terrance to whom she owed her loyalty… and her love and kisses if things developed that way.

Elisabet wasn't big on placing herself under obligation to another, but neither was she one for taking risks. She could not just launch herself away from Terence, who was a sure thing; in quest of Tom, whose feelings were unknown.

Saturday afternoon, the band was due to perform in Northcoast. Craig and Tom went ahead with the heavy gear, in the university bus. Elisabet followed in her car, with James and Vivione as passengers.

The performance went well. They played some traditional religious songs, and the selection of psalms Craig had prepared. The audience was devout; and aside from an aversion to anything loud and rocky, relatively uncritical. There was no clapping, because some people did not approve of clapping in a church, but the verbal thanks were sincere.

After the performance, the band were invited to mingle with the church goers. They were also offered simple refreshments. These consisted of fruit juice and vegetarian snacks, because the Reform Church followed strict dietary policies. However the nibbles were delicious. Vegetarian food could be quite acceptable when prepared well.

The next day after the two worship services, Elisabet was sitting with Terence, Anita and Larry, Craig and Luke. They were waiting for Tess to come and join them, when Larry asked how the band was going.

"The band is going well," Craig answered. "I am pleased. We have survived a membership reshuffle and gone on to perform as well as can be expected."

"I have been thinking," Larry said. "That perhaps you ought to enter the Christian band festival."

Craig switched to attention. "The Christian band festival? What is that?"

"It is a charismatic initiative," Larry said. "Held down at the big Hillsong Church in Sydney."

"Well, as the manager, I have to consider the costs," Craig said. "I take it this festival will have an entry fee?"

Larry nodded. "Unfortunately, yes. Hillsong is also a business concern."

"Then there would be travel and accommodation costs," Craig continued. "Tickets to Sydney wouldn't be cheap. And we might need to hire drums and amps down there to save taking our own."

"You might be able to get sponsorship from one of the local churches here," Larry said. "I will have a chat to the Chaplains."

"It sounds exciting," Elisabet ventured. "If a bit scary. Some of those bands will have been going longer than ours."

"We have talented, well trained musicians," Craig said. "And I would like to give my own compositions the wider exposure. Hillsong could even help me publish my music."

"It's certainly an option worth exploring," Terence said. "I would miss you Elisabet, but I think you ought to go and do it!"

"When is the festival?" Craig asked.

"Near the end of October," Larry said.

"And when do applications have to be in?" Craig probed.

"I will check," Larry said. "Mid-September, I think."

"So we only have a couple of weeks to raise the entry fee," Craig said thoughtfully. "Please speak to the chaplains immediately."

"I'll get right on it," Larry promised.

Monday, Elisabet organised a time with Cara to complete their weekly counselling skills task. When she listened to Cara, she learned that Cara was from Geelong, and was of Uniting Church persuasion. She had two outspoken Irish parents and one very traditional Presbyterian grandmother. Cara had a younger sister called Bede, who had just left for America with her boyfriend, Kaleb. Some of these things she had known already, but it was nice to put them all together into a profile.

In turn, Elisabet told Cara that she came from Byron Bay, where her parents ran an organic market farm. She had one brother, and numerous cousins. Her family was not overly strict, but believed in pulling together in the family business. Attending Silver Springs University had been Elisabet's dream, because she felt that she had a talent for literature.

Elisabet said that she wasn't sure whether she would end up returning to the family business, or pursue a career in journalism. She glossed over a few things, describing the family as 'gardeners'. Even so, Cara was impressed Elisabet had, as someone had once expressed, 'options'.

Tuesday was the first of September and the close of the Year Book competitions. Elisabet helped Tom empty the entry boxes with a sense of excitement. They read a few entries as they worked, but the real judging would occur during their regular meeting on Friday.

Then she said goodbye to Tom and hurried down to the gymnasium. Terence was officiating that evening, and he had asked Elisabet to come and keep him company.

After the game, Terence walked Elisabet back to the girl's dormitory and kissed her goodnight in a shadowy spot just before the door. The youth always appeared to enjoy their kisses, but this time, he seemed to notice something was wrong.

"Elisabet," Terence said, breaking off the kiss, "Is everything okay?"

"Yes, why?" Elisabet asked.

"I don't think the girl is meant to just stand there," Terence said.

"What do you mean?" Elisabet asked.

"At first I thought you were shy, but now I realise you are not kissing me back," Terence said.

"I know I look like I've dated, but I really haven't done a lot of kissing," Elisabet murmured. "Not even with Justin."

"Put your arms around my neck," Terence instructed.

Elisabet had to reach upwards to place her arms around Terence's neck. The action drew them closer together and Elisabet had to admit it was pleasant. It didn't change the kiss a lot however. Terence stopped again and regarded her thoughtfully.

"Is it because we are close to the door?" he said. "I'm getting the impression you might just not be into me."

"I do like you, Terence," Elisabet replied truthfully. Then she decided to insert a thin edge of the wedge of the issue into the conversation.

"Maybe I'm not ready to kiss you that way, just yet."

"I don't want to pressure you Elisabet," Terrence said. "But if we are heading into the friend-zone, I would prefer you just told me."

"I need some time to think," Elisabet said. She knew that Terence was attractive and popular, and could easily get another date for the next function. If she allowed him to move on, she would probably never be able to get him back. "I don't want us to be friend-zoned either."

Terence said goodnight, and Elisabet went inside the dormitory thoughtfully. It was true that she had never kissed anyone very deeply. She had wanted to with Justin, but he had been the one to hold back. Were things really so different with Terence, or was she afflicted with the tendency to want what she could not have? It was something she had been reading about in counselling theory that very week.

Wednesday afternoon, Elisabet and Cara met to complete their next joint counselling assignment. The lecturer had instructed them to talk about their relationships in the second session.

"Many people come to counselling because they want to resolve their relationship problems," the Counselling Lecturer had explained. "I want you to talk about what you know about relationships in general, and try to deduce some healthy principles. It's not about getting deep into the details of your personal life at this stage."

So Elisabet and Cara had pulled their chairs into position facing each other, and Cara had begun. "Outside of my family and friendships with girls, I've had two main romantic relationships," Cara began. "In my first relationship, Kaleb and I had good communication – at least until things began to break down. We had fun together and supported each other. We are still friends today, and he is going out with my sister."

"What do you think went wrong?" Elisabet asked.

Cara laughed. "That is easy. I didn't want to make a commitment. Kaleb needed a girl who was prepared to at least visit America with him, and I was happy here in Australia. I didn't have that travel lust."

"So you identify communication and commitment as important factors," Elisabet reflected.

"Oh yes," Cara affirmed.

"What is different with Dylan do you think?" Elisabet asked.

"Dylan is fun to be with, we have been friends for a very long time, and I'm not frightened of spending my future with him," Cara said.

"So friendship is important?" Elisabet reflected.

"Yes, very much so," Cara agreed. "And security. Perhaps a bit of timing and compatibility of situation."

"Do you associate settling down with 'settling'?" Elisabet asked curiously.

Once again, Cara laughed. "No way," she said. "Settling down means making a stable life with someone. 'Settling' is usually associated with giving up things that are important to you in order to have a relationship."

"I see," Elisabet said.

"It's your turn," Cara suggested. "What are your views on relationships?"

"Well, I used to believe that dating was about having fun, and that if you were careful, no one got hurt. Eventually you met the right person, and then everything would be perfect!" Elisabet admitted. "Recently I have learned that people do get hurt."

Cara nodded sympathetically. "Justin."

"Yeah, Justin," Elisabet admitted. "Like you – I believe communication is important, and I thought that Justin and I had that. It seemed the communication ceased before it reached the truth."

Cara nodded. "Some people are very self-protective that way."

"There is another thing I am learning about – the mystical attraction thing. It seems that a relationship is doomed if either party lacks that," Elisabet continued. "And the cruel thing is that it is not always mutual."

"Uh-um," Cara made a listening sound.

"Justin held back on the physical, and he said it was for appearances - for his ministry; but now I wonder whether he was simply more attracted to Joelle," Elisabet confided.

"You and Justin also had the international challenge thing going," Cara interjected. "Do you think your willingness to go to the UK with him was a factor?"

"I had not decided for or against the UK," Elisabet said. "I was approaching the issue from the point of view of the personal relationship."

"And yet, Joelle had already been to the UK," Cara observed. "In real counselling I would not know all this, but I do know that Justin and Joelle met in the UK. So perhaps, Joelle was not more attractive than you – just more committed to the UK?"

"It might lift a burden of hurt off me, if I began to think of it in those terms," Elisabet admitted. "But I'm still a little – err – ripped off. What if I had been able to develop such a commitment to the UK?"

"You have a fairly tight system going with your family and the business," Cara said. "Perhaps Justin could see that."

"Anyway, I've moved onto Terence now," Elisabet said. "And I'm afraid it might be him who will get hurt this time."

"Why so?" Cara asked.

"I don't think I'm attracted enough to him…" Elisabet admitted.

"You haven't been together very long," Cara observed.

"I know, and I would like to give feelings longer to grow," Elisabet said. "But Terence said to tell him if he was being 'friend-zoned'. What is the difference between 'friend-zoned' and friends? You said friendship was a major ingredient in your relationship with Dylan."

"I think friend-zoned is where the relationship is not heading in the romantic direction, and never will," Cara said. "To share a comparison with my situation, Dylan did feel friend-zoned when I would not go out with him, but he never gave up hope. And we weren't really friend-zoned, because we had never tested our chemistry. Which turned out to be very good indeed!"

"Terence and I have tested the chemistry," Elisabet murmured. She blushed. "Although not very far."

"And how do you feel?' Cara asked.

"I like him so much as a person, but…" Elisabet concluded.

"That could be friend-zoned," Cara agreed. "Look deep inside yourself. Be completely honest. Pray for understanding even. And if the answer is companionship, keep him as a friend before he becomes a bitter ex-lover."

"It's difficult," Elisabet murmured.

"I know," Cara said empathetically. "Well, I think we ought to close the session. You value communication, honesty and attraction in a relationship. I will skip some of the personal details in my report."

"And you value fun, commitment, communication and a little security," Elisabet said. "I will also skip the personal details."

Thursday evening, Elisabet went down to the gymnasium to watch Terence play basketball. The game went very well, and Elisabet's eyes dwelt on Terence's athletic form. He was so good looking, how could she not be responding to his kisses? However, as she was not, she had to do something about it. She felt very sad.

After the game was over, Terence suggested they go to the campus snack shop for a little junk food. Elisabet agreed. She hoped the relaxed atmosphere would make it easier for them to talk. They walked across to the lee of the cafeteria, where the snack shop operated. Terence bought a bucket of hot chips and two soft drinks.

"Do you want anything more?" he asked.

Elisabet shook her head. "No, we already had tea."

"The game makes me hungry," Terence admitted, tucking into the chips.

"You burn the calories," Elisabet agreed. She reached out and laid her hand on his free hand. The one that wasn't busy shovelling chips into his mouth. "Terence, I really, really like you."

"But?" Terence suggested.

"I don't seem to be able to give you what you want, at least not at the moment, so I feel I have to set you free to see other girls," Elisabet said.

"Set me free?" Terence repeated. "Is that a fancy way of dropping me?"

"No," Elisabet said. "The selfish part of me wants to keep going out with you. I value your friendship. We have fun together and I enjoy our dates. But you could be missing the chance to find the girl you are meant to marry while we continue to go out."

"Heavy," Terence said. "And what about the man you are meant to marry?"

"I suppose he exists somewhere," Elisabet dropped her eyes. They were filled with tears. "Just not here and not now."

"It is Tom Randall," Terence said, munching heavily on chips.

"I beg your pardon?" Elisabet said.

"You study with Tom more often than you go out on dates with me," Terence said. "I expect that you cannot get into kissing me, because you have feelings for him."

"I've never done anything with Tom," Elisabet objected.

Terence forestalled her. "I know that you have not betrayed me with Tom. I'm saying that you ought to think about it. I know that a girl like you is always looking further and further for her Mr. Right. You want someone taller, smarter - more exciting. Tom is a good guy. He is solid, faithful, a friend. You need to look at him properly."

"A minute ago you were accusing me of breaking up with you – now you are suggesting I go after Tom?" Elisabet cried in indignation.

"The reasons you were giving – they work for me, but not for you," Terence said. "I know you, Elisabet. You wouldn't break up with me for completely unselfish reasons. If it is not Tom, it is your impossible dream of Mr. Right, and I'm not prepared to step aside for a fantasy guy. If it's Tom, I will know you are happy with a good man."

"That's something of an odd point of view," Elisabet said.

"Perhaps it is," Terence said. "And perhaps it isn't. I don't see the difference between you telling me to date other girls. Either way, we are friend-zoned, and now I am speaking as your friend!"

Elisabet was vaguely angry with this outcome, but she did not dare say. Terence's logic seemed correct, and her own sensibilities seemed irrational. Feelings were not logical, but that was a private matter.

Friday afternoon, the Yearbook committee pawed through the poetry and photographs from the competition. There was no real prize, just the glory of publication. There was also no limit on the number of winners, except the space allowed in the book. So they set aside all the entries of good quality for inclusion. Then they settled down to working on layout. Elisabet avoided being alone with Tom, leaving the meeting in company with Stephanie.

At the Uniting Church vespers that evening, Terence did not sit beside her for the first time in weeks. The space was empty until Debbie and David sat down. Looking around the ladies' assembly area, Elisabet saw that Terence and Tom, Janet and Vincent, and a few of the other A grade basketball players were all seated together.

Saturday, the *Electronic Jive Classical Vibe Band* met for another practice. Craig and Vivione were working together very closely, and Elisabet wondered whether it was just about the music, even for Craig. Craig had been known to date occasionally, and she had no idea of the outcome of his counselling with Justin. In counselling skills, he was partnered with Luke, but she had no idea what was said there either.

Craig was also pushing James, because with the entry into the Christian band festival, they would be up against some of the most experienced Christian bands in Australia. Therefore Craig maintained that metrical perfection would not be enough.

James was trying very hard, but as a trumpet player, with brass band experience, he was highly attached to a regular expression of rhythm. He was going to have to learn to throw in some rolls and trills, and create variations known as 'bridges'.

Sunday was Father's Day and long queues formed as the students vied for the usage of the payphones in the dormitory foyers. Elisabet had placed her call home early, and also posted a card on Thursday, which she hoped her father would receive very soon. It had not arrived on Friday, but it ought to be there on Monday.

Monday was quiet, and a little dull. Music class was never as exciting as band practice, and the theory could be boring. Elisabet also had an assignment to do for education, and a tutorial to prepare for English. Her practice teaching portfolio needed work, and all her readings seemed to be due at once.

Tuesday, Elisabet presented her paper on James Joyce to the English class. To be honest, she hated James Joyce. He was difficult to read, and nothing like what she considered a 'modern classic'. However, she had to elaborate on the theory behind the Modernist choice to make meaning obscure, and talk about the challenges it posed to elicit an active readership.

She must have succeeded, because the English Professor gave her 8/10. It was a relief that now she had completed her essay on James Joyce, she would not be expected to complete the Joyce question in the exam. Elisabet felt that she had made a very prudent choice.

Wednesday, Elisabet and Cara met for another of their counselling skills sessions. This week the lecturer had stipulated that the couples talk about loneliness and solitude, another serious challenge to mental health. The girls set their chairs down, and Elisabet began.

"I swear the lecturer is spying on my life," she declared. "Now we have to talk about loneliness, and I am lonely after breaking up with Terence. If you can call it a break up - when it wasn't really a steady relationship."

"You and Terence were on your way to a relationship," Cara said. "Isn't that one reason why you broke up?"

"My fear of loneliness wasn't stronger than my conviction that a relationship ought to be the right one," Elisabet said. "But I had hoped we could remain friends."

"I think Terence is just giving you space," Cara comforted her. "And you have us girls. Why do you think you are alone, when you are surrounded by friends?"

"Because my female friends all have boyfriends," Elisabet said. "Because I cannot marry you girls and have children perhaps? Something makes us quest and seek for the opposite sex. I never admitted it before, but there is a lonely hole in my heart with no romantic relationship."

"That is a major admission," Cara said. "I expect a lot of people feel that way. These are the sort of observations we are meant to make for our notes."

Both girls scribbled a little, and then they swapped roles, with Cara as the speaker and Elisabet as the listener.

"I am not lonely here at university," Cara said. "But I expect I will be at Christmas. I never expected my sister to go to America, and I probably won't see a lot of her over the years. We weren't besties or anything, we even argued. However, it is like I have lost a sister."

"Do you hear from her?" Elisabet asked.

"Letters and email," Cara said. "Bede and Kaleb are enjoying America, but it's not the same. If she chooses to get married over there, I might not even get to the wedding."

"That's major," Elisabet said.

"You are luckier than most boarding students, Elisabet," Cara said. "Your family are so much closer, you have your own car and you can drive home every holiday. I didn't think about it until we began this session."

"We are supposed to be talking about you," Elisabet said in embarrassment.

"Well I guess I am observing that people can be lonely when they are separated from their families," Cara concluded. "We need more than just romantic relationships."

The girls made another note in their counselling journals. Then they packed up and walked across to the cafeteria for tea.

Thursday evening, Elisabet had an impulse urging her to go to the gymnasium and watch the men's basketball. She checked her inclination with Stephanie, and the roommate said she thought it might be okay to do so.

"You and Terence parted amicably didn't you?" Stephanie asked.

Elisabet nodded.

"And basketball is a huge part of campus life," Stephanie said. "I would have recommended you came with me and Cara the other day to watch Dylan play, however. None of the A grade players were there, and it would have been a safer choice."

"Will you come with me to the gymnasium then?" Elisabet asked.

Stephanie nodded. "If we are lucky, Tom and Vincent will be playing, and Terence will be busy," she said.

"Hmm," Elisabet muttered. She was avoiding the appearance of hanging around Tom, even more than the appearance of hankering after Terence, but she chose not to say.

Stephanie accompanied Elisabet to the gymnasium, and they watched the men's team play without incident. Terence was indeed busy, and Vincent's team were not scheduled to play that evening. They had a nice chat to Lacey who was also watching the men play.

At Friday's Year Book committee meeting, Tom had a sample layout the computing department had created for him. The team inspected the formatting and rearranged a few of the photographs, choosing positions that they thought aesthetically pleasing. After the meeting was over, Tom left with Ms. Louise to return the layout to the Computing Department and get some proofs made up.

Once, Elisabet might have accompanied Tom on his walk down to the Computer Department. Today she hung back, and constrained Stephanie to remain with her. Stephanie and Moira looked at her curiously.

"Is something wrong between you and Tom?" Stephanie finally asked.

"It's nothing," Elisabet said. "I just feel I have had enough dramas for the year."

"But you and Tom are not like that," Moira said. "You have always been good friends."

"He hangs out with Terence now," Elisabet said lamely.

"Nonsense," Moira said. "I saw you in the gymnasium yourself yesterday evening. You could easily have run into Terence then."

"That's different," Elisabet said cryptically.

She had never told anyone what Terence had said about Tom being her soul mate, but the idea was creating an embarrassment in her mind. If she hung out with Tom now, Terence might be proved right. If Terence were not right, and Tom rejected her, she might suffer a real heartbreak, and she did not think she could bear that.

Saturday the students were eating in the cafeteria, and Elisabet was about to pour herself a drink of cordial when a shout went up.

"There is smoke in the back paddock!" Vincent, who had been looking out the window that showed the campus all the way back to the bushlands, gave the alarm.

The Café Proprietor got on the telephone and called the fire brigade. He also called the Campus Farm Manager, who arrived looking grim.

"After all the spring growth, the fire danger is extreme until the rainy season cuts in," the Manager declared. "Only yesterday I sent some cows down into the paddock to eat the undergrowth down."

The students were perturbed when they heard animals were in danger, and Terence volunteered the A grade men's basketball teams to help herd the cattle back together. Although the university had a duty of care to all the students, most of the A grade players were seniors, and fit and organised, so the Farm Manager accepted the offer gratefully.

The majority of the students were instructed to return to their dormitories, and listen for the fire alarm, should it go off. The fire had some barren ground to cross before it approached the buildings, and the wind was blowing in the other direction, but it was best to remain alert. If the fire alarm sounded throughout the dorms, the next assembly area would be the student car park.

Stephanie, Cara and Elisabet retreated to girl's dorm, where they had to remain in the reception area, because they had Dylan and Andrew with them. They sat down on some comfortable chairs to wait. The two guys were regretting not joining the cattle muster, but they were also glad that they could comfort the girls.

"There is no way the fire will come all the way up here," Cara said sturdily, as the sound of the Fire Engine's siren passed by the building and went out around University Drive, to the little accessed gravel road. Cara worked in the grounds department, mowing the lawns regularly. She knew that a reasonable fire-break had been created between the farmland and the residential section of campus.

"It's not the fire coming to us that I am so worried about," Elisabet admitted. "But the fire threatening our brave boys."

Janet hastened to agree with her. "Terence and Vincent are so heroic," she said. "And all to save a few cattle."

"Those cows would have been trapped because of the fences," Stephanie cried. "And it's the kangaroos and koalas I am worried about."

"To say nothing of the birds, wombats and lizards," Cara added. "All wildlife suffers during a fire."

"If the fire-fighters can turn the fire, they may be able to stop it going into the rainforest behind the bush," Janet said optimistically.

"If they turn the fire it could come to us," Tess suggested timidly.

Andrew shook his head. "If they turn the fire, it will burn back on itself and run out of fuel," he declared.

It seemed as though they waited for hours, and the smell of the smoke was strong for a while before they were told that the fire was under control. Then the exhausted A grade basketball players came stumbling out of the back paddock, and began to make their way towards the boy's dormitory. Janet and the basketball girlfriends had posted a sentry to watch for this development.

Moira gave a squeal and the girls were alerted. They streamed out of the back door of girl's dormitory and across the lawn towards the boy's dormitory. Tired, sooty boyfriends who could barely stand on their feet were enveloped in great hugs and given enthusiastic kisses.

Elisabet had joined the basketball girlfriends. The first young man she saw was Terence, and she hugged him, much to his surprise. Then she looked around. "Where is Tom?"

Terence looked serious. "A snake came out of the bush and bit Tom," he explained. "Tom has been laid down in the ambulance for observation after receiving a dose of antivenin."

"Take me to him," Elisabet cried.

Terence was tired, but he took Elisabet by the hand and led her to where the ambulance was parked. Tom was surprised and pleased to see his friends, except his eyes lingered on their clasped hands.

"Thank you Terence," Elisabet said. She dropped onto her knees beside Tom's stretcher. "You were bitten by a snake?"

"They say I will live," Tom tried to joke, although he too sounded very tired. "The leg is swollen and bruised."

He stretched out the limb to show Elisabet, and she squealed in horror. His jeans had been cut off below the knee and the lower leg was bandaged. Despite the bandage, the area appeared swollen.

"If you don't need me anymore Elisabet," Terence said, "I want to go to the dorm to shower and rest. I believe we will all be getting a check over for smoke inhalation too."

"You can go," Elisabet murmured. Her eyes were on Tom.

Terence bid them both goodbye and left.

"I'm glad you two have made up again," Tom said. "You are a good couple."

"Oh no," Elisabet said. "It's not like that at all. Terence seems to know just how I feel about you."

"How you feel about me?" Tom's head was spinning with a combination of poison and antivenin. "I'm not sure what you mean."

"Tom, I've so nearly lost you," Elisabet cried. "That I have to tell you – when I said that I loved you – I didn't mean just as a friend."

"What did you mean then?" Tom was looking very confused.

"I meant as a best friend, as a man, as a soul-mate," Elisabet said. "As the Adam to my Eve, Isaac to my Rebecca, Jacob to my Leah, Boaz to my Ruth."

"That's quite a list," Tom said.

"Say something else Tom, please," Elisabet begged.

"I'm not sure I'm not hallucinating," Tom said. "Why were you holding hands with Terence then?"

"He just brought me over here," Elisabet said. "Honestly."

"If I find out otherwise, I will clobber someone," Tom said. "Which one of you, I don't know. You are both meant to be my friends!"

Elisabet leaned over and kissed Tom full on the lips. It definitely left her wanting more. Tom responded, and his lips clung to hers even though he was tired and sick.

"Get better soon," Elisabet said.

She jumped down out of the ambulance, because the medical crew had finished checking the other boys, and the driver was going to start the engine.

"I expect he will be home in the morning, miss," the Ambulance Driver said. "We are only taking him to hospital as a precaution."

CHAPTER ELEVEN: LOVE IS AN ATTITUDE

Sunday morning, Elisabet was pleased to hear Tom was about to be released from hospital. She organised with the deans to drive across to Northcoast and collect him. He wanted to rest, because his leg was extremely sore. The tissue that had been traumatised by the poison, and was showing bruising.

Elisabet drove past the student car park, and to the rear of the boy's dormitory. Then she parked the car and activated the brake. She eyed Tom shyly. Things had been said in the heat of the crisis the previous day, but they needed to be repeated in the cold light of normality.

"Thanks for coming to pick me up," Tom said.

"You are welcome, you know that," Elisabet murmured. She reached a hand out. "Tom?"

"Elisabet?" Tom reached out too.

They both leaned forward and met in the middle for a kiss.

"So I didn't imagine it." Tom whispered.

"Of course not," Elisabet said. "We will start going out as soon as you are well enough."

Elisabet hailed Dylan, who was waiting in the corridor, to assist Tom back to his room. Dylan also promised he would keep Tom company, and fetch him some lunch. After delivering Tom safely home to boys' dormitory, Elisabet hurried to the campus meeting hall to attend the church service.

At the Reform Church service, Elisabet caught up with Debbie and David, Luke and Tess. They were all very pleased to hear that Tom was back. When the service finished, the friends walked across to the cafeteria for lunch. They were joined by Andrew Grosvy and several other theology students.

"There is a rumour going around the boy's dormitory," David said after they were all seated. "I don't know whether either you or Stephanie have heard about it."

"I wouldn't know either unless you told me," Elisabet said. She was vaguely puzzled regarding why a rumour would concern the girls.

"They say that Jeffrey Mannington and Ms. Louise are engaged," Luke said. "I mean – it's just talk – and some of the blokes do talk nonsense."

"Ms. Louise did not say anything Friday," Elisabet said thoughtfully.

"I actually thought it was a bit sudden to be true," David said. "But Debbie reminded me they have been out together in the past."

"Briefly, but not so seriously I think," Tess said.

"Well, I still wouldn't know," Elisabet said. "And Stephanie tries not to listen to gossip. Especially gossip about Jeffrey." She turned to Andrew. "When are we expecting Kathy to arrive?"

Andrew's face lit up with joy. "Sometime tomorrow," he said. "The school holidays have already commenced, so she can take her time. Thank you so much again for having her stay in the room."

"You are welcome," Elisabet said. "Stephanie is away in Yandina so often that I practically feel as though I have the room to myself."

"I'm sure Stephanie will be home to see Kathy," Andrew said confidently.

It was late when Stephanie got back from Yandina that night. Kathy arrived half-way through Monday morning, and both girls greeted her warmly. There was so much to talk about, it was afternoon before Elisabet had a chance to repeat the gossip about Jeffrey and Ms. Louise. Moreover, when she did, she found both girls looked doubtful.

"Hmm," Stephanie said thoughtfully, "I doubt that marriage is Jeffrey's style. He always told me it wasn't, and Ms. Louise would have to have been mighty persuasive to change his mind."

"When I see Ms. Louise, I will look to see whether she is wearing a ring," Kathy said.

"Why?" Stephanie looked puzzled.

"If it is a half-hearted engagement, he wouldn't have bothered to spend money on a ring," Kathy said wisely.

Elisabet nodded in agreement. Being involved in the family business had taught her that the money trail tended to reveal the ugly truth.

"A fake engagement seems a lot of bother, even for Jeff," Stephanie said. "His sort of thing was always rumour and a-friend-of-a-friend mischief. Usually quite untraceable."

"Perhaps it is a 'keep up with the Jones' stunt because so many students have gotten engaged," Kathy suggested.

"You mean Garry and me specifically," Stephanie said. "Jeffrey should be over all that by now - I am."

"I didn't know him very well," Elisabet said, "But I always got the impression Jeffrey Mannington had a long memory."

Tuesday, Stephanie was due to present her English tutorial. The girl had chosen to focus upon Joseph Campbell, who outlined the hero motif and quest plotlines, a lot of which were drawn from folklore.

According to Stephanie, Campbell represented something of an alternate point of view. Ethnographic and anthropological approaches were almost the polar opposite to classic Modernism.

Elisabet enjoyed Stephanie's presentation, although she suspected her roommate was disappointed with the grade of 7.5/10 she received. Tom was also back in class, although he had a tendency to favour his uninjured leg. Elisabet was pleased to see him out and about.

Wednesday morning, the girls just happened to be in the ladies' toilets at the same time as Ms. Louise. Elisabet looked down at the basin where the lecturer was washing her hands. There was no engagement ring on her finger.

"So it's not true," she muttered. She hadn't intended Ms. Louise to hear, but the lecturer half caught her meaning.

"What was that Elisabet?" Ms. Louise asked.

"I'm sorry, Ms. Louise," Elisabet said. "But there is a rumour going around, that you and Jeffrey Mannington are engaged.

Ms. Louise fluttered her eyelashes. "You really ought to call him Mr. Mannington, Elisabet," she said. "Although he is not that many years older than you, he is a lecturer now."

"He graduated at the end of my first year at Silver Springs," Kathy said. "I graduated last year. He is hardly 'Mr.' to me."

"I guess not," Ms. Louise conceded. She laughed awkwardly.

"About you and Mr. Mannington," Elisabet prompted.

Ms. Louise fiddled self-consciously with her hair. "Jeffrey and I have know each other for some years now, and we are thinking about getting married. It's not a rumour, it is true. Some people say I'm too old for him… but it's really only a five year gap."

"I think you are pretty Ms. Louise," Kathy said. "You could have any man you wanted."

"Thank you Kathy," Ms. Louise said flattered. "Dating is really not that easy. Once you have graduated, you will not have hundreds of young men to choose from anymore."

Thursday the proofs for the Year Book were due back from the Computing Department. Elisabet accompanied Tom on the errand down to the Computing building. When they got there, Jeffrey Mannington pretended that he had never heard of the proofs.

Tom got a stubborn look on his face and persisted in insisting Mannington look in the filing cabinet. Sure enough, the proofs were there, corrected and adjusted perfectly.

"Thank you very much," Tom said with irony.

"You're welcome," Jeffrey Mannington said snakily, subsiding back into his protective shell.

"That gave me a fright," Elisabet whispered as they left the Computing Department.

"Jeff meant it to," Tom said. "The guy is a pain to work with."

"What if he had really lost the proofs?" Elisabet whispered.

"I knew he wouldn't," Tom said. "Jeff is a perfectionist so far as work goes. The project was too important for him to lose or sabotage. Giving us a fright was as far as he would go."

The Year Book committee met in the Art Department immediately after lunch to check the proofs carefully, and then the templates were sent off to the printers. The books were being printed overseas, so it would be several months before they received the physical volumes. However, approving the proofs gave the team an amazing sense of achievement.

Elisabet kept looking at Ms. Louise's left hand, thinking that the Art Tutor and Computing Lecturer could easily gave gone down to Northcoast and chosen an engagement ring to symbolise their commitment.

"Why hasn't Jeff bought you an engagement ring yet?" she asked Ms. Louise after a few of the committee members had left.

"Jeffrey doesn't believe in that sort of thing," Ms. Louise said. "He is very strict Reform Church."

"Perhaps he could buy you something else then, like a watch," Tom suggested. "I would be certain to buy my fiancé something."

Tom winked meaningfully at Elisabet, and her heart leaped. They had barely started going out, but they had known each other for a long time. Anything could happen.

"A watch would be nice," Ms. Louise looked wistful. "Although I am quite artistic and alternative and don't really need that sort of thing."

Ms. Louise and Jeffrey's arrangement did not sound much like an engagement, Elisabet thought to herself. Jeffrey was being careful not to spend any money on the woman. He was clearly up to his old tricks again. Ms. Louise deserved far better treatment than she was receiving.

Friday was the last day of the half-semester. Elisabet could not believe that it had come so soon. She had reading reports to hand in, and then she was free to go home. When she had asked Tom what he was doing, she had been slightly disappointed to learn he had already booked his tickets to Dubbo.

"I'm sorry Elisabet," he said, stroking her hand. "I bought them several weeks ago."

"I would have liked to have taken you home to meet my parents," Elisabet said.

"Perhaps you could drive across and meet mine," Tom suggested. "At least we both live in New South Wales."

"It's a big state," Elisabet observed, studying the map. "And a short holiday!"

Things were getting serious between Elisabet and Tom fast. It was as though they had been going out for years already - all the years that they had been close friends! With graduation coming up soon, they were reluctant to be parted for a moment. Now they had found each other, neither had any regrets regarding Justin and Joelle at all. As far as they were concerned, the other couple could do exactly as they liked.

In the end, it was decided Tom would contact the bus company and adjust his return journey, so that he returned via Byron Bay. Then they could drive the final leg of the journey to Silver Springs together.

Elisabet was happy to spend a few days at home. The mid-year break had been a working holiday really, so this was her first time to fully relax. Tom called almost every evening, once the subscriber trunk dialling rates had kicked in and telephone calls were cheaper. At the end of the first week of the holidays, he boarded the bus and made the journey across New South Wales to Byron Bay to join Elisabet.

Elisabet's parents liked Tom immensely. Her father said that he was just the reliable sort of young man that he had always hoped his daughter would find.

"Your mother and I have been mildly worried that with your search for perfection, you might choose a young man who would put himself and his achievements first," Elisabet's Father said.

"I think I almost did," Elisabet said, her mind going to Justin. Everyone said Justin was a nice fellow, but he had hardly been considerate of Elisabet's feelings. "Tom is truly special, partly because we have been friends for so very long."

"Yes, I think it is very healthy," Elisabet's Mother added. She gave Elisabet a warm hug. "Tom looks at you just right!"

"He does too," Elisabet mused. The light that came into Tom's eyes whenever he glanced towards her was reassuring. It told her that he was really into her. In fact, if she thought about it seriously, she suspected that Tom seemed to dote upon her, more than he ever had Joelle. "I am so happy!"

After the visit with her parents, the couple drove back to Silver Springs University together. It was pleasant to have company in the car, and instead of driving straight through, they stopped to enjoy a few breaks along the way.

When Elisabet and Tom arrived back at Silver Spring's University, they hurried to drop their luggage off at their dorms, and then met their friends in the cafeteria. After tea, they made their way to the recreation area to watch the news on the television. The evening bulletin was still full of the coup in Fiji. The new republican government had instituted military patrols and curfews were in place. Australian citizens were being warned against holidaying in the area.

David and Andrew suggested that they all pray for the residents of Fiji. The Indian population had been imported by the British colonial government as cheap labour. However, the current generation had been born on the islands and had nowhere else to go. It was always sad to see racial conflict in action.

Monday, classes commenced again. Elisabet greeted James, Jessie and Vivione in music. The first years had all had their initial taste of practice teaching during the holidays. James observed the children were inclined to play around in music; while Vivione reported that she had been obliged to attend two schools, because neither school offered enough music hours to support a full time music teacher. Jessie said she was lucky the school she had visited offered an exclusive instrumental music programme and attendance was viewed as a privilege.

"I think we will have to be independent to carve out careers for ourselves though," she said.

"Some specialist music teachers do run their own businesses," James observed. "It also depend upon your minor teaching field too, if you have one."

Elisabet was quite happy her major teaching field was English and that she also had history. Music was just great as an elective, but it would be challenging as a career. The morning flew and lunch time arrived quickly. After the meal, she did some reading.

Tuesday, Tom was due to give his tutorial presentation in English. He had chosen to present upon Dostoevsky, who was a structuralist critic as well as European author. Tom's presentation was very informative, and Even Stephanie was impressed!

Elisabet felt Tom had come to terms with Doestoevsky's challenging style quite well. The English professor gave Tom an assessment of 8.5/10, which was the highest in the modern literature unit so far.

Wednesday, Craig reported Larry had successfully lobbied the Chaplains to get the *Electronic Jive Classical Vibe Band* sponsorship from several regional churches and one of the larger Brisbane congregations.

"It is unusual for the Reform Church to get involved," Craig said. "But apparently the Northcoast congregation liked our music so much that they took an offering for us. The contributions arrived just in time to cover the entry fee!"

"That is wonderful," Elisabet enthused.

"We still have travel and other expenses to cover," Craig said, "The churches are looking into helping with those!"

"It is very exciting," James said. "And to think it is happening in my first year!"

"I won't be around to organise you next year," Craig said. "So enjoy the experience!"

"There will be the university choir and orchestra," Vivione observed. "But it won't be the same as having our own band - and we will miss you Craig."

Vivione laid a hand on Craig's arm. He had relaxed a lot lately, and Elisabet thought that it was due to his peer counselling with Luke.

"I will miss you too," Craig said. "But there is a wide world out there waiting to recognise my talents."

"This competition might just be the right place to start," Elisabet said determinedly. "I did a bit of research. The Christian Life Church have helped some musicians' careers immensely…"

"Indeed," James agreed. "You can even take music lessons through them."

The practice continued. As the students had just returned from a break, it took a couple of songs to groove them into playing together again. Craig looked concerned, because there was only a fortnight to the competition. He asked whether the members could spare some extra time to practice several times a week.

Thursday afternoon, Elisabet spent her time working on her education essay, which was due on Friday. Stephanie was at her afternoon biology practical, and it was dull work sitting in the room alone; but Elisabet reflected that it would be good to have the essay out of the way for the semester.

Friday afternoon, Tom and Elisabet walked across to the Art Department to see whether Ms. Loiuse had heard anything about the Year Book. Ms. Louise assured them that she had received an acknowledgement that the proofs had arrived safely via airmail.

"They are in the queue for printing," Ms. Louise said. "I think we can rest assured they will be shipped back in time for distribution."

"That's good," Tom said. As leader of the Year Book committee, he felt a strong sense of responsibility for the success of the project.

"I can't wait to see the printed book," Elisabet said. She surveyed Ms. Louise, who appeared somewhat restless that afternoon. "Are you alright Ms. Louise?"

"Yes," Ms. Louise sighed. "I'm just waiting for a call from Jeffrey. He went to Brisbane to pick up his new mobile telephone, and I don't know when he will be back."

"A mobile phone," Tom exclaimed. "Aren't they very expensive?"

"It cost him around $3,000," Ms. Louise admitted.

"That is a lot of money," Elisabet observed.

"Well, mobile phones are very new," Ms. Louise said. "Jeff wanted one for work, however."

"I suppose it will be tax deductible," Elisabet said doubtfully.

She glanced at Ms. Louise's hand and wrist. There was still no engagement ring, and no watch either. Jeffrey Mannington could afford to get a mobile telephone, but not buy Ms. Louise an engagement present.

That seemed pathetic in Elisabet's estimation.

"We will see you at vespers Ms. Louise," Elisabet said.

Ms. Louise nodded absently.

Tom took Elisabet by the arm and steered her towards the recreation area, where they could hang out.

"I wonder why Jeffrey did not take Ms. Louise to Brisbane with him for an outing," Elisabet whispered. "Lunch and a drive would have made a nice date, and Ms. Louise did not appear to have any classes to teach this afternoon."

"Well, it's only my humble opinion," Tom said. "But I suspect Jeffrey might be up to something he doesn't want Ms. Louise knowing about."

"Like what?" Elisabet asked.

Tom shrugged. "I dunno, the usual is another woman, but it could be anything. Travel perhaps. Hence the mobile phone."

"She said it was for work," Elisabet objected.

"It could be handy for a lot of things," Tom said. "But if it was really for work – chances are the Computing Department would supply one. If Jeff is buying his own, that would mean he wants to keep it. He is clearly into the high tech stuff."

Saturday, Craig had booked another band practice. He was inclined to treat the previous practice as a mere warm-up and push the members hard. There were compositions that he wanted the band to learn, and he had been studying the style of music favoured by the Charismatic churches.

"Unlike the Reform Church, the Christian Life community like rock," Craig observed.

"It is because they focus on youth ministry," Tom commented. He had accompanied Elisabet to practice, because he was curious as to whether Craig would allow the roadie to come along on the trip.

Elisabet played through the pieces Craig had put in front of her. Several were new, and one or two had tricky rhythms. James accompanied her tentatively on the drums, and Vivione strummed her bass guitar.

"Turn it up please, Vivione," Craig ordered.

Vivione gave Craig a questioning look. "Do you know what this guitar can do through that amp?" she said. "If we aren't careful, we will be getting noise complaints."

"I don't care," Craig said. "The students like a bit of rock, and I want you playing more aggressively."

"Okay," Vivione obediently turned her volume control up.

"Now James," Craig ordered. "Hit it!"

The *Electronic Jive Classical Vibe Band* ran through everything again with greater energy. James got into the swing of the beat, and began to put his shoulders into the drumming.

"That's better James," Craig commented. "And vary the rhythm please. No one likes a metronome."

James attempted to comply. Vivione matched and surpassed James, while Elisabet's fingers romped on the keyboard. When they were finished, they were sweating from the effort. Craig crossed the room and activated the air-conditioning unit.

"That is better," Vivione said. "The humidity was making everything sticky."

"Perhaps the rain come early this year," James said.

Sunday after attending the morning services, and lunching with their friends, Elisabet and Tom decided to walk down to the suspension bridge. It was something that they had done a hundred times before, but this was the first time alone as a couple. They strolled along hand-in-hand, admiring the green grass along the river bank.

"The sprinklers must have run last night," Tom said. "It looks very fresh along here."

"There won't be snakes will there?" Eliabet asked anxiously.

"I don't think so," Tom replied. "It's been mown."

October was snake breeding season, and even the keenest walkers had learned to avoid the brush-lined tracks, where the snakes came out to sun themselves on warm days.

"We don't want any more close encounters," Elisabet said tenderly.

"Once in a lifetime is enough," Tom observed. It had been almost a month since the bite, but he still remembered the pain.

"Snakes should be like bees and die if they bite someone," Elisabet declared viciously.

"I dunno," Tom mused. "I've always been sorry for the poor bees."

"Stephanie would say they are an essential part of the environment," Elisabet added. "And far less dangerous than snakes."

"Unless you are allergic of course." The couple had come to the suspension bridge. Tom pulled at her hand: "Come on."

"What for?" Elisabet asked puzzled. Most of the students loitered on the campus side of the bridge. There were staff houses across the other side. It was also a short cut, but only if you knew where you were going.

"I'm going to kiss you in the centre of the bridge," Tom said.

"That sounds like fun," Elisabet giggled.

They crossed to the centre of the bridge, and Tom turned to face Elisabet. He held onto the rope with one hand, and put the other around his girlfriend. "Are you ready?"

Elisabet nodded. She took a secure grip on the rope with one hand, and placed the other on his shoulder. Tom leaned in for a kiss and Elisabet closed her eyes. Conscious that they were on a shaky bridge, she tried to remain very still. The kiss was special and they held it for a few minutes.

"Watch out you two," it was Jeffrey Mannington that interrupted them. He was walking along the staff side of the river, with his expensive new mobile phone in his hand.

"Sorry, Mr. Mannington," Elisabet stammered conservatively.

Jeffrey laughed. "Don't Mr. Mannington me, Elisabet," he said. "It's not so long since I was a student too."

"I know," Elisabet said.

Jeffrey turned to Tom: "You play A grade basketball, I hear. I used to play B grade myself."

"I think I remember," Tom said. Tom really had a very good memory, but it was safest to seem casual around a guy like Jeffrey.

"I wouldn't want to drop this in the river," Jeffrey said ostentatiously, tucking his mobile safely in a pouch attached to his belt.

"Of course not," Tom agreed.

Jeffrey passed them on his side of the riverbank and walked up to the staff house he had been assigned. He climbed into an expensive car and drove off.

"I wonder what that was all about?" Elisabet said.

"Just showing off I reckon," Tom concluded. "It is funny - Jeffrey has been seen more often without Ms. Louise, than he has been seen with her lately."

"Are they still engaged?" Elisabet asked.

"As far as I've heard," Tom said. "I doubt they will get married though."

"What makes you say that?" Elisabet asked.

"Well," Tom said. "Jeffrey's lecturing appointment was only temporary. Filling in while the regular professor was overseas. He will be back soon. Then I believe Jeffrey will return to his job in Brisbane."

"That is only an hour away," Elisabet observed.

"And yet, an hour is a long way for someone who makes as little effort as Jeffrey does," Tom observed. "And likes to have his head in a computer all day and half the night, or so I hear."

Monday afternoon, Craig had organised another practice for the *Electronic Jive Classical Vibe Band*. He had good news because the Brisbane congregation had raised enough money to cover travel to Sydney. In addition, the Baulkham Hills congregation might be able to billet the students during their stay, and save them hotel costs.

Once again, Craig asked Vivione to turn her bass guitar up, and he also pressured James to ham the drumming. "I want a few rolls," he said. "Smoke on water sort of thing!"

James frowned. "I know what you mean," he said. "But it is so far from my brass band training."

"You wanted to take over the drums," Craig said severely.

The two boys nearly came to blows over the issue. James was stubborn in his way; while Craig, on the other hand, was passionate about winning fans at the festival. It got to the point where James nearly walked out. Elisabet and Vivione had to beg them to stop arguing.

Tuesday after class, Cara and Elisabet met to complete another peer counselling session. This time, the Lecturer had assigned the topic of 'stress'. Cara began by talking about the stress of study.

"I think that everyone will agree assignments and exams can be stressful," Cara said. "They may have challenging topics, and also deadlines. If you don't do well, there is always the fear of failure."

"Is there anything else about campus life that might be stressful?" Elisabet asked.

"Um, the routine can be boring and the attendance requirement demanding," Cara said. "Especially if you get sick."

"What about socially?" Elisabet suggested.

"I was considering that a separate area," Cara said. "But socially, there is fitting in, surviving bullies and trying to make friends. All of which aren't major problems for us fourth years."

"I agree, we are comfortable and settled," Elisabet said.

"That will change at the end of the year with graduation," Cara said. "Change is another source of stress the lecturer mentioned."

"I don't worry much about it," Elisabet said.

"No, but maybe some people do," Cara observed.

Then it was Elisabet's turn to speak and Cara's turn to listen.

"I'm going to bring up the subject of break-ups," Elisabet said. "I'm past my break-up and happy with Tom now, but that was stressful for a few weeks."

Cara nodded.

"I tried to put it out of my mind," Elisabet said, "But some people really cry and unravel. Even become depressed."

"There was one week you were particularly bad," Cara reminded her friend.

"Yeah," Eliabet said. "After Justin moved on with Joelle. But I was not so much sad, more like angry."

"Still very stressful," Cara reflected. "And what about loneliness while you were broken up?"

"I felt some of that," Elisabet admitted. "On campus there are lots of people, but it would be worse if you lived alone."

The girls continued to chat for a few moments about their own experience, and what they had observed of their peer's break-ups.

"I feel like we ought to be able to find a few other sources of stress to talk about," Cara said finally.

"Well, money is a source of stress for most people," Elisabet suggested.

"Students are poor," Cara agreed. "Although, once we pay our boarding fees, everything is provided. Food, accommodation etc…"

"I think there are people out there who do it worse," Elisabet said. "Young families, the elderly, the homeless."

"Not knowing how to pay the bills would be very stressful," Cara agreed.

CHAPTER TWELVE: THE CHRISTIAN BAND FESTIVAL

Wednesday Craig had scheduled another band practice. It seemed like a lot of rehearsal, but even meeting every second day, they would fit a maximum of five or six more practices in before the Christian band festival.

"I would like to play our music to the students," Craig said. "Get an idea how an audience responds."

"You have the guitar turned up, and James drumming as hard as he can," Elisabet said. "We would risk getting shut down for being rocky."

"I'm surprised no one complains about the noise coming out of the Music Department," Vivione said.

"I think people expect noise to come from the Music Department," Craig said wryly. "And the buildings are set apart deliberately."

"Why don't we busk?" James suggested. "It would be an outdoor practice really, but we would probably need permission, because of the cords and things."

"I like the idea," Craig said. "We could set up along University Drive. Students would be free to stop and listen, or pass by. Even the extra volume would not be a problem outdoors."

"I'm in," Vivione said promptly.

"Elisabet, I'll need Tom's help setting up out there," Craig said. "After I get permission, I'll ask you to let him know."

"Okay," Elisabet said.

The band returned to their instruments, but they were excited about the new idea. Busking was something different to do, and would be good preparation for the festival. Everyone was pleased James had the idea.

Thursday Elisabet felt the beginnings of a cold. She took some Vitamin C and ate healthy fruit and vegetables at the cafeteria, hoping for a quick recovery. Being sick on campus could be very miserable, not to mention missing tests and getting behind on assignments.

Friday morning, Elisabet's symptoms were worse and she decided to stay in bed. Stephanie fetched food from the cafeteria, and the girl had to miss a band rehearsal. She climbed out of bed and showered just before vespers, but decided it would be best not to go in case she was germ ridden. She also asked Stephanie to explain to Craig that she might be missing band practice.

That Saturday a disability awareness event had been organised in honour of the 'Special Olympics' coming in November. The experience was held down at the gymnasium, where students would have a chance to try to play basketball from a wheel chair, complete an obstacle course blind-folded, and participate other consciousness raising activities. Elisabet was beginning to feel a bit better, so she visited the event with Tom.

Sunday, Elisabet attended the second worship service and was pretty much her usual self. Craig had scheduled a band practice for the afternoon, although Sunday was their free day usually. However, he said they needed to make up for lost sessions, and prepare for the busking activity, which had been approved for Tuesday afternoon.

After tea, Elisabet was also keen to spend some time relaxing with Tom in the recreation room, because she had seen less of him during her illness. They watched some evening comedy television shows and joked around with other students.

Monday, the news of an international stock market crash reverberated across Australian television screens. Most of the students had not had any funds to invest in stock, but the clever ones suggested that the financial crisis would still affect them.

"Debbie and I will be looking to buy a house," David said. "After we get married sometime… and with people losing confidence in stock, they will put their money into property instead, making it harder for the first home buyer."

"Phoebe and Hank are lucky they have already bought," Stephanie said dreamily. "Garry has been looking around since he has been working. Although we are not sure whether we want to be in Yandina permanently. Wollongong might be better in the long run."

"I'm just sorry for all those that have lost money," Elisabet said. "Some of our parents perhaps."

Elisabet's family had put most of their money into the farm, however there might have been a little left over for stock and shares. Any loss hurt.

"I think my parents had some shares," Andrew admitted. His family were from Canberra, and were the clerical types who might have something to do with share trading. "Safe companies mostly."

"No one was safe from this," Debbie pointed out.

"Very true," Stephanie agreed. "Perhaps if they hold the shares, they will recover."

"But if they hold onto them and they drop further, the loss might be greater," Andrew objected.

"It is a difficult one," David said. "Generally, it's safer to hold. But it does depend how long you are able to hold. And if the whole company should go bust – you would get nothing."

"It sounds as though you have been reading up on it," Elisabet observed.

David nodded. "I like to learn about things," he said. "And I was checking whether trading was moral."

"God said to weigh everything with fair scales," Andrew observed. "Leviticus 19:36."

"Didn't he say not to charge interest?" Cara asked.

Andrew nodded. "Exodus 22:25, 'You shall not charge interest to your brother'."

"That would only work in a society where nobody charged interest," David said thoughtfully. "And the use of someone else's money for a period must have value. Deuteronomy 23:19-20 says you can charge interest to a foreigner."

"But not a usurious value," Andrew concluded. "See Proverbs 28 – the whole chapter. It is not fair to cause financial pain and drive another into the ground because they came to you in need."

"Exactly," David said.

No announcement had been made about a concert, so Craig and Tom were the subject of a lot of curious questions when they began to set the band equipment up alongside University Drive. By the time Elisabet arrived, they had already gathered a bit of a following. This was without even playing a single note.

"What are they doing?" one student was whispering.

"Busking," another student replied.

"What's that?" the first student asked.

"A street concert," someone replied. "I've seen it happen in my capital city."

"What about lunch?" one hungry student asked.

"Have your lunch in the cafeteria as usual," Craig announced. "We will be playing out here after you have finished!"

The majority of the students followed Craig's advice and went on into the cafeteria to collect their food. A few lingered to see what the *Electronic Jive Classical Vibe Band* was up to.

"Food first," Craig said. He left Tom and Elisabet in charge and went into the cafeteria for his meal.

"Have your meals," Elisabet reiterated. "We won't be starting until Craig is back." The spectators followed the band leader inside.

It didn't take Craig long to eat his lunch and he emerged refreshed. He was followed by a few students.

"I will go and get my lunch," Tom said to Elisabet, who had eaten earlier. "Good luck!" He kissed her and disappeared into the cafeteria.

Craig picked up the microphone. "You may have heard a lot of noise coming from the Music Department lately," he said. "I would like to share the news that it was us! We are practicing to enter a Christian band festival and compete against a lot of other Christian bands."

More people emerged from the cafeteria. Seeing Craig holding a microphone, they stopped to look. Craig nodded to Vivione. She and James began to strum and drum. The heavy rifts of 'smoke on the water' drifted across the quadrangle and over the grass. The guitar chords were a universal signal, announcing the commencement of rousing music. A few students clapped in excitement.

At Craig's signal, Elisabet began to play one of their latest performance pieces. Vivione and James adjusted what they were doing to match her. The concert had begun.

The new pieces were simpler than some of their older pieces, and relied on repetition and rhythm. They worked up to a crescendo and kept repeating key words. Craig had done some research, and he had learned this style of music was immensely popular where they were going.

At the end of a couple of pieces, the band paused to get an audience reaction. The spectators clapped.

"You are getting more rocky," someone cried.

Craig decided to address this impression. "We are matching our style to the event," he said. "Because we perceive that will give us the best chance of success. But we retain our full range of style."

At Craig's signal, the *Electronic Jive Classical Vibe Band* began to play a psalm. This piece was a favourite around campus and had been included specifically to allay any staff concerns about their music. The last thing they needed was to be shut down just before the festival.

"Very nice," muttered a couple of lecturers who had wandered out of the faculty dining room. "Almost traditional."

The *Electronic Jive Classical Vibe Band* continued to play until they had performed each of their festival pieces several times. The group of students watching them fluctuated in numbers, as some students arrived, and others who tired of standing, decided to move on.

There was a general consensus that the new pieces were interesting and a bit different. Many students were excited to hear the band would be representing Silver Spring's University at a major Christian music event, and everyone wished them luck. A very few preferred what they remembered of Craig's earlier compositions, which they said were truly poetic.

Wednesday and Thursday, the band members were busy with practices and also their studies. As they would be travelling to Sydney on Friday, anything that was due before the weekend would have to be handed in early. The Music Master was also very strict and would not authorise any extensions due to musical activities. The students were expected to be able to manage their time wisely, and juggle all their commitments.

Friday morning, Elisabet rose early. She packed a few outfits, and made sure that she had her sheet music. She wished that she was taking her familiar keyboard, but one would be supplied down in Baulkham Hills by the festival organisers. Craig was taking his violin, and Vivione was taking her bass guitar. However, they would also be using borrowed drums, microphones and amps.

Luke dropped them off at Northcoast station using the mini-bus because of the suitcases and instruments. They checked their luggage and boarded the train. An hour and a half later, they arrived in Brisbane and caught a shuttle bus to the airport. There was a short wait to board the plane, and then they flew from Brisbane to Sydney.

In Sydney they caught a shuttle bus once again, which took them to Central Station. This was a huge transport node, from where they boarded a train headed out on the correct line. A representative of the festival organisers met them at the station.

Elisabet was glad to see a friendly face and have a guide at last. They piled into a mini-bus owned by the 'Youth Alive' social group and were taken straight to the festival venue.

"It's huge!" Elisabet whispered to Tom. The Silver Springs University students were accustomed to a large church, because the university congregation was composed of residents and faculty as well as the students. However, this church made their own look moderate.

"I wonder where everyone came from," Tom mused.

"I can answer that," said their guide, whose name was Timothy. "Most of the congregation have come from other denominations in search of a more vibrant and expressive worship style."

"That is very interesting," Elisabet said. "Do you do much grass roots evangelism amongst the unchurched?"

"I'm not sure what you mean," Timothy replied. "The Christian Life Church does offer an appealing alternative for today's youth, if that is what you mean. The music can even attract people off the streets."

"That is what I like to hear," Craig's face was enthusiastic.

They signed the register that formalised their arrival, and the guide led them towards their rostrum position. They were relieved to see the loan equipment waiting on the podium.

"You will have a while to set up and tune your instruments," Timothy said, then he left them.

There is a lot to do," Craig said. "And I'm glad we brought Tom. The extra pair of hands will be invaluable."

"It's going to be massive when all the bands are in here," Vivione observed. "Let alone the congregation."

"There is a possibility we might even be televised," James said. Pointing towards some camera equipment mounted on tripods.

"Better and better," Craig said. "I can't wait to finally meet Geoff Bullock, their music pastor. Imagine having a minister just for music!"

Tom got busy connecting cords and amps, while the musicians tried out their hired equipment. Elisabet wished for the Music Department keyboard, where she was familiar with every setting and every stop, but she guessed she would know this one pretty well by the end of the weekend.

James tapped cautiously at the drums. They seemed slightly worn and quite different from the Music Department set, which was lovingly maintained.

"Okay," Tom said. "Everything is connected."

"Test it out," Craig instructed.

Elisabet and Vivione both powered up their instruments. Elisabet wasn't sure about the initial sound, so she adjusted a few settings. The keyboard started to sound much more like the one back at Silver Springs.

James tentatively tapped the drums: "Sweet."

"Let's play a piece," Craig said.

The *Electronic Jive Classical Vibe Band* struck up a tune, and commenced one of their new pieces. Everything sounded different in the new venue, and a few competing strains arose from the adjacent band. So far as they could tell, the instruments were in tune. They just had to get over their nerves and accustom themselves to the situation.

A mature surfie-type stuck his head around the corner. "That sounds good," he commented. "Where are you guys from?"

"Silver Springs University," Craig replied. "About an hour north and slightly east of Brisbane."

"Ah yes, a lot of talent comes from South-east Queensland," the surfie said. "My name is Trevor, and I'm one of the assistants here."

"Pleased to meet you Trevor," Craig said.

Craig offered his hand to Trevor, who shook hands all around.

"Good luck with the festival," Trevor said. "I will be keeping my ears open – I might be organising something big next year – and I could use a few good Christian musicians."

"We will be busy with our studies," James said, speaking for himself and Vivione.

"I will have graduated," Craig said. "I would be keen to be involved in anything that is happening. Depending what other work I am offered of course."

"Who is the songwriter of the group?" Trevor asked, and Craig looked proud.

"Me, of course," he said.

"Craig is our major talent," Elisabet added supportively.

"We must catch up later," Trevor said. He waved goodbye and strolled off to greet some of the other bands.

Craig turned to his band members with shining eyes. "Do you know who that was?"

"No," Elisabet said shortly. She half wished they had brought Larry along with them. Tom's presence was comforting and solid, but Larry had actually done a pastoral practicum at the Christian Life Church and would know his way around. "I'm at a loss."

"I think it was Trevor King," Craig said. "From the Andy Gibb band."

"One of the Bee Gees?" Vivione was incredulous.

"No," Craig said. "Andy was the younger brother. He belonged to a few different bands."

James frowned. "I thought Andy Gibb's drummer was Trevor Norton," he said.

"Perhaps they used some extra musicians," Elisabet said. "I don't see why he would make the claim if he hadn't been."

"Anyway, Trevor King is very influential now," Craig said. "And I believe he hangs around with David Moyes of *Air Supply* and Jeff Beacham from *Black Feather*."

A couple of hours later, all the bands were set up, and the congregation filled the interior to capacity. Elisabet was glad they merely had to play a few set pieces in unison with the other bands, and support the official Christian Life group that evening. Original compositions by individual bands would be presented later.

After the evening was over, Elisabet and Tom were collected by the family that was going to billet them. They ate a late supper and tumbled into bed, in separate rooms of course. In the morning, Elisabet found that she was very nervous.

"I can't believe that we are up against people who have been actual stars," she whispered. "And I'm not even a music major."

"I wouldn't worry about that," Tom said. "I was chatting around last night, and not everyone has formal training. In fact, you guys might be an exception for being more classical in background."

"Doesn't that make it worse?" Elisabet cried.

"How do you normally get through a performance?' Tom asked.

"I don't know," Elisabet said. "Once the music starts – I'm alright."

"So let's get you there and get the music started," Tom said sturdily. "Craig is so good, I don't think you guys can go wrong. If you do get knocked out of the competition early – you have less playing to worry about!"

The kind family that were providing the billet drove Elisabet and Tom to the venue, where they reconnected with Craig and Vivione, who had both been staying with another family. Craig wanted to do an early run through of their pieces, and then they sat waiting for the programme to commence.

Elisabet counted about twenty bands seated around the venue at the commencement of the competition. There were some preliminaries, during which the Christian Life Church's official band played some introductory pieces. These were followed by an announcement to the effect that this semi-formal event was being held to encourage the composition of original music to the glory of God. By the evidence of their surroundings, music was very central to Christian Life worship theology.

Each band commenced presenting their first song, one by one. Some were just average, but others were really quite impressive. Elisabet was so busy listening that she barely noticed when it was *Electronic Jive Classical Vibe Band's* turn to play.

Her fingers slid into the familiar notes of one of Craig's new compositions, and Vivione's guitar boomed beside her. James drummed as he had never drummed before, and he seemed to have finally lost the last vestiges of brass band style that always haunted him. Craig sang like an angel, although he was making an effort to roughen the timbre of his voice to match the musical style. Once their piece was finished, Elisabet was able to sit back and relax, enjoying listening to the other bands.

The festival programme paused for lunch, which was provided in the adjoining hall. Craig was very pleased when one of the organisers came around to their table to tell them that the *Electronic Jive Classical Vibe Band* had been selected to go into round two, and would be required to perform a second and third piece during the afternoon programme.

After lunch, about fourteen of the participating bands took their places on the rostrum to present their original Christian compositions. The overall standard of the afternoon performance was higher, and the listeners gathered more of an impression of each groups' unique style.

The audience clapped and swung their arms around, and generally got excited. At first Elisabet was put off, because she was used to congregations that listened quietly, but she began to adapt. By the time the *Electronic Jive Classical Vibe Band* was required to execute their two new pieces, she saw how cleverly Craig had composed everything to fit right into this environment. The realisation gave her confidence and she played well.

During the tea break, Craig received the news that they had reached the top ten, and were qualified to participate in round three. The next segment involved presenting one new composition, while they got the option of repeating one of the pieces played in a previous round. This was designed to give the judges a chance to analyse their compositions.

By now, Elisabet was feeling tired. She had been sitting on the rostrum all day, with the exception of interval breaks and meal breaks. Vivione and James were also feeling stiff and cramped. Only Craig appeared comfortable, buoyed up by his excitement.

When it was their turn, the *Electronic Jive Classical Vibe Band* performed their fourth original composition, and repeated the very first song they had played. This was one of the best of the new songs, and Craig had chosen it as their opener for that reason. It was good to be able to repeat it during the performance.

At the end of round three, they received the disappointing news that they had not been selected for the finals.

"I don't mind," Elisabet said. "It means that we can sit and relax during tomorrow's worship."

James and Vivione agreed, but Craig looked crestfallen.

"I guess we knew this was coming," Craig said mournfully. "Our first multi-band event and all that."

"I think we have done very well," James said. "For a group that has only been together for a few months, and puts most of its energy into academic studies anyway."

The Silver Spring's University students went home to their billets to sleep for the night. In the morning, they were ferried back to the venue. James, Elisabet and Vivione settled comfortably into seats amongst the congregation, but one of the worship pastors approached and took Craig away from his companions.

Craig looked pleased and promised he would be back, but a few moments later, he appeared on the raised area amongst the successful artists.

"I think Craig has been invited to continue on as a soloist," Vivione whispered.

"Surely not," Elisabet said. "I mean – he is good enough – but we are his accompaniment."

"I think it is simply that this morning's divine service is not part of the competition," James observed. "Craig's talent has been noted, and is being acknowledged, but it doesn't affect the festival outcome."

As it turned out, James was right. Craig had indeed been noticed and had formed some important professional musical connections. However, there was no intention of promoting him further without his group.

The afternoon program was fun to watch, as the final six bands sung it out to take their position on the festival leader-board. There was no monetary prize as such, but the possibility of cutting a Compact Disk was on offer, if the winning group had enough original pieces prepared. The runner's up would be included in mixed CD featuring different Christian groups.

As soon as the festival had concluded, the students were taken across to the train station, where they bid goodbye to their host families. They caught an evening flight from Sydney to Brisbane, and another train to Northcoast, where Luke collected them in the university mini-bus.

Monday morning, Elisabet was tired, but she forced herself to get up, and go across to the cafeteria with Stephanie. They sat with Larry and Anita, Jessie and James, and Andrew. Jessie, who shared music with them, asked Elisabet and James how the weekend had gone.

"We made it into the top ten," Elisabet said. "But not the final six."

"Oh," Jessie sounded disappointed. "We thought you guys were good."

"We were," Elisabet said. "Just some others were better!"

"What did you think of it really?" Larry said, his eyes glinting mischievously. "Different isn't it?"

"I expect Craig will be keeping in contact with Christian Life," Elisabet said. "I'm more comfortable with my home church. Nice and traditional."

"A theology based almost purely around music is interesting," James began. "I wonder whether there are enough references in the Bible to warrant it, however."

"Music is an excellent outreach tool," Larry challenged.

"Oh – I could see that," James agreed.

"The Psalms say to sing, dance and make a loud noise before the Lord," Andrew said. "And Revelation says we will sing with the angels… but that is an interesting question."

"David's reference always meant brass band to me," James said. "He even mentions cymbals."

"God loves music, that is for sure," Larry said. "And you guys - Craig especially - with your talents ought to use them!"

"We intend to," James said. "Well, we have classes – coming Jessie?"

James and Jessie left the cafeteria and Elisabet sighed. "I don't have a seven-thirty, but I will need to get a move along. Study awaits."

"We will see you in counselling skills," Larry and Anita said.

"Me as well," Andrew said. "Have a good morning. Elisabet."

"Thanks," Elisabet said. "You too."

Tuesday Elisabet sat an education test. In the afternoon, she went to watch Tom play basketball. His team was progressing well under Vincent's direction, and there was a good chance that they might make it to the semi-finals that season. They won the match easily, and then Tom joined Elisabet on the bench to watch the B grade boys play.

Terence was in the gymnasium as well, and he gave the couple a cheery wave. The basketball administrator had taken to hanging out with Lacey lately. Tom observed that Lacey was a very nice girl, and he hoped Terence would make her very happy.

Elisabet felt a mild, but almost pleasurable stab of jealousy when Tom said this. Tom and Lacey had been 'good friends' when Tom was between girlfriends, but Elisabet knew her boyfriend loved her completely. Lacey was not a threat, but it still reminded her she ought to value what she had.

Wednesday, Cara and Elisabet met for another peer counselling session. The Counselling Skills Lecturer had specified that the topic was 'the life cycle', but the girls had drifted into discussing the excitement of Elisabet's participation in the Christian band festival the previous weekend.

"I think Craig hopes to get in with them," Elisabet said.

"Do you think that would be a good career move?" Cara said.

"For someone like him, perhaps," Elisabet said. "But Craig has a lot of classical training – I hope he doesn't drop teaching."

"I don't expect that he will," Cara said comfortable. "What about him and Vivione? Anything happening there?"

Elisabet shook her head. "I think they are just good friends," she said. "Craig talks in terms of missing her after graduation, but he always paints a picture of a solitary future."

"We had better get back to the topic," Cara observed.

"I didn't think we were that far off, Elisabet said. "After childhood comes partnering and career. Not necessarily in that order."

"And then children and middle age," Cara said. "Retirement, grandchildren and old age."

"Which stage do you think is best?" Elisabet inquired.

"They all have their positives," Cara said. "But I like our current stage – I've found Dylan and we have our lives before us. You have found Tom, and you can do fun things together, like participate in music festivals."

"Yeah, it was fun," Elisabet agreed. "And I'm so glad Tom came along. To think that I resisted his becoming our roadie at first!"

CHAPTER THIRTEEN: THE END OF THE BASKETBALL SEASON

The regular Computing Lecturer returned from his conference tour, on Thursday, and consequently Jeffrey Mannington was due to leave Silver Springs. The faculty threw a luncheon party to farewell him on Friday, and the *Electronic Jive Classical Vibe Band* were booked to provide light background music during the event.

It was short notice, but the band played Craig's earlier compositions, and their selection of Psalm music, which pleased the staff very well. Craig deliberately avoided the rocky pieces he had written for the festival, as these were not so much to the faculty taste.

During the luncheon, Elisabet noticed Ms. Louise eyeing her ring-less left hand thoughtfully. Once Jeffrey left, the Art Tutor would have no reminder of their relationship, and no evidence of commitment. The lack of a ring might not have been an issue before, but the woman appeared to be getting worried.

The Uniting Church Chaplain toasted Jeffrey with sparkling grape juice and wished him all the best for the future. Then Jeffrey rose to his feet and thanked everyone.

"I have enjoyed working here immensely," he said. "Feel free to call upon me any time you need me again."

"Hear, hear," the Professors cried.

"I love my job in Brisbane," Jeff said, "And I know I am leaving you in good hands while the Computing Lecturer is in charge."

"Hear, hear," the Professors cried. They began to sing: "For he is a jolly good fellow." When the professors had run out of words, the Reform

Church Chaplain took over and began to pray, asking for a blessing on Jeffrey and his return to Brisbane.

"There was no mention of Ms. Louise and their engagement," Elisabet observed later to Tom.

"I noticed that too," Tom said. "And without a ring – it is like it never happened."

"We will see whether he comes back here to visit Ms. Louise," Elisabet mused. "I think she could do better than Jeffrey Mannington."

"Most certainly," Tom concurred.

That weekend the campus was Jeffrey-free, and Stephanie heaved a sigh of relief. While the room-mate had insisted that his presence was having no effect, she had been inclined to avoid social situations that would involve contact, just as a precaution. Everyone who knew him agreed Jeffrey had a long memory, and was capable of holding a grudge.

Stephanie took advantage of the peace to remain on campus and complete the machining on her bridesmaid's dresses. Then she called both Cara and Cathy up to the room for a fitting. The girls looked very pretty in the taffeta frocks.

Sunday, the first of November, was All Saints Day. The Uniting Church Chaplain revived the cute tradition of lighting a candle for a loved one, and the ladies assembly area remained open all day for the purpose. Elisabet accompanied Stephanie to the chapel, where they lit a candle for Bradley, who had died two years ago.

Elisabet said a prayer of her own, but her prayer was for the future, as she did not believe in praying for the deceased. Stephanie she said that her candle represented gratitude for the memory of her loved ones.

Monday, Tom received the welcome news from Ms. Louise that the yearbook was on its way. It had been printed and freighted to Brisbane, where it was awaiting a courier to pick it up. All the members of the committee were immensely excited in anticipation of seeing the finished product.

"Just imagine unpacking the boxes," Stephanie sighed. "It will be like Christmas!"

Elisabet laughed. "You do take pleasure in little things, don't you?" she observed.

"Why not?" Stephanie said.

"Only one book will be yours," Elisabet said.

"But we will have the fun of giving them out," Stephanie enthused.

"Next thing you will say 'just like Santa Claus'," Elisabet joked.

Stephanie looked indignant. "That Santa is a commercial construct!" she said. "But you have to admit giving is a lot of fun!"

"I have to agree a volume designed specifically by us is a satisfying achievement," Tom agreed.

"To be sure," Elisabet agreed. "I was simply amused by Stephanie's childlike joy."

"I want to remain young at heart forever," Stephanie asserted. "There is nothing wrong with that!"

Elisabet laughed. Glimpses into Stephanie's fun side were rare. The girl had learned to be guarded over the years, due to bullying she had experienced. However, the fun-loving Stephanie did exist, bottled up inside and occasionally peeking out.

Tuesday was Melbourne Cup Day. Silver Spring's University did not hold with horse racing, because it was associated with gambling. This meant that there were no fun games or dress-ups in the cafeteria, but the televisions in the recreation area could be tuned to broadcast the race, so a few students gathered to view the significant race known as 'the cup'.

Elisabet had a sneaking fancy for horses, which she considered magnificent creatures, and the fashions that the ladies wore to the race-track were legendary. She persuaded Tom to linger in the recreation area, until it was time for her to go and complete her shift on the Student Services desk.

Wednesday Garry arrived on campus just after the cafeteria had finished serving tea. He was looking very pleased with himself, and drew Stephanie aside for an intimate word.

The roommate clapped her hands in delight: "Accept it!" she exclaimed loud enough for the other students to hear.

"That's what I was thinking too," Garry said. "It is settled then!"

He turned to the other students. "I have been offered a job I applied for in the technical department of Sydney Water, based near Illawarra Lake. I start in the New Year, when my contract with Queensland Rail expires."

"That's fantastic!" Elisabet exclaimed.

"Congratulations mate," David said. He looked a little envious. Graduate placements had not been announced, and none of the Theology students knew where they might be assigned work.

"You deserve it," Andrew pronounced. Garry had worked very hard and he was something of a selfless person, so it was satisfying to see good things flowing his direction.

"There is a house Stephanie and I looked at during the break," Garry said. "I have been saving most of my wage, and with permanent employment, I might be in a position to make an offer on it."

"The house is above Wollongong," Stephanie said. "An older place, so it has been on the market for a while, but we will enjoy renovating it. According to the builder's report, it is worth the effort."

"How exciting," Elisabet observed. "And you won't be too far from Garry's parents."

"That is another good thing," Stephanie said.

On Thursday the courier delivered some large boxes to the Student Services Office. Tom called the Year Book committee together, and they broke open the packaging. Tom lifted the first sample out and placed it on the table. The group gathered around and exclaimed over every page.

"I cannot believe how good it looks," Stephanie exclaimed.

"I am particularly happy with the way the photographs printed," Ms. Louise observed.

"Christopher's devotional looks good," Felipe observed. "As does my article about the science programme."

"The sports pages have turned out well," commented Moira.

"I am happy with the poetry," Stephanie concluded.

"Now Stephanie," Tom instructed. "You can have fun getting them all out of the box."

"Yay!" Stephanie exclaimed. She began to scrabble eagerly and was soon surrounded by piles of books.

Tom laughed. "It's not a game Stephanie," he said. "I need you to check the quantity. We ordered 500 copies, so they have to be counted exactly. And checked! Any copies with flaws will have to be returned to the company."

"I hope there aren't too many like that," Stephanie's voice was muffled from her position on the floor beside the boxes.

"So do I," Ms. Louise said. "Returns are such a nuisance. But we have to keep the printer accountable!"

"Oh exactly," Stephanie said. "You can trust me." The quiet girl secretly loved responsibility. "Today's Biology is a research project. I can go to the library later."

"I will help," Moira said, squatting down too. "The counting could get boring Steph."

"We will make piles of 50," Stephanie said. "That way it will be easier."

"I have to practice my music," Elisabet said. She picked up a copy of the Year Book to take with her, but Stephanie snatched it back.

"No you don't," she said. "Not until the stock-take is completed."

"Meanie!" Elisabet teased. "Just tick it off your list."

"No," Stephanie was comically officious. "I can bring yours to the room later."

By Friday afternoon, the books had been counted. Tom had organised a table to be set up in the cafeteria lounge, where the committee volunteers sat with a complete list of the student body. As each scholar collected their copy, their name was marked off. Additional copies were available for a price for friends and family.

They took turns sitting at the table, which would remain operational throughout the evening. After that, the remaining stock would be stored at the Student Services office, and Elisabet would be in charge of special orders.

Distributing the Year Book in this orderly fashion wasn't as much fun as Stephanie had imagined, and the girls got bored sitting on the table. They passed the time collecting autographs on their personal copies. Elisabet was glad when both she and Tom were finally free to go for a romantic afternoon drive through the warm spring rain.

Sunday morning the downpour had become heavier, and it was literally pelting. Elisabet and Stephanie dressed for worship and huddled under large umbrellas as they ducked between buildings. Their shoes got soaked, and Elisabet regretted wearing the pretty new courts she had bought during the holidays. The drenching would reduce the shoe's life dramatically. She lined them up against the wall to dry and changed into everyday shoes.

Someone reported that the river was rising, and a group of students braved the weather to go down and look. The water certainly was flowing merrily, bubbling away gleefully and lapping at the banks.

Monday evening, Tom's team played in the men's basketball semi-finals. Elisabet and Stephanie went down to the gymnasium to watch and cheer. Tom's team was playing Terrence's team, who were universally acknowledged the best on campus; so the most they could expect was to present a good challenge.

Vincent gathered the guys together before the match for instruction, and they set to play using as much strategy as possible. His team won the toss, and Vincent pushed his advantage by knocking the ball towards Tom. Tom was prepared to collect the ball, and headed directly towards the goal. They had the advantage of surprise, and scored immediately.

After that, Terrence's team gained control of the ball. The veteran players pounded up and down the court, trying for goal after goal. Vincent's team were active in defence, attempting to block them at every mood.

Vincent's team succeeded in minimising the score, and even fought their way through to achieving a couple more goals of their own. At half time, the score was near even, but by full-time, Terrence's team had pulled well ahead.

Terrence clapped Vincent on the back. "Good work mate," he cried.

Vincent glowed. "Thanks," he said. His journey from outcast to successful captain was complete, and his adoring girlfriend, Janet, clapped from the spectator bench. "Congratulations man, I hope you win the finals," Vincent returned generously to Terrence.

Tom came trotting up to Elisabet. "Well that's basketball finished for me," he joked. "I can get back to surfing."

Elisabet laughed. Tom had never ceased his early morning surfing expeditions with Dylan. Both boys claimed the activity helped them get through the rest of the day. "Let's go to the canteen to celebrate," she suggested.

Tuesday Elisabet's counselling skills journal was due. She spent most of her free time adding final observations and reflections, and summarising what she had learned about herself as a counsellor. This had to be referenced against at least three texts outlining the theoretical approaches they had studied, so it was a serious project.

Stephanie was also hard at work finalising her journal. Because the assignment had been practical and progressive, this was not something that Stephanie had been able to do ahead of time, even though that was the studious girl's preference.

Both girls added the final touches to their work, and decided to walk across campus to the submission box. They ran into Debbie and David on the way to completing the same errand. The students all agreed the project had been a good change from the usual pen and paper exercises. David observed that the subject was especially relevant for the theology students who might undertaker pastoral counselling in their parishes.

Wednesday evening, Stephanie invited Elisabet to accompany her to watch the women's basketball finals, because Cara was playing. Elisabet invited Tom to accompany them, and Dylan accompanied him. Vincent was also there to watch Janet play.

Cara's team performed brilliantly and succeeded in winning a place in the finals. After the game finished, the two teams went up to the canteen and indulged in ice-cream to celebrate. Several of the boys asked for soft drink mixed with their ice-cream, and exclaimed in amusement as the 'spiders' bubbled over. It was a fun evening.

Thursday Elisabet settled down to finish her assignments. The lecturers required class-work from the graduating class be presented in advance. This allowed time to mark everything before the graduation ceremony. Several of Elisabet's papers had already been handed in, but a couple of reading reports remained.

Stephanie was busy down at the Science Department, completing her final biology practical for the semester. The following Thursday was actually scheduled to be her 'prac exam', which the Biology Master often scheduled independent of exam week. She arrived up at the cafeteria late for tea, and Elisabet comforted her by observing they had almost reached the culmination of four years of effort.

"I know," Stephanie said, and sighed. "I will almost miss it."

"Miss it," Elisabet exclaimed. "No way!"

"I will tell you a secret," Stephanie whispered. "I have applied to do a Master's degree next year at Wollongong University."

"Really?" Elisabet was astounded. "In what field?"

Stephanie looked serious. "Health promotion," she said. "I love English – but I think I could do more good running Health Education programs in the community. I've put as many years into my biology as my English really... and I enjoyed the volunteer work I did at the nursing home during our second year."

"You and Garry are not planning to start a family straight away then?" Elisabet asked.

Stephanie shook her head. "I'm a couple of years younger than the rest of you remember – plenty of time for that later."

"It's an interesting idea," Elisabet was thoughtful.

Elisabet enjoyed the Uniting Church Vespers programme on Friday evening. The Chaplain had decided to screen a film of an interesting motivational preacher. After the film had concluded, Tom and Elisabet sat talking to Cara and Dylan. Elisabet was curious about their plans for the future and asked where each had applied to be sent.

"North New South Wales," Cara replied promptly.

Elisabet was surprised. "I thought you might like to go back to Victoria?"

"Perhaps," Cara said. "But – it's a great secret really – Dylan has had holiday work in the agricultural industry for the past several years. Food technology sort of thing… and the company offered to take him on permanently."

Elisabet knew that Dylan had worked during the holidays, but she had never been told exactly what his job was. For Dylan to keep so quiet about his employment, it was probably something the Reform Church would not approve, perhaps in the meat or wine industries. However, many other churches were not as strict regarding dietary matters, and after graduation, Dylan would be able to do as he liked.

"That's great," Elisabet said. "Will you be getting married?"

"When we are ready," Cara said. She blushed. "Dylan and I have talked about it, and we thought we might take another year to have fun first. We both like camping and hiking and that sort of thing."

"Surely you can do that after marriage?" Elisabet suggested.

"Yeah," Cara said. "But maybe not the same once kids come along. Anyway, Dylan and I only became 'official' last year, and we see no need to rush to catch up with the other couples."

Elisabet nodded. She and Tom were in the same sort of situation, but even more so, because they had only just begun going steady.

On Saturday, Tom and Elisabet celebrated their second month anniversary. Neither was quite sure whether they counted their relationship from the day of the fire, or the following day, when Elisabet had picked Tom up from the hospital and they confirmed their commitment.

Elisabet wasn't as sentimental as some of the girls, but she was very pleased when Tom presented her with a bunch of red roses. She laughed and kissed him, and generally made him feel loved.

In the evening, Ms. Louise and the English Professor took the members of the Year Book Committee out to dinner at the Chinese restaurant in Northcoast as a 'thank you' for their hard work. Partners had been invited too, so Stephanie was bringing Garry.

Felipe and Moira had developed a close friendship working together on the Year Book, and they were shaping up to be one of the latest couples on campus. They were very sweet to watch, billing and cooing as they guided each other through the menu.

None of the party had eaten Chinese food very often. Elisabet chose stir fried beef in plum sauce, and Tom ordered apricot chicken. Ms. Louise ordered one of the vegetarian fried noodle options, and the English Professor ordered the most conservative looking dish on the menu, the seasonal vegetables.

"Have you heard from Jeffrey Mannington, Ms. Louise?" Cara asked politely, noticing that their hostess was unaccompanied, although the English Professor had brought his wife along.

Ms. Louise sighed. "I'm afraid that Jeff is not very good at keeping in contact," she said. "And he has been so busy settling back into work he has not even wanted me to visit."

"I guess he has friends in Brisbane?" Tom ventured.

Ms. Louise nodded. "That is another problem," she said. "Jeff's friends are sort of… I don't know how to describe it."

"Cliquey," Stephanie said from further down the table. "That crowd always was a bit exclusive."

"That is the word, thank you Stephanie," Ms. Louise said. "I feel they do not welcome me. They also don't understand art and the things I stand for."

"You need someone who appreciates you, Ms. Louise," Tom observed.

"Yes," Ms. Louise's face brightened. "On a more cheerful note – I heard from another colleague – and they invited me to join a tour of the Holy Land."

"It sounds lovely," Cara said.

"Yes," Ms. Louise said. "The tour runs over the long break. Imagine celebrating Christmas actually in Bethlehem…"

"Fancy that!" Tom agreed. "I cannot think of anything more amazing."

"Would this colleague of yours be a single male by any chance?" Stephanie asked.

"They would," Ms. Louise admitted. "And someone I have been out with once or twice over the years too. But there is nothing going on – I would have to finish with Jeffrey for that."

"It might be worth considering," Tom said. "I can't imagine Jeffrey wanting to go to the Holy Land. Maybe London, or New York, or even Hawaii perhaps."

"You are right," Ms. Louise said. "Jeff didn't want to go on the tour. He said that his work would be too demanding. Even over Christmas!"

The English Professor interrupted the conversation to call them to attention and congratulate the Year Book team on the excellent quality of their publication, and their ability to work independently. He was a busy man and had been appreciative of how smoothly things had progressed with Ms. Louise in charge of the everyday details.

Everyone clapped, and Tom proposed a toast to Ms. Louise. "The best staff adviser ever," he said.

"To Miss Louise," the others agreed.

It was late when they arrived back on campus, and the female students had to use their electronic keys to access the building through the security system, but that was alright because they had been under staff chaperonage.

Sunday morning, Elisabet attended both worship services and enjoyed lunch in the cafeteria. After lunch, Tom suggested they find a quiet place to talk. Elisabet felt slightly nervous hearing this, although she was secure in their relationship. She obediently followed Tom into the lounge, and sat down. Tom took her hands and gazed into her eyes in all seriousness.

"I know what must be thinking," he said. "The other couples are all far, far ahead of us."

"Not all of them," Elisabet admitted. "Kathy and Andrew are still 'engaged to be engaged' as far as I know. And Luke and Tess have been going out forever, but have not got engaged yet."

"Last night the English Professor mentioned a Christian publishing position to me," Tom said. "He recommended I apply for it… but it is in Brookvale."

"Sydney?" Elisabet asked.

"Northern Beaches," Tom said. "Not as expensive as North Shore. We might be able to afford a unit or even something a little better."

"I think I could live with that if we weren't in the centre of the city," Elisabet said. "Please go ahead and apply."

"I know that you are interested in journalism too," Tom said.

"I am," Elisabet said. "But we might hear about more media opportunities once we get down there."

"They are interested in me because I anchored the Year Book production this year," Tom said.

"It was valuable experience," Elisabet agreed. "For both of us - I'm glad you asked me to join."

So it was agreed that Tom would apply for the job. He would also ask around and see whether any suitable positions might be available for Elisabet.

Monday evening was the men's A grade basketball finals, so Elisabet and Tom joined the spectators. It was raining outside, but warm and steamy in the gymnasium. Terence ran around adjusting the ventilation before the match began so everyone would be more comfortable.

Both teams played well, but Terence's team won as many had predicted. After the prestigious A grade match was finished, the B grade and C grade finals were fought out simultaneously on alternate courts. This made quite a long evening for those who stayed to watch all the matches.

Tuesday, the women's A grade finals were played, also followed by their B and C grade counterparts. Elisabet and Stephanie watched the A grade to support Cara, who ended the match heated and flushed.

"You played well," Elisabet said.

"Thanks," Cara said. She picked up her water bottle and took a long draft. "In this humidity, you sweat, but it doesn't cool you much."

"I'm almost used to the warm rain," observed Stephanie, who originally came from Adelaide, which had a much cooler climate.

"That was my last university match," Cara said.

"You will play basketball again" Dylan assured her.

"Community basketball perhaps," Cara said. "It won't be the same."

"Every ending represents a new beginning," Dylan insisted.

"Oh of course," Cara said. "And I enjoy a challenge. Just now, I need a shower. Walk me back to the dorm girls?"

Wednesday evening was the Basketball Tea. Tom and Elisabet were seated on the A grade table along with Vincent and Janet. Now that several female basketball players were dating male players, the men's and women's teams were somewhat intermingled.

The meal was jovial, with a selection of pita breads, dips, salsas and fillings that the students could use to create their own 'wraps'. This was complimented by a tray of chicken wings and traditional barbecue fare. Sparkling apple juice had been provided as a celebratory drink.

Terence rose and presented several trophies, including 'most improved' to Vincent, who had grown into his captain's role. The 'best and fairest' award went to a solid member of Terrence's own team. The captain of the opposing team presented the A grade trophy to Terence, then Janet rose to present the women's trophies.

After Janet had finished, Terence stood up again. "Now I come to a special category of player," he pronounced. "Our fourth years, including Tom, Dylan and Cara, will not be playing with us again next year. We will miss them very much."

Everyone nodded. There was the usual detachment between classes, but many of the third years had become friendly with the fourth years.

"I think I can remember the way to come and visit," Dylan shouted, and a few people clapped.

"Big words," Terrence taunted. "Make sure you do as you say."

The hospitality students served fruit salad and ice-cream, before the A grade captains cut the gigantic cake. A good time was had by all the students involved in basketball, and many who just enjoyed being spectators. After the tea was over, Tom walked Elisabet back to the girl's dormitory and kissed her goodnight.

Thursday was the last day of classes, before the commencement of study vacation and exams. It was also the day of Stephanie's practical examination. Stephanie confided no matter how hard she studied, the Biology Master always managed to trick the students.

"He is just sadistic," Stephanie declared.

"Surprising, he seems easy going every day," Elisabet mused.

"Outside of class, yes!" Stephanie agreed. "And he makes life fun with all our excursions."

Elisabet wished her roommate luck: "Do your best, Steph, I will see you at tea when it is all over."

Stephanie waved and left to make her way across to the Science Department. A few hours later she was back, resigned and relieved, just as Elisabet had expected. Cara and Dylan were also pleased that their biology practical programme had concluded.

CHAPTER FOURTEEN: CALLINGS AND DIRECTIONS

Friday, Saturday and Sunday were independent study days during which the students were expected to manage their own revision activities. Worship services provided a welcome change of pace, but organised social activities were kept to a minimum. Along with the rest of the fourth year class, Elisabet and Stephanie applied themselves to make the best use of the time before exams commenced.

Monday, the girls both sat their counselling skills and English exams. On Tuesday, Elisabet had education and the music theory exam, while Stephanie also had education and biology exams. These exams had all been scheduled early to facilitate marking before the graduation ceremony.

Wednesday morning, the girls began the process of packing their personal effects and cleaning their rooms. Stephanie was planning on keeping her gear in storage until after her wedding in January; while Elisabet was planning on taking everything back to her parent's house at Byron Bay until she knew what she was doing next.

Starting Thursday, the fourth year students began anxiously keeping their ears open for the names being called over the public address system, as graduate work placements were being announced.

Luke and Tess were one of the first to receive their calling. Luke, who had his bus licence, had been called to Alice Springs. This was a placement where a pastor with a range of skills might be invaluable. Tess was philosophical about the selection, announcing that it would be an adventure, even if they did not stay outback forever.

"It will be hot," Elisabet said with a shudder.

"I'm prepared for that," Tess said. "And appointments usually last about four to six years. We can apply for something different after that."

"They say the outback gets into your blood and then you don't want to leave," Luke said. He had the sturdy ability to make the best of his situation, the way he always did at Silver Springs.

"I think I will just wait and see about that," Tess said sweetly. She was wearing an engagement ring now, because Luke had proposed as soon as he had heard about the placement. The theology student said that he could hardly take Tess into the outback with him unless she was his wife, and after years of uneventful courtship, the couple were suddenly fast-tracking the wedding.

They lodged the paperwork with the Uniting Church Chaplain that very day, and as it was the 25th of November, they would be eligible to get married on or after the 27th of December. This gave them a fortnight for a honeymoon; before Luke took up his position as a Northern Territory minister in the middle of January. A few people glanced suspiciously at Tess' stomach, but she laughed merrily at any suggestion that she might be pregnant.

Tess' parents had flown in for graduation, and her mother took her to Noosa where the girl found a wedding dress she described as "just perfect". Debbie was going to be her bridesmaid, wearing a simple burgundy dress that would also look nice for a pastor's wife to wear to church.

Larry and Anita were the next to receive their calling. Larry had drawn a position as assistant pastor to a Pentecostal congregation in Parramatta. It was such a large congregation that being assistant pastor there carried the same prestige as sole pastor at a smaller parish. Anita would be working at a school nearby. Their wedding plans were progressing steadily.

The next call was for Andrew Grosvy. With typical dedication, Andrew had indicated he was open to work in the mission fields. However, to his surprise, instead of being called to Papua New Guinea, or the Aboriginal lands, he was directed to Tasmania. This caused him some soul searching, because the island state was far from Kathy's parents in Armidale, and his own parents in Canberra, yet did not qualify in his mind as an incredibly needy cause.

Andrew spent some hours cloistered with the Theology Lecturer, who explained to him that Tasmania was isolated from the mainland, and in need of good pastoral staff. Then he had a long telephone conversation with Kathy, who was confident that she would find some teaching work around Hobart.

By the time Andrew finally accepted the call, he was aglow with holy joy because he had convinced himself that he was fulfilling God's will. He had also begun to study maps and sought out Craig for his knowledge of the area.

Elisabet generally avoided talking to Justin, but Saturday at lunch she heard him confirm he was returning to his regular parish in the UK, and taking Joelle back with him. Joelle had developed her music connections over there when she had visited the previous year, and appeared very excited by the opportunities that would be open to her in England.

Saturday night, a special dinner was served to the graduating class. Many of the girls wore the white gowns they intended to wear under their robes for the graduation ceremony, and were very careful to keep them spotlessly clean.

Stephanie was wearing the dress Bede had entered into the Man Made Fiber competition, which was doubly special because it had been a winner.

The gown was truly beautiful, with its boat shaped neckline flattering Stephanie's slim shoulders, and extended peter pan collar with matching peplum on the hip.

Elisabet had a fully-lined designer gown of crepe de chine. It was shift style, with a bow on the left side of the waist. She realised it was one of the plainer graduation gowns, but it's elegance suited her well. The dress had been expensive, but her mother had bought it as a gift, saying her little girl would only graduate from her first degree once.

The food was traditional, a choice of meat or vegetarian dishes, served with beautifully cooked vegetables. Although the fare was simple, the hospitality students had outdone themselves in their attention to quality. The hospitality class were graduating too, and were celebrating by presenting the best food they could.

The dinner included the presentation of awards for participation in campus activities. These were practical awards that were quite independent of academic excellence. Terence and Janet received volunteer service awards for their contribution to the campus basketball programme. Joelle received an award for playing the organ for worship services, while Larry revived a leadership award for his role on the worship committee.

The final award went to Tom for work on the Year Book Committee. Elisabet was immensely proud of him. She knew that he had been through a bit that year, but throughout it all, he had managed to impress the faculty with his willingness to serve.

Desert was a simple set-and-chill fruit compote, which was absolutely delicious. At the end of the evening, Tom walked Elisabet back to the girl's dormitory and she lovingly clasped his arm. Their kisses at the door were warm and tender, and filled with excitement.

Sunday morning, Elisabet and Tom, Stephanie and Garry, attended the Reform Church service. By now, there were two distinct groups forming on campus, the undergraduates who still had exams to worry about, and the graduating class who had already finished everything.

In the afternoon, the friends decided that they would laze around the pool. Elisabet was sitting dangling her legs in the water, while Tom swam up and down.

"Tom," Elisabet began when her boyfriend stopped swimming, "Have you heard anything about the Christian media position?"

Tom hauled himself out of the water and sat on the pool edge beside her. "I put my application in for it," he explained. "I also had a phone interview. It seemed to go well."

"Good," Elisabet said. "When do you think you might hear more?"

"It's unlikely I would receive an answer in less than a week," Tom said "And it will be awkward if I am offered anything else in the meantime, because I won't not know whether to accept it."

"I've been wondering about something you said," Elisabet ventured.

"What?" Tom asked lazily.

"That we might be able to afford a unit…"

"I meant it," Tom sounded stubborn. "I don't want to be parted!"

"I don't see how we could live together unmarried," Elisabet said cautiously. "If you have a Christian employer – you could lose your job!"

"We could have separate rooms," Tom suggested.

A thundering wave of disappointment descended upon Elisabet. Things had been going so well for them, but now it seemed Tom did not want to make a full commitment. They exchanged a few angry words and Elisabet began to cry.

"Who would believe we had separate rooms?" She asked shakily. "Even if you didn't lose the job – I would lose my reputation. And there would be no possibility of Christian employment for me."

Tom eyed her seriously. "Isn't that stuff for kids?"

"Perhaps it ought to be," Elisabet said. "But I think you will find it's not!"

"It's too soon for me to propose, if that is what you are getting at," Tom returned snappily. "We have only been dating for a couple of months!"

Tom looked at her helplessly, and seemed to have nothing more to say. Elisabet turned to go back into the girl's dormitory. Being seen cry around campus was fodder for the worst type of gossip.

Tea time things were still tense. Tom was sullen and sulky, and Elisabet was puzzled as to what she could do to change things. As far as she knew, she had been right. Living together was the worldly way, and couldn't be pulled off without harm in Christian circles. According to some psychologists, it damaged the relationship too, and she was not willing to risk losing something so precious.

Seeing that Tom was impossible to talk to, Elisabet retreated to the dormitory room to continue her packing. Her mother phoned that evening to say they would be arriving on campus Friday, just in time for graduation and staying at a hotel in Northcoast.

Elisabet was surprised her mother took Tom's side in the argument.

"I think you are both right, dear," Mother said. "You in saying that you cannot ignore the social implications; and Tom in viewing things in a practical light."

"We can't both be right," Elisabet objected. "We have opposite points of view."

"But like Tom said, you aren't children anymore," Mother observed.

"Granted," Elisabet conceded.

"It is likely Tom will have to go ahead to start work and find a place," Mother said. "Then you could join him. And by then – you might be ready to get engaged."

"I can't even begin to guess how long Tom might need before he is ready to propose," Elisabet said. "He doesn't seem keen. If he feels pressured – maybe never."

"I don't think he is like that dear," Mother said. "When you went down to Sydney for the Christian band competition, you stayed somewhere together. Where was that?"

"We were billeted with local Christians," Elisabet admitted.

"What about doing that again?" Mother suggested.

"It wouldn't be a good long term solution," Elisabet said. "And Tom wants to get a unit."

"But for a visit, or while Tom is house-hunting, it might be an option," Mother said.

"Maybe," Elisabet conceded.

"I think both you and Tom have taken a gigantic leap ahead in your thinking," Mother submitted. "You have forgotten that there might be some in-between steps, and other choices to make while you are getting established."

"Even a share house situation would be better," Elisabet mused. "It would help with the bills for a while, and we wouldn't be alone."

"There you go," Mother said. "Put some of those ideas to Tom and see whether it breaks the impasse."

"Thanks, Mum," Elisabet said. "It could even be fun!"

"See how it goes," Mother said. "I'm sorry your father and I cannot make it to Silver Springs until the weekend. You know how it is in the garden business, always a lot of work to do."

"It is fine, Mum," Elisabet said. "I am looking forward to seeing you."

Monday morning at breakfast, Elisabet invited Tom to go for a drive to talk things through. They headed towards the mountains, where Elisabet stopped and gave Tom the wheel, because she did not like the windy dirt tracks. Finally, Tom pulled the car over into a parking area beside a romantic lookout.

"I guess we ought to clear the air," he grunted grudgingly.

Elisabet produced some cookies she had purloined from the cafeteria. "I'm surprised we found it so difficult to agree," she said. "That gave me a shock."

"Me too," Tom admitted between munches. "I really don't want a long separation."

"I had a talk to Mother and she pointed out that we won't necessarily have a place of our own immediately," Elisabet said.

"What did she mean?" Tom asked guardedly.

"You might have to go ahead and house hunt," Elisabet said.

"True," Tom said. "Although I was hoping for some guidance from you."

"Temporary accommodation might be necessary," Elisabet suggested.

"Also true," Tom said. "I can see what your mother meant – I had jumped forward in my mind about six months, to when we had a place already."

"And so had I," Elisabet admitted.

"I might be staying with one of the bosses for a few weeks," Tom admitted. "They suggested it would be a good way of getting me settled."

'There you go," Elisabet said.

"And the family have asked me to look after my cousin, who is starting at Sydney University," Tom said slowly. "Although she might want to stay in the dorms."

"If she doesn't stay on campus – we could get a three bedroom place and share with her," Elisabet suggested. "It would be nice to have a friend in a strange city."

"I suppose," Tom said. He looked more cheerful.

Elisabet felt there were still a few unanswered questions about the future, but the current conversation had been much more satisfactory than the previous one. She took a large bite out of her cookie. "These are good," she pronounced. "When can I meet your cousin?"

"At Christmas I expect," Tom looked amused. "If you can drop by Dubbo for the celebration."

Tuesday, David and Debbie were called to Port Douglas, which suited David well enough because he was originally from North Queensland. Debbie, who was from Gosford, hoped that they would not stay there all their lives.

"I've heard it is a beautiful place to visit," Debbie whispered. "But honestly, it will be a little too tropical for me."

"Think of it as an extended holiday in paradise," Elisabet advised. "And it can't be that much different than the Central Coast can it?"

Debbie rolled her eyes. "I think their rainy season will be more severe," she said. "I am afraid of flooding."

"But Gosford must be subject to flooding too," Elisabet said. "It's set on all those lakes."

"Not in the best bits," Debbie asserted. "And the people there know how to manage."

"I'm sure you will get used to Port Douglas," Stephanie said. "And like you said, David might not be posted there forever."

"He will probably ask for somewhere in the Queensland hinterland after that," Debbie said. "I wouldn't mind that."

"I have heard the mountains are cooler." Elisabet agreed.

"But I doubt I will be going back home to NSW," Debbie sighed.

"That is part of getting married," Stephanie agreed. She was trading her native South Australia for permanent residence in Wollongong, and she seemed comfortable with the prospect.

Wednesday, Tom got the big news for which they had been waiting. He had indeed been offered the job in Christian publishing, and would be expected to start in the New Year. Tom told the friends at lunch, and they all cheered for him as they waited in line. The cafeteria was crowded and service was slow because of the number of parents visiting for graduation. By Friday most of the accommodation in Northcoast and Eumundi would be full.

"Luckily Northern Beaches is not too far from Wollongong," Stephanie, exclaimed. "You will be required at the wedding."

"That will probably be my first visit," Elisabet said.

The friends looked at her curiously. "Won't you be with Tom?"

"I will be staying with one of the directors for a few weeks," Tom said. "Before finding a unit of my own."

"Then Tom's cousin will be starting university in Sydney," Elisabet said. "And I will join them."

"What will you be doing about a job?" Garry asked curiously.

"My parents business is always very busy over summer," Elisabet said. "Plenty of work for me there… but I'm still waiting for news about a placement."

"What if you got something that was not close to Tom?" Cara asked.

"I don't think I would take it," Elisabet said. "There is plenty of work around Sydney."

"Oh to be sure," Dylan agreed.

"Are you guys getting engaged?" Stephanie asked.

Elisabet blushed and looked down at the table. "Not yet," she admitted.

"You have plenty of time," Cara said. The sporty girl threw a warning glance at Stephanie not to pursue the subject. Tom continued chatting to the boys about what he expected from his career in the publishing industry. It all sounded very positive. Except for the moment when Elisabet had to admit they were not getting engaged. She knew that it was too soon, and yet it rankled.

Thursday was the last day of exams for the undergraduates, and James had his education exam. He was stressing about it at breakfast, and Elisabet tried to empathise, but really, her mind was too full of the future.

After she had eaten her meal, Elisabet hurried back to the dormitory, where Stephanie was experimenting with hairstyles for the graduation ceremonies. Stephanie's long brown hair was stubbornly straight, and she usually had to tie it back or plait it to make it do anything.

Elisabet laid back on her bed and broached the subject she had on her mind. "I read once in a magazine that if you live with a guy before marriage… he is less likely to marry you in the long run," she announced.

"And you are worried about living with Tom?" Stephanie reflected.

"Yes," Elisabet admitted.

"Well, firstly, I think that magazine meant 'defacto'. With Tom's cousin staying - you wouldn't be 'living as married'," Stephanie said.

"That's what I was hoping," Elisabet said. "We could always ask her to move into the university dormitories if we wanted to get married of course."

"Exactly," Stephanie said. "And those magazines – they are hardly scientific."

"Yes," Elisabet agreed. "I read them for the fashion pages really."

"There are a few guys who never want to marry," Stephanie said thoughtfully. "So if a girl agreed to live with one of them – that would twist the statistics."

"Maybe," Elisabet said thoughtfully. Her mind went to Craig, who would probably fit into the category of a man who would be happiest never marrying. And yet he was a very nice guy. Females sometimes liked him; and even more occasionally, Craig liked them back. He would probably have a great career as a musician, and this would attract him more admirers.

"What are you thinking?" Stephanie asked, seeing the faraway look on her roommate's face.

Elisabet shook herself back to reality. "How would I find out exactly how Tom feels about marriage?"

Stephanie laughed. "Ask him," she advised. "I had to learn not to be scared to ask Garry about stuff long ago."

The rest of the day passed in a whirl of last visits to familiar spots on campus and other sentimental moments. Elisabet and Tom were accompanied by their friends, and Elisabet had little opportunity to initiate a serious conversation with him.

Friday afternoon Elisabet's parents arrived for graduation, and in the evening the opening service commenced. Elisabet and Stephanie donned their white frocks, covered by their voluminous black robes. They completed their outfits with mortarboard hats and sashes.

Now that the moment had finally come, Elisabet could hardly believe it. She stood in line with her classmates waiting to enter the gymnasium, which had been filled with seating for the occasion. The organ commenced a selection from Saint Saens' *Symphony Number 3 in C Minor*, and the whole line moved forward, heading down the central aisle.

As they settled into their chairs, Craig turned around from his position directly in front of Elisabet and beside Joelle. "Every other year I have been with the orchestra," he whispered nostalgically.

"Perhaps it's time to move on," Elisabet whispered, but she understood his sense of disorientation. When she had attended previous years, she had been seated with the congregation.

"I've been replaced already," Joelle whispered, nodding towards where Jessie sat concentrating on the organ.

"She is not you," Craig said comfortingly. "And she never will be."

"Oh you are sweet," Joelle whispered back. She and Craig had been friends and classmates since their first year.

"Shush you two," Stephanie said from beside Elisabet. "Talk later."

Elisabet reached down and clasped Tom's hand. They had the same major, and had consequently been lucky enough to be seated beside each other.

The first service was mostly devotional. The proceedings were designed to welcome the parents onto campus, as well as congratulate the graduating class on their achievements. They listened to an address form the Chancellor and short readings by the Chaplains; then they filed out of the building to the accompaniment of orchestral music, this time the pleasing notes of William Walton's *Crown Imperial*. After the service, there was much hugging and kissing of visiting parents, and then the elders returned to their booked accommodation.

Saturday morning brought another large ceremonial service. The graduands entered the gymnasium to the rousing sound of Martin Luther's *Almighty Fortress*, and sat still through another round of speeches. Today's celebrations included remarks from most of the department heads, and special thanks to God for guiding the students through their years of study. At the end of the proceedings, the graduands marched down the aisle to Rimsky-Korsakov's *Procession of the Nobles*.

After the service, Elisabet's parents took her into Northcoast for a special dinner at a restaurant. They invited Tom and his parents to accompany them, so that the two families could get to know each other. The party ended up at a local pizza and pasta house, where there was something available to please everyone.

Seeing that their parents were getting along well, Elisabet and Tom relaxed, and began to have a good time. Tom chatted proudly to Elisabet's father about his new job, and Elisabet took the opportunity to ask Mrs. Randall about the young cousin who might be coming to live with them in Sydney.

"You will love Emilia," Mrs. Randall said to Elisabet. "She is a very sweet girl. And my sister would be so grateful if you were to take her under your wing."

"I will do my best," Elisabet said.

Mrs. Randall nodded: "My sister worries because Emilia will surrounded by so many secular influences at Sydney University," she said.

"Not everyone is lucky enough to attend a Christian University like Silver Springs," Elisabet replied.

"The course Emilia wanted simply wasn't available here," Mrs. Randall said. "But we do hope she will find Christian friends, and maybe even meet a Christian young man."

"You never know," Elisabet said. "I will keep an eye open for her."

"That is all we can ask," Mrs. Randall looked pleased.

Saturday evening, both sets of parents visited the cafeteria to sample the university food. They had to stop at the door and buy meal tickets, while Elisabet and Tom were able to walk straight through to the servery.

"Tomorrow Dylan and I are going for one last morning surf," Tom said to Elisabet. "Cara is coming along, and I was hoping that you would join me."

"But tomorrow afternoon we graduate," Elisabet began to object.

"What else do you have to do?" Tom objected. "Spend the whole morning on hair and make-up? Live a little Elisabet!"

Elisabet had actually been looking forward to a morning spent pampering herself, but she had to admit Tom had a point. Her beauty routine did sound tame compared to a farewell visit to the ocean.

Cara, who was a few steps ahead with Mr. and Mrs. O'Brien, turned and gave Elisabet a wink. "It would be nice to have the company," she said.

"I will come then," Elisabet agreed.

The plan was explained to the parents, who all decided to go straight to worship in the morning and not stop by the dormitory to hunt for errant offspring. They would all find each other somehow later.

"You must all enjoy your last day," Mrs. Randall said understandingly. "Graduation is a major milestone."

Stephanie was an early riser, so Elisabet simply opened her eyes when she heard her roommate moving around. Instead of turning over for a few more minutes sleep before breakfast, she sat up and yawned.

"Is it time?" she asked.

"Afraid so," Stephanie said. "Welcome to our last day on campus!"

"Happy graduation to you too," Elisabet exclaimed. She decided that surfing on a full stomach would be a mistake, and headed for the shower instead. A few minutes later, she felt refreshed and had a small bag packed ready for the expedition to the beach.

Cara knocked on the door, and the two girls tiptoed through the dormitory so as not to wake other girls who wanted to spend their last morning in slumber. They crossed University Drive and walked towards the student car-park, where all travel in Dylan's Suzuki LJ to save taking two cars.

It was something like a twenty minute drive to Noosa, where even Elisabet had to admit, the early morning beach was appealing. Tom and Dylan unpacked their surfboards and headed out into the water, eager to catch the swelling waves. Cara pulled a more modest body board down off the roof rack.

"I thought you were going to sit and watch with me," Elisabet objected.

"I changed my mind," Cara said. "It's our last morning and all, so I might as well get wet!"

"I'm going to enjoy the sun before it gets hot," Elisabet smiled.

Cara followed the boys into the water and paddled around at a more modest depth. Elisabet spread out her towel and shrugged out of her coverall. She was wearing her bathing suit underneath, so she laid down to tan herself in the early morning sun.

A little while later, Tom startled her out of her pleasant dreams by dropping his surfboard down beside her with a thump. "I've finished my serious surfing," he said. "Come into the water with me."

"I didn't really want to swim," Elisabet objected, worrying about the effects of salt on her hair. She had worn her bathing suit for appearances more than anything else.

Tom caught her by the hands and dragged her to her feet. "It's our last day," he cried. His eyes were sparkling and his blonde curls dripped water. His relaxed charm was impossible to resist.

Elisabet laughed, "Why not!"

Tom escorted her to the edge of the water, where they jumped a few shallow waves. Then suddenly, the sand bar dropped away, and they stepped into a channel. Elisabet was neck deep in the water, and had to hang onto Tom when the larger waves crashed into them. The surfer was taller and stood quite comfortably. "Isn't this fun?" he said.

Elisabet nodded, and Tom bent to kiss her, his mouth salty against her lips. Elisabet returned the kiss, enjoying the sensation of closeness and the wash of the surrounding water. "It is," she said.

"We will go to the beach together every weekend when we live on the Northern Beaches," Tom said.

"Yes," Elisabet cried. "Every weekend."

A wave pounded in and she clung tightly to Tom for support. The moment was a little frightening and incredibly stimulating. If she were alone, she would have been seeking calmer waters.

"I've got you," Tom said. "You will always be safe with me."

Elisabet felt loved, but she still wanted what all the other couples were having. An engagement, marriage and eventually, children. She renewed her resolve to talk to Tom about the need for commitment.

CHAPTER FIFTEEN: GRADUATION AT LAST!

Around eight-thirty, Dylan and Tom reluctantly packed up their surfboards and headed back towards Silver Springs campus. Dylan parked the Suzuki in the student car park, and they all headed towards their respective dormitories.

Elisabet collected her toiletries and went straight to the shower. She used a good quality shampoo and conditioner, thoroughly washing the salt out of her hair. The brittle surfy-look was very nice on Tom, but she wanted to keep her hair smooth and shiny.

She hurried her beauty routine somewhat, setting her hairdryer and curler on high, even though a slower setting generally gave her hair greater body. Then she applied some light make-up and slid into a summery dress for the Reform Church service, where she hoped to connect with her parents.

The gymnasium was full, so Elisabet and Tom stood in the doorway, looking around for their families. Finally they spotted them, and weaved their way to a couple of vacant seats within reach. Elisabet's mother noticed their arrival and waved.

After worship, the graduating students and their relatives made their way to the cafeteria for their last lunch on campus. Her food finished, Elisabet hurried back to the dorms to change into her elegant dress and graduation regalia.

Outside on the lawn, Elisabet and Stephanie joined the queue of graduands waiting for the important processional into the hall. Camera's flashed all around, as parents and friends took happy-shots to remember the day. Tom slid into line beside Elisabet and she squeezed his hand, although she knew she would have to let go for the march.

"How do you feel?" Stephanie whispered.

"I hope I don't trip going to get my testamur," Elisabet whispered. Her court shoes were very nice, but had a pointed stiletto heel, as was the fashion.

"You will be alright," Tom assured her.

"I can't believe graduation is really here," Stephanie said. "It only seems yesterday I watched Jeff and his class' ceremony at the end of my first year."

"It's been three more years and a lot of work really," Tom observed.

The organ began to play Gustav Holst's *First Suite in E-flat*, which was their cue to begin moving. Elisabet reluctantly let go of Tom's hand and tried to walk daintily along with the column. It seemed a long way down the aisle and into their reserved seating.

The graduation ritual was solemn and inspiring. First the Uniting Church Chaplain rose and thanked God for the blessing of another generation of workers. Then the Reform Church Chaplain spoke about the gospel commission and the ministry of service, which they would soon enter. All could render unto the glory of God, whether they were employed as pastors, teachers, administrators, scientists, or artisans. The commission also applied to their roles as husbands, wives, parents and key members of the community.

The spiritual message complete, the Chancellor began reading out the graduating class titles. One by one, the candidates climbed the steps onto the stage to collect their degree parchments.

The theology students were called first because preparing candidates for the ministry was Silver Spring's University's primary function. Then the teaching classes began to be called, according to their major subject area. The first classes to be called in alphabetical order, were accounting and art. Next came biology. Cara, and Dylan, along with Garry, who had returned just for the ceremony, received their degrees. Then the chemistry and computing classes received their awards.

When the English class was called, Elisabet, Stephanie, Phoebe and Tom rose to their feet. Elisabet's heart beat hard in her chest, as she led the way, but she smiled and nodded to the chancellor, and paused momentarily to face the parents, as she had been instructed. Stephanie, Tom and Phoebe received their testamurs in turn, and stood lined up, beside Elisabet on the stage. Cameras and flashes exploded all around them. Then they retreated down the steps, back to their seats.

The next groups to be called were the geography, history and home economics majors. They were followed in sequence by mathematics, then music, physical education, physics and technology majors.

After the four year degrees had been conferred, the three year diplomas were distributed. Finally came the one year certificates. Elisabet was able to relax and enjoy this part of the proceedings, because her moment in the spotlight was finished.

At the end of the ceremony, the Uniting Church Chaplain rose and closed with prayer. The orchestra began to play the *Henry VIII Suite March* composed by Sir Arthur Sullivan. The graduands filed solemnly out of the gymnasium to this tune, and then broke formation to mill around across the quadrangle and the lawns.

Tom and Elisabet's parents collected their offspring, and began asking them to pose for photographs. The students were photographed alone, and with their families. They were photographed as a couple, and also with as many classmates as they could gather.

Finally, Mrs. Randall asked Elisabet and Tom to remove their flowing graduation gowns, to pose with Elisabet in her white dress and Tom in his black suit.

"Beautiful," Elisabet's Mother breathed.

"It's almost as though they were getting married," Mrs. Randall exclaimed.

"Isn't it just?" Elisabet's Mother agreed. She gestured to her husband. "Take some more photos dear."

Elisabet felt a shiver of unease despite the happiness of the day. Mrs. Randall was viewing her as a bride; yet she knew Tom was not ready to propose. She glanced at Tom, but he was smiling and indulging his mother in her maternal pride.

"We have to talk later," Elisabet whispered.

"Of course," Tom agreed.

The two sets of parents eventually tired of photography, and decided to attend the gala afternoon tea. Once inside the cafeteria, Elisabet and Tom said goodbye to all their classmates.

They hugged Debbie and David, Luke and Tess, Stephanie and Garry, Cara and Dylan, and Andrew along with his girlfriend Kathy – who was visiting. Larry and Anita, together with Hank and Phoebe, promised to keep in touch. Felipe solemnly wished them well in whatever they did.

The salutations exchanged with Justin and Joelle were more restrained, but graduation was far too momentous an event to be affected by past grudges.

Then the couple circulated amongst the undergraduates, magnanimously wishing the third year students, especially Janet and Vincent, along with Lacey and Terence, all the best of luck with their studies the following year.

In return, they received congratulations regarding graduation. Christopher thanked Tom for working with him on the Year Book, and Mathew wished them a blessed future together.

Finally, Elisabet and Tom rendezvoused with their parents, and made their way out to the car park. Most of their luggage had already been stowed away in the rear of the automobiles.

Elisabet's parents climbed into their family car to lead the way, Mr. and Mrs. Randall were second; with Tom and Elisabet bringing up the rear in Elisabet's vehicle. The cavalcade turned out of University Drive and headed towards the Bruce Highway.

As they left campus, Tom cheered merrily. "Goodbye Silver Springs - hello world!"

Elisabet laughed, but she was busy steering.

"What did you want to talk about?" Tom asked curiously, but Elisabet shook her head.

"I can't now – I'm driving."

"Oh, okay," Tom turned the radio up loud. The station was considered 'popular', but not overly rocky. It broadcast ideal travel music. The three cars headed for Brisbane where they stopped at a cafe for a late supper, before continuing on the journey. Tom's parents followed them down the highway, because the Randall family planned to stay overnight in Byron Bay.

The next morning, Elisabet and Tom walked hand in hand along the sandy beach where she had run and played as a child. It was incredibly romantic, and every moment was precious, because after lunch, Tom would continue on to Dubbo with his parents.

Tom turned Elisabet to face him, and pulled her close for a kiss. Elisabet returned the kiss with feverish intensity, but when they had finished, she found herself blinking the tears away.

"Is everything alright?" Tom asked tenderly.

"I felt weird yesterday when your mother talked about us getting married," Elisabet said. "It's nothing really."

"She was simply being a mum," Tom insisted. "But if it made you feel strange, it can't be nothing…"

"Well, it reminded me of the argument we had the other day," Elisabet replied. "When you said that you didn't want to propose?"

"Oh that!" Tom said. He laughed nervously. "Well with Joelle, I was scared to propose, because I knew she would have turned me down flat!"

"And with me?" Elisabet asked.

Even amongst Christians, she had heard of couples whose courtship had lasted many years and did not eventuate in marriage. She felt she needed some reassurance her relationship was going somewhere.

"I'm still a bit nervous," Tom admitted. "Someone like me feels proposing is a big deal. I need to develop the confidence."

Elisabet still had to check they were on the same page. "You do believe in marriage?"

"Of course I do," Tom said. "Maybe in six months or so - I will be bold enough… to make a certain request…"

"Hush!" Elisabet blushed.

Six months wasn't so long to wait. It was almost as good as being asked that special question.

Tom pulled Elisabet tightly against him and kissed her again. "Was there anything else?"

"No," Elisabet said. "All is good now."

"Be anxious for nothing, but in everything by prayer and supplication, with thanksgiving, let your requests be made known to God; and the peace of God, which surpasses all understanding, will guard your hearts and minds through Christ Jesus."

Philippians 4:6-7 New King James Version

ABOUT THE AUTHOR

Cecelia spent some years volunteering as a counsellor. She hopes that sharing her insights (in fictional form) can help empower modern youth. Life is all about being true to yourself – and maintaining your deepest beliefs.

Cecelia is also the author of:

Special Pictures to Talk About (ISBN: 978-0-646-97235-0), which developed out of her work on language delay and speech development in Kindergartens.

Silver Springtime (ISBN-13: 978-0-6481160-1-1), the first of a series of period romances following the developmental struggles of a group of teenagers attending a Christian university in the 1980s.

Faith and Love (ISBN: 978-0-6481160-3-5), the second "Silver Springs University" Christian college romance story.

Love Always Hopes (ISBN: 978-0-6481160-7-3), the third "Silver Springs University" Christian college romance story.

All for Love: on the Charity Dating Show (ISBN: 978-0-6481160-2-8), the first of a reality television spin-off series.

Mystic Evermore (ISBN: 978-0-6481160-0-4), the first of the fantasy series "Nevermore Parables".

Saints and Sinners (ISBN: 978-0-6481160-4-2), the second of the fantasy series "Nevermore Parables".

Autumn Secrets (ISBN: 978-0-6481160-5-9) the third of the fantasy series "Nevermore Parables".